JUST A LITTLE SEDUCTION

MERRY FARMER

JUST A LITTLE SEDUCTION

Cover design by Erin Dameron-Hill (the miracle-worker)

ASIN: B089KS79ZV

Paperback ISBN: 9798668482757

Click here for a complete list of other works by Merry Farmer.

If you'd like to be the first to learn about when the next books in the series come out and more, please sign up for my newsletter here: http://eepurl.com/RQ-KX

 Created with Vellum

CHAPTER 1

L ondon – June, 1890

Whenever there was a vital task to be done, David Wirth could be counted upon to do it. It had been true from David's earliest childhood, when his hard-working parents handed him the responsibility of keeping his younger siblings out of harm in their rough-and-tumble, working-class neighborhood. It stayed true when his father had earned enough to move them onto a quieter, middle-class square in Belgravia. It had been true all through university as David paid his own way by tutoring his higher-born classmates. And it had been true ten years ago, when he and John Dandie banded together after leaving university to form the law offices of Dandie

& Wirth. David was always the man people could count on to make even the most impossible tasks possible. He was a man with something to prove.

That had never been truer than as he walked from table to table in the dining room of Stephen Siddel and Max Hillsboro's newly-established orphanage in Earl's Court, interviewing the recently rescued children who had been victims of a kidnapping ring.

"Your name is Jimmy Hollis?" he asked the frightened boy of six who sat on the lap of Annie Ross, a woman who had worked side-by-side with Stephen at the orphanage in its old location and who had relocated, along with her mother, to the new site.

The boy nodded, his eyes wide with fright.

"And you were taken off the street in Limehouse?" David asked on, making his voice as soft as he could and smiling, in spite of the seriousness of his questions.

Again, Jimmy nodded.

"Do you have a mama or papa who is looking for you?"

Jimmy shook his head.

David's heart squeezed in his chest, and he met Annie's eyes. "Another orphan?"

"He must be," Annie said with a sigh. "Or, if not an orphan, his family must be bad enough that he doesn't want to go back."

David had heard the same story too many times in the last few days. He and Lionel had been working to reunite the rescued children with their families, but more often than not, the poor things either didn't have any or didn't want to go back.

A swell of determination filled David. "We'll find a place for you, lad." He rose, ruffling Jimmy's already messy hair as he did. He had to prove that he was competent and capable of so much more than people assumed a boy from his background, a boy just like Jimmy, was capable of. "Mr. Siddel's orphanage is for girls, but Sister Constance is willing to take in any boys."

"And Lord Hillsboro has been pressing Mr. Siddel to start an orphanage for boys across the square," Annie added.

"That's a good idea." David smiled and stepped away, heading to the next table and the next group of rescued children.

The child kidnapping ring had been broken, thanks to the efforts of actor Everett Jewel and Patrick Wrexham, not to mention the weeks of work David himself, and his business partner, Lionel Mercer, had put into tracking down the ringleaders. The work wasn't over yet, though. Not only were there dozens of children to return to their families or to find homes for, the ringleaders—all three of them noblemen of high rank—had disappeared when the police raided Castleford Estate in Yorkshire. Enough evidence had been secured to arrest Lord Castleford, Lord Eastleigh, and Lord Chisolm for their crimes, but the men were still on the loose. Rage rolled through David's gut every time he thought about how easily the nobs had gotten away. The same nobs who looked down on men like him simply because of where they were born. They wouldn't get away entirely, though. Not if he had anything to say about it.

A chorus of light laughter broke the gloom of David's thoughts, and he turned toward a table of slightly older girls at the other end of the room. Lionel sat among them, reading from a leather-bound book, a pair of spectacles balanced on his nose. His expression was as grave as a minister's, but the girls all beamed at him as though he were a clown performing magic tricks on a stage.

A hitch formed in David's chest as he watched Lionel. The man was dressed impeccably, as usual, in a dove grey suit with a lavender cravat. Not a hair on his head was out of place. His pale face was splashed with just enough color to make him seem lively. The way his lips moved as he read to the girls hinted at humor, even though David was too far away to hear what he was saying. The gentleness of Lionel's face was in direct contrast to the broad lines of his shoulders and the decidedly masculine, though slender, set of his body. Lionel was an erotic blend of masculine and feminine that never failed to leave David breathless. Which was inconvenient in a room filled with children.

He sucked in a breath, forcing himself to stop watching Lionel and get on with his business. But the second he resumed walking to the next table, Lionel darted a covert look at him. He managed it without moving a single muscle, only his eyes, and the effect had David breaking out in prickles down his back. It was no

4

surprise to him that Lionel was aware of him staring. Lionel always knew when David was watching him. Possibly because David was always watching him.

David cleared his throat and sank into a free chair at a table with three boys who looked to be between nine and eleven. "Hello," he said, holding out his hand as though they were adults. "I'm Mr. David Wirth. Has Mr. Siddel explained who I am?"

"You're the man trying to find people's families," the boy with ginger hair said.

"That's correct. Can you tell me anything that might help us search?"

"Fred here cries for his mama in his sleep." The ginger boy stuck his thumb out at the mousey boy sitting next to him.

"What's her name, lad, and where are you from? I'm sure we can find her and reunite the two of you," David said.

"She's dead, sir," Fred confessed, lowering his head. "Trampled by a horse two years ago. I got no other family."

David let out a sympathetic breath and reached out to pat the boy's hand. He'd been hearing the same story over and over from the remaining children. Everyone who had a family they could be reunited with had already been taken home. The ones who were left had no homes to go to.

The sensation that thought brought with it was oddly familiar, tender, aching, and emotional. David glanced across the room to Lionel, feeling it acutely in his chest. Lionel was still reading and the girls around him continued to giggle, but there was a distinct tension in the air, tension in the distance between him and Lionel, a barrier keeping them apart in spite of the pulse of emotion that throbbed between them.

David let out a breath and leaned back in his chair, rubbing a hand over his face.

"You all right, guv'nor?" the ginger boy asked.

David lowered his hands and sent the boy a lopsided smile. "I honestly have no idea."

And he didn't. In the last few weeks, his life had gone from business as usual to a jungle of intense and conflicting emotions, and all because of Lionel. He didn't try to hide the way he stared at his partner and thorn in his side. He'd never hidden the way he felt about Lionel from himself. Lionel captivated him. He had almost from the moment John had hired him four years before, right before he left for Manchester and a new life. Lionel was brilliant, powerful, and beautiful. It was impossible not to want him in every way. And for a while there, David had been convinced he was on the verge of having him at last.

Until Everett Jewel had blasted into the picture, like a cannonball tearing down a wall.

No, that wasn't fair. Jewel wasn't interested in Lionel and hadn't been for years. Besides which, Jewel was happy as a clam with Patrick Wrexham now. But Jewel was also under Lionel's skin somehow, as evidenced by the very public argument they'd had at The Chameleon

Club a fortnight ago. An argument that had proven to David that there was no place for him in Lionel's heart as long as he still carried a torch for Jewel.

Nothing destroyed a man's pride faster than being hopelessly in love with a man who loved someone else.

But there was something else, something David couldn't put his finger on. He couldn't shake how uncharacteristically upset Lionel had become during the argument with Jewel or some of the vague things Lionel had said. There was something Lionel wasn't telling him, something important.

"Oy!" The ginger boy snapped his fingers at David, startling him back to attention. "You gonna stare at the girls all day or you gonna try and find my folks?"

David burst into a smile in spite of himself. "You're a cheeky one, aren't you?" He sat straighter, sending Lionel one last look before focusing on the boy. "What's your name and where are you from?"

"Mick Lang," the ginger boy said. "And I'm from Poplar."

"Alright, Mick." David nodded, charmed by the scamp. "Who are your parents and where can we find them?"

"My dad's Prime Minister Gladstone and mum's the washerwoman," Mick said, then burst into laughter. The two other boys laughed raucously with him.

David smirked, figuring Mick was just as much of an orphan as every other child in the room, but one with a wicked sense of humor. "Well then, Mr. Gladstone," he laughed. "We'll see what we can do about getting you settled."

He leaned in, ready to ask more questions, but a commotion in the doorway snagged everyone's attention. As Jack Craig, Lord Clerkenwell, Assistant Commissioner of Scotland Yard, strode into the orphanage's dining room, every adult who knew who he was rose in respect, David along with them. The urge to prove himself to someone he admired flared so potently in David that he almost laughed at himself. Lionel stood as well, passing the book he'd been reading to one of the girls and stepping away from his table.

"Excuse me, lads," David murmured, doing the same.

By the time David reached the dining room doorway, Stephen and Max had also left their work with the orphans to converge on Lord Clerkenwell, along with Lionel.

"It's an honor to welcome you to our establishment, my lord," Stephen greeted the man with a firm handshake.

"Mr. Siddel." Lord Clerkenwell nodded and smiled as he shook Stephen's hand, then moved on to Max, and then David. "Gentlemen. I've come to see how much progress you've made in settling the children."

When Lord Clerkenwell reached for Lionel's hand, rather than offering his, Lionel bowed. "They are perfect darlings, as you can see," Lionel said with a smile over his shoulder for the girls, who continued to beam at him and giggle.

Lord Clerkenwell chuckled, then turned to Stephen. "I take it the ones who remain are in need of new homes?"

"Correct, my lord." Stephen nodded. "But we're doing our best to accommodate them."

"Good," Lord Clerkenwell said. "And in the meantime, we can move on to the more pressing matter of tracking down the men responsible for their sad state and bringing them to justice."

"As I mentioned the other day, my lord, Lionel and I are at your disposal and would relish the chance to hunt the men down," David said, bristling with the energy to show Lord Clerkenwell what he could accomplish.

Lionel glared sideways at him. "You're speaking for me now, are you?" he asked in an undertone, perhaps intending for only David to hear, as Lord Clerkenwell continued to speak to Stephen and Max.

David flinched, gut filling with indignation. "I'm speaking on behalf of Dandie & Wirth," he muttered in return.

"Oh, of course." Lionel rolled his eyes dramatically. "Because you always speak on behalf of *Dandie* & Wirth."

David turned more fully toward him, crossing his arms. "What in blazes is that supposed to mean?"

"Only that you seem to have elected yourself spokesman for the both of us without consulting me first." Lionel's back was ramrod straight, and his usual aura of calm power crackled with irritation.

David gaped at him. "What has gotten into you these last few weeks?" he asked, trying to keep thing between them but too startled by the bitterness of Lionel's attitude to contain himself.

"Nothing," Lionel said in a hoarse and haunted voice. "Nothing has gotten into me in quite some time, as you well know."

David snapped his lips shut, clenching his jaw, no idea whether Lionel was trying to make a joke about his self-imposed celibacy or drive home the point that they were not lovers, in spite of knowing how David felt about the possibility. Beyond that, the feeling that Lionel was holding something back from him twisted David's gut. He'd never kept secrets before. As badly as David wanted to prove to Lord Clerkenwell that he was competent, he wanted to prove to Lionel that he adored him and could be trusted with his heart even more.

Lord Clerkenwell cleared his throat, glancing between David and Lionel in a way that proved he, and everyone else, was listening, then on to Stephen and Max. "Regardless," he began warily, "time is of the essence when it comes to hunting down Chisolm, Castleford, and Eastleigh." He sent a cautious glance in Max's direction.

"My father only has so many means of escape," Max said, color splashing his cheeks. There was no love lost between him and his father, Lord Eastleigh, but it was plain for all to see how ashamed he was of his own flesh and blood's involvement in the kidnapping ring. "To be honest," he went on, "I have reason to believe Father might be in London."

"Truly?" David's brow shot up. His feud with Lionel was momentarily forgotten.

"What makes you so certain?" Lord Clerkenwell crossed his arms and stared at Max. "The most recent information Scotland Yard has places him in Southampton, attempting to book passage aboard a ship bound for his Caribbean holdings."

Max shrugged. "I spotted my brother, George, in town just yesterday. George detests London in the summer. Only something monumentally important would drag him out of the country at this time of year, especially with my mother and sisters in residence in Hampshire."

"Is there any way to prove Eastleigh is in London?" Lord Clerkenwell asked. "Any way to contact him or your brother?"

Max sighed and shook his head. "I've been utterly disowned by my family." He exchanged a look with Stephen, who took his hand and squeezed it comfortingly.

A slight grimace pulled at the corner of David's mouth. Max wasn't the only man like them to be disowned when their true desires were exposed. He still had a sore spot in his heart from the last time he'd spoken with his father.

"Surely, there must be some way we can make contact, though," Stephen said supportively.

"I doubt it." Max rubbed a hand over his face, then glanced to Lord Clerkenwell. "I'm sorry I can't be of more help."

"You may yet be able to help." Lord Clerkenwell frowned in thought. "If not in the search for your father, then in our attempts to capture the other two."

"Do we have any idea at all where they are?" Stephen asked.

"Castleford was last spotted in Liverpool, attempting to leave England through that port," Lord Clerkenwell said. "Though our latest intelligence suggests he's gone inland, perhaps to Manchester, to wait things out for a while."

David's gut clenched at the mention of Manchester. He had never visited the city, but he had ties to it. Definitive ties. Specifically, John Dandie. He peeked sideways at Lionel, unsurprised to find Lionel eyeing him with equal parts wariness and hurt. Though it was hypocritical in the extreme for Lionel to look so emotional, given the way he'd behaved with Jewel.

"Chisolm has gone north," Lord Clerkenwell went on, "though we're not certain where at this time. I've dozens of men working on the case, however. Even a man like him won't be able to hide forever."

"We'll find him," David said, glancing to Lionel. He nodded, acknowledging Lionel as his business partner, rather than whatever other mess stood between them at the moment.

Lionel's eyes widened slightly. "So you're including me in your endeavors now, are you?"

A new wave of frustration crashed over David. He clenched his fists at his sides before he could stop himself. "You were always included, Lionel. Any exclusion has been your own creation."

"Oh, yes." Lionel's voice dripped with sarcasm. "I am the cause of all my own problems, and I get what I deserve because of it."

David's brow furrowed in frustration. "What the devil are you talking about?" There was more to Lionel's irritation than one of his usual, occasional bad moods. He hadn't been right since the confrontation at The Chameleon Club.

"Never mind me," Lionel went on with a wave of his hand. "I know very well where I rank in your estimation these days."

David's mouth dropped open, but he couldn't think of a blasted thing to say in reply to Lionel's peevishness. It was utterly out of character for a man who was usually in control to the point of being icy and aloof, as if Lionel had turned as hot and bristling as the summer heat that had invaded London and made the place miserable.

"Are the two of you going to be able to work together on this?" Lord Clerkenwell asked, glancing between them, like a headmaster who might have to separate two obstreperous students.

"Yes," David answered.

"Of course," Lionel said at the same time.

The two of them exchanged looks of challenge. David's nerves were frayed enough from the sea of emotion that had grown so stormy between them in the past few weeks. He would almost have rather they return to Lionel's habit of teasing him incessantly and arousing him to such a degree that he'd resorted to relieving himself while picturing Lionel in any number of compromising positions. Being lured into a state of intense sexual frustration and left hanging was infinitely easier to deal with than the flat-out rejection David had been subject to since that blasted argument with Jewel.

"There isn't a millimeter of room for error in this endeavor," Lord Clerkenwell went on. "Eastleigh, Castleford, and Chisolm must be found and brought to justice. I don't have the time to entrust things to men who cannot get along long enough to hunt them down."

The sting of having Lord Clerkenwell question his abilities sobered David in a hurry.

"David and I get along perfectly well," Lionel insisted, tilting his chin up.

David waited for him to add something snide to the end of his sentence, but the comment never came. That didn't mean he couldn't see it implied in the angle of Lionel's chin or the tension in his jaw.

"Whatever personal difficulties we might have," David added, standing straighter and projecting as much of a sense of confidence as he could, "I would never let them interfere with business."

David could tell by the slight flare of Lionel's eyes,

the twitch at the corner of his mouth, and the way he turned his head infinitesimally toward him that Lionel had a whole wealth of things to say about his comment. It was a miracle he refrained.

"Good." Lord Clerkenwell nodded. "In that case, gentlemen, I leave the search for the ringleaders in the capable hands of Dandie & Wirth." He turned to Stephen. "And I leave the responsibility of finding homes for the rescued children in your continuing care."

"We will endeavor to do our best for you and for them, my lord." Stephen nodded.

"Gentlemen." With one final nod, Lord Clerkenwell turned and left the room, Stephen and Max trailing behind him to extend their goodbyes.

David watched them go before crossing his arms and facing Lionel. He arched one eyebrow, as if asking Lionel what the hell his display of pique had been all about and what he planned to do to curb his temper. But instead of finding anger and challenge in Lionel's blue eyes, what he saw was fear. It was only there for a second before Lionel cleared his throat and pulled himself to his full, imperious height, but David knew what he'd seen.

"I suppose we'd better do as Lord Clerkenwell says," Lionel said in a thin voice, then turned and walked away.

CHAPTER 2

*E*ven in the most tranquil of times, Lionel's mind was a whirlwind of thoughts and ideas. It spun like a room full of tops being kept in motion by an army of squirrels, and had ever since he was a boy. Those ideas usually served him well, helping him to make connections between seemingly disparate elements of whatever case David was attempting to crack. As he walked back to the table of darling orphan girls he'd been reading to, heart racing faster than it should have, his mind buzzed. He was already contemplating ways to have the girls trained as governesses and listing respectable families they could find places with, while simultaneously searching for ways to prove Lord Eastleigh was in London and to ferret him out of hiding.

But all of the gears in his normally well-oiled machine of a mind grated and scraped as though they were rusty, and his thoughts flapped around like loose ends he couldn't grab hold of. This was, of course, because of David and the infinite and ever-present distraction the man was for him. He'd lived with the constant ache of desire for David for as long as he'd known him. That was nothing new, in spite of David's sullen attitude of the last few weeks. Not a moment in the day went by where he didn't want to touch or tease David or drive him to distraction just so that he could see the fire of lust burn in the man's eyes. Now more than ever, though, David was as far out of his reach as the Sahara.

"Have you continued the story without me?" Lionel asked, a carefully-crafted, spritely grin on his face as he painfully resumed his seat at the table with the girls. It took all of his concentration to appear calm and at ease when his body felt as though it were falling apart.

"We couldn't possibly do that, Mr. Mercer," Betsy—one of the older girls and perhaps the cleverest of them all—said with a cheeky grin. "You read as beautifully as any actor."

"Perhaps I should have considered a career on the stage," Lionel said, striking a pose designed to make the girls laugh, which, gratifyingly, they did.

"You should have, Mr. Mercer," Ivy said, clapping her hands. "You would have been spectacular."

"Do you think?" Lionel batted his eyes, playing along with the charming girls. In fact, he would rather have died than take to the stage. Not only was the theater Everett Jewel's realm—and heaven already knew how much of a disaster it was for him and Everett to be anywhere near each other in the best of times—but Lionel preferred to play out his dramas in private performances.

"I want to be on stage someday," Merrily—one of the girls who had been rescued after the kidnapping ring had been uncovered—said, imitating Lionel's pose.

"I dare say you would make a delightful actress," Lionel told her. He meant it, though he would never voice his reasons for thinking so. Merrily had been rescued from a brothel, and it was clear to Lionel that she'd learned the art of pretending to enjoy herself while secretly seething that so many theatrical professionals had.

That thought magically set the gears in his mind working once more. Inspiration crackled through him like a Roman candle. Of the three villainous noblemen at the center of the kidnapping ring, Castleford was the one who adored the theater, but Eastleigh had just as much of a fondness for spectacle. If he was in London, he wouldn't be able to sit idly by, locked away in some shuttered townhouse. He would want to be entertained, no matter what the risk. Lionel knew more than a few men who enjoyed private entertainments of the kind Eastleigh enjoyed, men who might have seen Eastleigh recently and been sworn to secrecy as to his whereabouts.

Secrecy, however, had never stopped Lionel's particular friends from telling him whatever he wanted to know. In fact, Lionel had made his way through university and through life using a steady currency of charm, pleasure, and secrets. The connections he'd established in years past continued to serve him well, even though he had long since given up that game.

That thought dashed the moment of hope and cleverness that had put a mysterious grin on his face, driving his awareness back to the writhing discomfort in every fiber of his body. Pleasure and secrets had their price, and he would be paying it for the rest of his likely short life.

"My darlings." He stood, putting every last ounce of effort into making the motion look smooth and graceful when, in fact, the simple act of moving made him want to grind his teeth in pain. "I'm afraid you'll have to continue this reading on your own. I've just realized that I might have resources as my disposal to track down the horrid men who have put you and your friends in danger."

Betsy and Ivy groaned in disappointment, but Merrily looked suddenly grave, her eyes burning with a desire for vengeance.

"I promise you I will return as soon as I can," Lionel went on, stepping away from the table.

"I hope you find them, Mr. Mercer," Merrily called after him as Lionel searched to see where David had gone.

Lionel glanced over his shoulder, meeting Merrily's eyes as though she were as much of an adult as he was. After all she'd been through, she was. "Don't worry." His voice dropped to a deadly timbre. "They'll pay."

Merrily nodded in understanding, and Lionel

moved on, heading across the room to where David had resumed interviewing a table of children. The men responsible for the kidnapping ring would most certainly pay, and for more than just their most recent crimes. Eastleigh and Castleford were some of the vilest creatures Lionel had ever had the displeasure to know, but Chisolm existed in his own category of evil. Bringing Chisolm to justice and making him pay was more than a mission he'd been sent on by Lord Clerkenwell, it was personal. So, deeply personal.

"I need you to pay a call on an old friend with me," Lionel said when he reached the table where David sat.

David glanced slowly up at him, irritation at being interrupted in the middle of his work flickering around him as though he were circled by tiny, dancing flames. "I beg your pardon?" he asked in the voice he usually reserved for noblemen who thought they were better than him.

Lionel fought hard not to be stung by David's coldness. It was understandable, given what he was certain David thought was its cause. "I've just had an idea about how we might be able to find Eastleigh," he said, back stiff and chin angled as arrogantly as he could. It was better to have David think he was merely being an arse than to have him know the truth.

"Excuse me, boys." David nodded to the children at the table and stood. Lionel stepped away from the table, and David followed, crossing his arms and glaring at him.

"You want me to pay a call on an *old friend* with you?" His voice dripped with bitterness and hurt.

Lionel felt that hurt deep in his chest, right along with the physical pain that had been keeping him up nights. "Yes. Eastleigh isn't the sort to sequester himself, even for his own good, if he feels there are entertainments to be had. I know a man who might just have seen him at entertainments of a particular sort."

David's crossed arms tensed and his eyes burned. "It isn't Jewel, is it?"

Lionel let out an impatient breath. "My, but we're fixated, aren't we?"

"I don't know, are *we*?"

Lionel pressed his lips together and glanced off to the side for a moment, debating whether it was easier to let David persist in believing he had lingering feelings for Everett. He didn't—especially not now that he'd seen how happy Everett was with Patrick Wrexham—but letting David believe that had served its purpose.

He focused on David once more. "I was referring to Lord Roebuck," he said, keeping his voice down in spite of the fact that the children surrounding them wouldn't have the first clue who Roebuck was or what sort of entertainment he enjoyed.

David's countenance softened by a hair. Lionel watched, fascinated as usual, as David's expression flashed from emotion-driven to businesslike. Watching the interplay of thought and feeling David was prone to was as good as a cabaret, as far as Lionel was concerned.

21

"You think Roebuck might have some sort of information about Eastleigh's whereabouts?" David asked.

"If Eastleigh is, in fact, in London, I believe Roebuck will know about it," Lionel answered.

"What makes you think so?" David started for the door.

Lionel marched after him, his muscles relaxing and his mood improving as they slipped into the familiar pattern of work. "Most gentlemen attend bacchanals and tableaux of the sort Eastleigh enjoys for the pleasures of the flesh." He kept his voice down as they passed near the table with Betsy, Ivy, and Merrily, then continued out to the hall. "Roebuck attends for the pleasure of watching other men make fools of themselves. He says it's far more entertaining than what's on display."

"He's not wrong about that," David agreed.

A faint smile tugged at the corner of Lionel's mouth. Once again, he and David were in step with one another, figuratively and literally, as they waved a quick goodbye to Stephen and Max on their way out of the orphanage and as they reached the street. He liked feeling as though he were in accord with another man, as though they were parts of a single machine working in unison. It was why he enjoyed sex so much. There was nothing so soothing or satisfying as symbiosis with another soul, and that went double where David was concerned. Triple, even, and sex had nothing to do with it. He would have traded every ounce of the certain kind of prestige he'd built up over the years to be in permanent mental, emotional, and physical synchronicity with David.

Which was why it was a tragedy that his machine was so hopelessly broken.

"Are you certain Roebuck is in London?" David asked as they strode toward Cromwell Road to flag down a cab. "Aren't most of his set at their country houses this time of year?"

"He would be, had he not been forced to sell his country estate to an ambitious industrialist three years ago," Lionel answered. "He uses gout as an excuse not to travel out of London these days, but the truth is that he has nowhere else to go."

David huffed a laugh. "A fate shared by more than a few members of the once-shining nobility."

"Times are changing," Lionel agreed with a shrug as a cab spotted his raised hand and slowed to pick them up. "I predict we'll see the end of the golden age of the British nobility before the end of our lifetimes."

"You think so?" David held the cab's door open, sending Lionel a curious look.

"I'm certain of it," Lionel said as he hopped into the carriage.

It was all so simple, all so blissfully ordinary. They weren't fighting, and they weren't flirting. They were just two men who worked together and cared about each other, having an inconsequential conversation as they went about their day. And even though Lionel had to hide his wince as he settled himself gingerly into his seat, terrified of finding new sores once he finally reached home that evening and shed his clothes, he wouldn't have traded that moment for the world.

"My brother is the lucky one," he continued the conversation after giving the driver directions to Roebuck's home in Mayfair.

"Who, Phineas?" David asked.

"Phin is a genius." Lionel nodded. "Either that or the luckiest bastard England has ever seen. Not only has he made quite a pretty penny with his salacious novels, he married an American dollar princess and secured our middling gentry family name for generations to come."

"And does he support you with any of that hard-earned income?" David asked, one brow raised.

"Darling, I support myself," Lionel said with a look of mock offense.

David laughed. Lionel's heart threatened to turn to jelly in his chest and his cock stiffened. It was a miracle that burst of movement didn't cause him to growl in pain, but there was no denying the progress of his affliction. And it wasn't as though he could do anything about an untimely erection one way or another. All he could do was settle back in his seat, seeking out the most comfortable position possible, breathe in the scent of David in the enclosed space, and listen to him chatter about the income Dandie & Wirth had received due to the investigation into the kidnapping ring and the new cases he'd taken on as their reputation for untangling Gordian knots grew.

By the time they reached Roebuck's townhouse, Lionel was almost happy. He managed a cheery smile that was close to genuine as David offered him a hand down from the carriage—a brief moment of physical contact that he treasured—and walked with him to Roebuck's front door.

As expected, all Lionel had to do was give his name to the butler, and within a minute, he and David were being escorted through the somewhat threadbare townhouse to a private, family parlor near the back of the once-grand home.

"Lionel Mercer, as I live and breathe." Roebuck limped across the cozy parlor to greet them, wearing a huge smile and a summer suit that had been fashionable five years ago. "What a pleasure to have an unexpected visit from a dear, old friend."

"Michael, you must forgive me for being a bad friend," Lionel said, fully in character.

He met Roebuck's outstretched arms of greeting with a hug of his own and a quick buss on Roebuck's lips that was certain to have David green and writhing with jealousy. Roebuck lingered in the hug, sliding his hand subtly down Lionel's side in a gesture that brought up a wealth of bittersweet memories. Lionel's body reacted on its own, like it always had, but he stepped away, ignoring the urges he'd denied for years.

Sure enough, David's expression had gone stony, but Lionel ignored that as well.

"Come, sit down," Roebuck said, gesturing toward

the room's faded furniture. "Introduce me to your handsome friend and tell me why it's been so long since I've seen you." His tone and the way his eyes traveled quickly over Lionel's form implied the word "naked" at the end of his sentence.

"Michael, this is my dear friend and business partner, Mr. David Wirth." Lionel made the introduction.

"From the law offices of Dandie & Wirth," David said with a clenched jaw and an outstretched hand.

"Law offices?" Roebuck shook David's hand, lighting up at the strength of David's grip, then gestured for David and Lionel to sit. He sat himself on a chair opposite their sofa. "Am I being sued?"

"No, no, nothing of the sort," Lionel laughed. He shot a sideways glance to David, who was not amused by his easy manor or the flirtatious glances he sent Roebuck. "Mr. Wirth and I are spearheading an investigation," he said, leaning his elbow on the arm of the sofa and gazing at Roebuck with carefully calculated adoration. He'd always caught a great deal of flies with the honey he served in his previous occupation than he had with the sort of businesslike directness David preferred to use. "I believe that you might have vital information that could crack our case wide open." He poured every bit of innuendo he could into his words, fingering the upholstery of the sofa as if he were running his fingers over Roebuck's delicate parts.

David was as tight and brittle as a bundle of kindling beside him.

"What sort of information, my boy?" Roebuck asked, licking his lips and sweeping a glance over Lionel.

Lionel let him look, shifting slightly to give him more to look at—though the man would be horrified if he could see what was under Lionel's finely-tailored suit.

David clenched his hands together in his lap and writhed, radiating anger.

"I need to know if Eastleigh is in town," Lionel said, cutting right to the heart of the matter. It would have been cruel to drag things out, both to David and to Roebuck. Roebuck wasn't going to get what he wanted out of the interview, and David would only suffer from the spectacle if Lionel teased Roebuck into thinking he might.

"Eastleigh?" Roebuck pretended to ponder the question, but the glint in his eyes and the smile he couldn't hide told Lionel everything he needed to know. Roebuck knew, and Lionel knew how to get him to share.

"You don't happen to know which hole he's hiding in, do you?" Lionel chose his words carefully, meeting Roebuck's eyes with a coquettish smirk, biting his lip.

Roebuck hummed, pretending to think. He squirmed in his seat, obviously aroused by the interaction. "I didn't think Eastleigh was the sort to hide in holes," he said.

Lionel continued to grin as though Roebuck might be handsomely rewarded for his information, but inwardly he huffed with impatience. He wasn't in the game anymore, and surprisingly, he didn't want to be. "Eastleigh, Lord Castleford, and Lord Chisolm are responsible for kidnapping children and selling them into sexual slavery," he said outright, without sugar-coating the truth at all.

Roebuck's flirtatious expression hardened. "Good Lord." He thought for a moment, then repeated, "Good Lord," with more feeling. "I thought the man was escaping creditors. I had no idea it was something so...so odious."

"I'm afraid so." David took over the conversation, sitting forward. "Enough evidence to convict Eastleigh has been gathered by Scotland Yard, but the man himself has gone into hiding. Anything you can tell us that might help capture him would be greatly appreciated."

Roebuck's mouth hung open. He glanced from David to Lionel. "I only wish I knew his exact whereabouts," he said. "I saw him at Gavin's theatricals just the night before last."

"So he is in London?" Lionel asked, shifting forward and changing his tactics to show deepest empathy for the sudden emotional distress Roebuck was under.

"He was two days ago."

"You poor thing. This must be such a fright." Lionel slipped off of the sofa, barely managing not to wince, and sank to his knees on the carpet in front of Roebuck's chair. He took the man's hand and patted it, glancing sympathetically up at him.

Roebuck sucked in a breath, his face splotching with color, his gaze heating. They'd been in those relative positions before, and it had always ended well for Roebuck. Very well.

"I *wish* I knew where Eastleigh was," Roebuck said, clasping Lionel's hands with both of his. "You must believe that I would tell you in an instant if I knew, dear boy."

"I know you would, I know." Lionel softened his voice, speaking to Roebuck as though he were in trouble and needed comfort.

Roebuck grinned at him, his expression turning fond and hazy.

David cleared his throat and stood. "We really shouldn't dawdle," he said in clipped tones. "Time is of the essence in this investigation."

Roebuck's grin took on a knowing edge. He leaned closer to Lionel. "Is he your someone special these days?" he asked, quietly, but not so quietly that David couldn't hear.

"No." Lionel leaned closer to Roebuck and whispered, "He's still mad about his former lover."

David flinched, as though he'd heard the comment, even though Lionel had whispered.

"Ah, I see." Roebuck leaned back, then moved to stand. Lionel stood with him, still holding Roebuck's hand. "In that case, you wouldn't, er, like to come by one evening to relive old times?"

Lionel gave Roebuck the fondest smile he could with David standing right behind him, making his presence known in every fiber of his body. "I'm no longer in business," he told Roebuck with a wink, patting his hand, then letting it go. "Haven't been for years."

"More's the pity," Roebuck chuckled. "It's a shame to let that gloriously perfect body go to waste."

David choked, then fell into a coughing fit.

Lionel sent Roebuck a flirtatious wink before stepping away. How woefully mistaken the man was. There hadn't been anything gloriously perfect about his body for years.

"Thank you so much, dear friend, for the information you were able to give us," he said. "You've no idea how useful it will be."

David continued to cough. Lionel stepped over to his side and thumped his back. That only caused David to glare at him and flinch away, stomping out of the room. Lionel laughed, pretending the whole thing was amusing, but inwardly he groaned. He would pay for his methods of extracting much-needed information from Roebuck for days, by the look of things. Just because David knew all about his colorful past and said he accepted it didn't mean the man wasn't ragingly jealous when faced with it.

"If you will excuse us," Lionel said, as graciously as possible, following David to the door.

"Oh, just one other thing." Roebuck stopped them as they reached the hall, hurrying after them. "You mentioned Castleford."

Lionel's pulse quickened. David stopped coughing and turned back to Roebuck.

"He's in Manchester, you know," Roebuck went on.

Lionel exchanged a look with David. In an instant, they were back in symbiosis, all business. "Isn't that what Lord Clerkenwell said?" Lionel asked.

"It was." David turned to Roebuck. "Do you know where?"

"I've never been to Manchester myself," Roebuck said, looking as delighted as a puppy at being able to share important information. "But there was some chatter at Gavin's about how droll it was that Castleford had taken up residence at a brothel called The Silver Serpent."

"The Silver Serpent." David repeated, as though committing the name to memory.

"I thought both the name and the fact that Castleford was in residence at a brothel named after an animal—what with that ridiculous menagerie he used to keep—was notable," Roebuck went on. "I trust you can find something useful in that?" He clutched his hands together in front of him as if saying a prayer.

"I'm sure everything you've told us is invaluable, Michael." Lionel broke away from David long enough to approach Roebuck for a quick kiss. "It was such a pleasure to see you again. I only wish we had more time to spend together." He stepped away, returning to David's side. It wasn't exactly a lie. Roebuck was a good sort and appreciative as a lover. But even if those days weren't far, far behind Lionel, there was the tangle of his relationship with David to deal with.

And that was a tangle he had to deal with sooner rather than later.

"That was a ridiculous and shocking display," David mumbled as Roebuck's butler escorted them out of the house. He all but vibrated with fury and jealousy.

"Don't pretend you don't know who I am and what I was," Lionel snapped as they reached the street. "Jealousy is not becoming on you."

David grabbed his arm, yanking him to a stop before Lionel could move closer to the corner and hail a cab. The sudden stop ignited his already inflamed skin, and he winced.

"There's something you're not telling me," David growled.

Guilt and dread at being caught quivered through Lionel, but he jerked out of David's grasp and stood straighter. He wasn't caught. He'd been careful. There was no way David knew he was sick.

"Darling, there are a great many things I'm not telling you," he said with practiced calm, eyeing David the way he had Roebuck. The difference was that the desire and the longing Lionel felt for David was real. It was the most real thing in his crumbling life. David opened his mouth to snap a reply, but Lionel cut him off with, "Fortunately for us, there are a great many things that Roebuck has told us. And if we're smart, we'll use those things as swiftly as possible to bring Lord Clerkenwell's investigation to a close."

He knew he'd won the point when David clamped

his mouth shut and huffed out a breath through his nose. "We're not finished talking about this," he said, stomping on and holding up an arm to wave at passing cabs.

Lionel watched David's back for a moment, watched the strong lines of his shoulders and the fierceness of his gait. His heart ached within him. David was beautiful in every way, healthy and hale. Lionel would have given anything to wrap himself around the man and show him every trick he knew, bring him every drop of pleasure he'd learned how to share in his past. He would have kept David sighing and happy for the rest of his life and poured his whole heart and soul into it. But that possibility was gone now with no chance of recovery. The only thing Lionel could hope for now was revenge on the man who had destroyed everything.

CHAPTER 3

*H*e was being childish, behaving like a green boy with his first lover. David scolded himself for the pointlessness of his jealousy as a cab drew close to the curb and he gave the driver directions to The Chameleon Club. Lionel was right. He'd known who Lionel was and how he'd made his living before John hired him from the very start. He knew how remorseless Lionel was about his past dalliances as well, how proud he was of the connections those dalliances had formed, how useful they'd been in any number of private investigations, and how they'd helped untangle hundreds of sticky situations for Dandie & Wirth's clients.

Knowing solved nothing.

"Are you going to look like an alligator who's swallowed a lemon tree the entire way to the club?" Lionel asked as he settled into the carriage's backward-facing seat. He winced slightly as he leaned into the cushion.

David wouldn't even have noted the expression except that Lionel almost never let any sort of discomfort show.

"I do not—" he started, but gave up, huffing a breath through his nose. He crossed his arms and stared out the window with narrowed eyes as the carriage lurched into motion, thinking himself the worst sort of fool. He'd wanted Lionel for years. How could he not? The man was elegance and power wrapped up in a gorgeous package, and he knew it. Lionel was arrogant, but he deserved that arrogance. He was a tease, but he was never cruel. The electric attraction that had existed between the two of them for years was enough to explode the new, incandescent lightbulbs being installed in homes and businesses all over the city. David had always been uncomfortable with Lionel's past, but that discomfort had existed in the back of his brain, out of sight, out of mind.

Until the confrontation with Everett Jewell had dragged the past out into the open.

"I heard what you said to Roebuck back there." David shifted to stare at Lionel—who was, of course, staring hard at him with an unreadable look in his deep, blue eyes.

"Yes, dearest, I believe hearing what I said to Roebuck is the cause of your horrid mood at the moment," Lionel said with a sharper than usual edge to his voice.

David clenched his jaw for a moment before forcing himself to relax and lower his arms. "I mean what you said about John, about me still being in love with him."

"Aren't you?" Lionel arched one refined eyebrow, the sharpness in his eyes like a drawn sword, ready for battle.

David wouldn't be intimidated. "Aren't you still in love with Jewel?"

"No," Lionel answered without pause. He held David's gaze for another moment before sighing and rubbing a hand over his face in an uncharacteristic show of exhaustion. "Could we please let the fucking past die?" he asked, pinching the bridge of his nose. "And I mean that literally."

More than anything, David wanted to fight—not because he wanted to keep the past at the forefront of his mind, but because at least fighting with Lionel would represent the sort of intense, personal interaction that he craved with the man. "Things have changed between us in these last few weeks," David found himself saying, against his better judgement. "Neither of us can deny that. Jewel is at the heart of it."

"Everett has nothing to do with it," Lionel said, voice weak, shoulder sagging, as he glanced out the window.

David ignored the comment. It felt too much like a theatrical way to divert his attention. "We can have only one focus right now," he said. "We need to put every last drop of our energy into hunting down Eastleigh, Castleford, and Chisolm. Lord Clerkenwell is counting on us. Those children are counting on us. It would be unforgivable if we let our personal struggles get in the way of that mission."

"Agreed," Lionel said, glancing at David. His head

was still lowered in apparent exhaustion, and the way he looked across at David came off as vulnerable and strangely erotic.

Which was the last thing David needed in the confined space of the carriage, the scent of Lionel's cologne tickling at his nose, and too much at stake to pause to appreciate it. His reputation as a man who could get things done was on the line. And yet, he wanted Lionel to give in and trust him, love him, even more than he wanted to prove to the world he was worthy.

"I'm not still in love with John," he said. "I'm only saying that once, so that it's out in the open and we can move away from it."

He studied Lionel's expression to see whether the man believed him, but, as always, Lionel was difficult to read.

"Eastleigh is in London," he went on. "Castleford is in Manchester. We have corroboration of that now."

"So you believe Roebuck's word?" Lionel straightened, his expression registering victory.

David clenched his jaw. "The man seems sincere enough. I don't know his character as well as you do," he paused before admitting, "but I trust your judgement when it comes to the measure of a man's character."

Surprise registered on Lionel's porcelain-pale face for a moment before settling into a pleased grin. "I'm glad we've settled that, then." He sat a bit straighter, more like his usual self, and cleared his throat. "I'll go talk to Phineas as soon as possible."

"Phineas?" David frowned. The carriage lurched to a halt near the door to The Chameleon Club. He almost wished the club was farther from Mayfair so that their conversation could have continued. "What does your brother have to do with it?"

"Eastleigh is in London," Lionel said, as though David were dense. "And Hillsboro said his brother, George, is in London as well. I doubt Eastleigh will come out of hiding, but George Eastleigh is a drunken degenerate who cannot resist a good party, especially one where the wine and spirits flow freely."

The driver opened the carriage door, and David shifted to step out. When he turned to wait for Lionel, he caught Lionel's face pinched with discomfort once again, but only for the briefest of seconds.

"What does Phineas have to do with any of this?" he asked, offering Lionel a hand.

Lionel stared at his hand as though it might burst into flame, but he grasped it anyhow. "Phin's delightful, American wife hosts the very best parties," he said, stepping down to the pavement. "If Lenore throws a party and invites George Eastleigh, it will be child's play to corner the man after he's imbibed more than his fair share and to pry information about Eastleigh's whereabouts out of him."

David registered surprise as the two of them walked up to the club's discreet front door and let themselves inside. "That's not a half bad plan," he said.

"It's a brilliant plan," Lionel said off-handedly.

They nodded to the attendant at the front desk, then headed through the marble entry hall and up a small flight of stairs to the main corridor of The Chameleon Club. In spite of its drab appearance from the street, The Chameleon Club was one of the most elegant locations in London. It was the unofficial home of The Brotherhood, an underground organization for men who loved other men. Unlike the ribald molly houses and less than reputable establishments dotted throughout the city for men like them, The Chameleon Club was a safe gathering place for social and business interaction. Indiscreet activities were strictly discouraged, although the club did host the occasional ball or musical entertainment where those who felt inclined could dress as whatever gender they preferred.

David liked the place because of the aura of seriousness and normality it conveyed. He'd transacted more business in the club's vast dining room, where he and Lionel headed for a bite to eat, than he had on the premises of his own law office. David suspected that Lionel enjoyed the place for its many social benefits, as evidenced by the number of men who waved in Lionel's direction in greeting as they made their way to the buffet table, where lunch was waiting for any paid-up member of the club to enjoy. Still others, like Niall Cristofori, the celebrated playwright who sat at one of the tables to one side of the room, notebooks and papers strewn across the table in front of him, enjoyed the club because of the safety it provided for men like them, who lived in constant wariness of the Labouchere Amendment and the trouble it could cause.

"Wirth, Mercer. I hear congratulations are in order." David was stopped as he approached the buffet table by a dark-skinned man of striking appearance.

"Percy." David nodded to him in greeting, taking Samuel Percy's outstretched hand when it was offered. "I'm not sure what you're congratulating me about when it's you who deserves the praise, or so I hear. Is it true your latest symphony is to be performed at the Royal Albert Hall?"

Percy shifted to shake Lionel's hand. Lionel smiled at the man, though he seemed distracted by a man in a grey suit who had just risen from a table in the corner. The man nodded to him before heading out of the room.

"Gentlemen, if you will excuse me," Lionel said, stepping away without another word.

David's mouth hung open at the unusual rudeness of Lionel's exit. Lionel never passed up an opportunity to bask in praise or to court artistic types, like Percy. "Sorry about him," he told Percy. "I don't know what's wrong with him these days."

"Perhaps it's fatigue from your efforts to bring down that notorious child kidnapping ring," Percy said, gesturing for David to join him at the table where Cristofori was set up. "News is all over London about your part in foiling the ring. Well done, man." He thumped David on the back as he sat.

"The work isn't done yet," David said, nodding to

Cristofori in greeting. "We still have to catch the men who spearheaded the whole vile endeavor." Cristofori had been an integral part of the plot to attempt to capture those men in Yorkshire. Judging by the dark expression that came over his usually friendly face, he wanted them captured as badly as David did.

"You'll do it, I'm sure," Percy said, all smiles and encouragement.

"If Lionel and I can avoid murdering each other," David added under his breath, glancing across the room to where Lionel and the man in the grey suit had fallen into conversation.

David would have given anything to know what the two were saying. A completely irrational part of him was convinced Lionel was arranging some sort of assignation with the man, in spite of the fact that they wore absolutely serious expressions. He cursed himself for even entertaining the possibility. What business was it of his anyhow? He needed to rein in his ridiculous emotions.

Far too late, he realized the table had gone silent and Percy and Cristofori were staring at him. He sighed, face heating with embarrassment at letting his feelings show, and turned away from Lionel.

"Forgive me, but that's not the look of a man about to go to war with someone," Percy said.

Cristofori chuckled. "Then you're not seeing it correctly. David and Lionel have been at war for years now."

David's brow flew up in surprise. "Have we?"

41

Of course, they had, but he'd never dreamed their friends and acquaintances had witnessed the heat and tension between the two of them.

Cristofori set down the pen he'd been twirling between his fingers and sent David a frank look. "You don't need eyes to see a conflagration like the one that exists between you and Lionel Mercer."

For a split-second, David considered arguing the point and claiming he and Lionel were merely business partners. It would have been a pointless argument that only made him look foolish, though. He couldn't afford to look foolish. Not when the majority of his clientele were men from The Brotherhood. He needed them to see him as an indomitable force, not a lovesick puppy.

"It doesn't make a lick of difference," he said. "Lionel isn't interested in me, and even if he were, he's taken a vow of celibacy."

That seemed to surprise Percy, but Cristofori shrugged. "Celibacy is a convenient way to say you're exhausted by maintaining a busy social life and are looking to settle down," he said. His expression darkened by a hair before he added, "I know the feeling."

David leaned back in his chair, taking that into consideration. He knew enough about Cristofori to know the man had never had anything close to Lionel's sort of "social life", though David recalled the man having a lover or two over the years.

"Perhaps your friend simply needs a little nudge," Percy said, humor flashing in his dark eyes.

David laughed weakly. "Nobody nudges Lionel. He does whatever the hell he wants, whenever he wants. Or doesn't do it," he added as an afterthought. The idea brought far more melancholy to David than he thought it would.

"Why accept that as an answer?" Cristofori asked with a poorly concealed grin of amusement. "I've seen the way he looks at you. It's almost as blatant as the way you look at him. You're both dying for a fuck."

David arched one eyebrow at Cristofori, trying to decide whether to feel irritated or sheepish, then peeked at Percy.

Percy was fighting a smile. "If you ask me, the two of you should break a few vows and possibly a bed as well, if only once. Lay all your cards on the table, bugger each other senseless, and see how you truly feel."

David blinked at Percy, wanting to be offended by the suggestion. He certainly wasn't used to his friends talking to him so bluntly. Not in the way Lionel was used to it. Lionel could have an entire conversation where every third word was innuendo and flirtation without so much as cracking a smile. David felt his face heating at the barest hint that he and Lionel should work out their differences horizontally.

And yet, a deep part of him felt that was exactly what he and Lionel needed to do to address whatever it was between them. He needed to stop being such a prude and get Lionel naked and on his back, the way he wanted him, as soon as possible. Maybe then he could get the arrogant peacock out of his system and return to what really mattered—business.

Although, if he were honest with himself, Lionel would never be fully out of his system. His cock wasn't the organ most interested in the infuriating man, his heart was.

"Seducing Lionel would only cause trouble at work," David mumbled, crossing his arms and staring at the tablecloth.

"Correct me if I'm wrong, but don't you already have trouble at work?" Cristofori asked.

David didn't answer with words, but he did shoot Cristofori a narrow-eyed look across the table.

"What is the worst that could happen?" Percy asked, genuine in spite of the fact that his eyes sparkled with mirth. "You're already at loggerheads with each other. A bit of an experimental fuck couldn't make things worse, could it?"

It could make things much worse, David thought to himself. It could also break through the infuriating barrier that only seemed to be growing thicker between them. If they could diffuse the boiling tension between them by giving in to the lust they both felt, then perhaps they could move beyond it and focus on bringing Eastleigh and the others to justice.

"Gentlemen, you've given me a great deal to think about," he said, thumping the table and standing. "Thank you."

"Don't thank us until you're sighing in satisfaction

after bedding that handsome partner of yours," Percy said.

David clenched his jaw, wishing Percy would keep his voice down. He darted a glance around, but fortunately, no one seemed to be listening.

"Do whatever needs to be done," Cristofori said, far more circumspect. "Just don't lose focus on what is truly important. I visited Castleford's estate last week. I saw the things those three men are capable of. Catching them is a top priority for all of us."

The gravity of Cristofori's words went a long way to making David feel if not better, then at least normal. "We won't let you down," he said.

He turned to march out of the room in search of Lionel. They hadn't had their lunch yet, and they needed to discuss their plans not only for drawing Eastleigh out, but going to Manchester to locate Castleford and figuring out where exactly Chisolm was up north. It was one thing for Lionel to fly off to pay a visit to Roebuck when it provided them with useful information, but David didn't know who the man in the grey suit who Lionel had snuck off with was.

His suspicions had only just begun to weave themselves into stories of what Lionel might be up to when David stepped out into the main hallway. Lionel and the unknown man stood close together all the way at the far end of the hall. Lionel reached into his pocket, took out his wallet, and handed the man a bill. In turn, the man passed Lionel a small, blue medicine bottle.

As soon as David saw the exchange, he jumped back into the dining room, careful not to be seen.

"Laudanum?" he murmured to himself. There was no way to tell. Medications of all kinds came in blue bottles. So did other kinds of narcotics. Earlier that spring, he and Lionel had been involved in a case where a member of The Brotherhood had been accused of dealing in opium. It had been a false accusation, but David had learned a few things about how opium was taken in the process of having his client exonerated.

He blinked. Lionel had been a fountain of information about opium during that case. At the time, David had written it off as a remnant of Lionel's former life, but that sort of addiction could explain why Lionel had been behaving so out of character in the last few weeks. Perhaps he was right and it had nothing to do with Jewel after all.

But no, Lionel was far too fastidious to take opium. Or so David assumed.

He leaned out into the hall, hoping to see something more that would decide the matter one way or another, but Lionel and the man in the grey suit were gone. David stepped farther into the hall, craning his neck as though looking harder would make Lionel suddenly materialize at the end of the hall. He gave up in short order, though. Lionel wasn't there. Instead, David was left with the feeling that far more things were wrong than he had imagined.

CHAPTER 4

$\mathscr{L}$ionel's brother's London home was only a short walk across Hyde Park from The Chameleon Club. Phineas had used all of the profits from his secret literary endeavors, as well as the sizeable income he'd received from his delightful and enigmatic dollar princess bride, Lenore, to purchase the stately Kensington Home. It was a far cry from the crumbling edifice in Hampshire that the two of them and their sisters had grown up in.

Lionel couldn't help but smirk as he climbed the stairs and knocked on Phin's artistically designed front door, then stepped back to await the butler. What the Mercer family had lacked in ready money in their early years, they'd made up for in cleverness, ingenuity, and a devil-may-care attitude. Lionel had made his money and pursued his interests one way, Phineas in an entirely different way, and their sisters in still other ways. They were all exceedingly proud of themselves and each other, no matter how shockingly unconventional and downright immoral their methods were.

Which was why Lionel felt an immense sense of relief as Phin's butler, Jameson, invited him into the house and escorted him to the bright and airy family parlor at the back of the mansion.

"Lionel." Phin rose from his ornate writing desk beside an open set of French doors that led to a courtyard garden. "This is an unexpected pleasure. I don't usually expect visits from you during working hours."

"Is that Lionel?" Lenore called from the garden. Lionel strode over to greet his brother with a warm embrace and spotted an extremely pregnant Lenore attempting to hoist herself out of the cushioned chaise where she'd been reading. "What are you doing here on a Tuesday afternoon?" she asked, waddling into the parlor, a hand on her back.

"I've actually come on business, Princess." Lionel greeted his sister-in-law with a wide smile, though he hugged her only gingerly. Logic told him there was no way he could transfer his illness to Lenore or to his unborn niece or nephew, but emotion refused to let him take the risk.

"Business?" Phin arched one eyebrow, looking wary. "It's never good news when a solicitor comes calling on business."

"Fortunately for you, I am not a solicitor," Lionel said with a smirk.

"You might as well be, what with the way you practically run that office." Phin crossed to the center of the room, where several chairs and a sofa were arranged ideally for conversation. He gestured for Lionel to have a seat on the sofa.

"Try telling David that I run the office and see what he has to say about it," Lionel laughed, though his emotions bounced around his chest like they were a rubber ball thrown by a child, ricocheting madly out of control, as he spoke.

"I dare say David would have more than a few choice things to say about you, if I asked him." Phin's mouth twitched in the corner. The man knew too much. He always had. It was what had made his career as an author of erotic fiction so successful and what had gotten him into trouble more times than Lionel could count.

"I believe I shall leave the two of you alone for this conversation," Lenore said as she waddled toward the door, her eyes sparkling with mirth and mischief. "Something tells me it isn't going to be appropriate for delicate, female ears."

"It most certainly will not be." Lionel matched her look of mischief with one of his own. "You must do everything possible to keep those ears of yours as pristine and innocent as possible."

"Of course," Lenore said as she swept out of the room, blowing Phin a kiss as she went. In fact, Lionel knew as well as anyone that Lenore was as far from the angelic, domestic ideal of a gentry wife all of the educational pamphlets put out by ladies' improvement societies said a woman should be, as Lucifer was from Gabriel. She'd been downright wicked in her pursuit of Phin, and Phin, for his part, had encouraged and outmatched her wickedness. Which was why Lionel loved the both of them so desperately.

All the same, as soon as Lenore left him and Phin alone, Lionel's fond smile vanished. He took the seat Phin had offered him, not bothering to hide his discomfort as he did. There was no point in hiding anything from Phin anyhow.

Phin's expression turned grave as he settled into one of the chairs. "Do you need an extra cushion?" he asked. "Or a stiff drink?"

Lionel laughed. "No, I've got everything I need, thank you very much." He patted the pocket of his jacket where the bottle of Dr. Sullivan's latest experimental mixture of herbs and mercury was nestled.

Phin narrowed his eyes slightly and studied Lionel. "It's come back, has it?"

Misery of the sort Lionel had hoped he would never know roiled through his gut. "I believe so," he said, sitting stiffly and staring at his hands, folded in his lap. "The sores started to appear again several weeks ago. I held out hope that they were the result of bad fish or something equally insignificant."

"You don't think they are?" Phin arched one eyebrow.

Lionel shook his head, feeling far too much like he was confessing some sort of inner filth to his brother.

Phin, more than anyone, knew all of the vagaries of the life he'd lived in his earlier years. They'd had the same tastes and the same penchant for experimentation, though they carefully and deliberately avoided running in the same circles. Phin knew exactly what sort of dangers a life like that could leave one prone to. He'd taken the risks himself, and he had never judged Lionel for anything.

Lionel raised his eyes slowly to meet his brother's. "The dormant period is over. I have to accept that. And we both know what comes next."

Phin winced, shifting in his chair and pinching his face in sympathetic distaste. "Have you visited a doctor? Are you certain it's...you know?" The fact that his brother couldn't even bring himself to speak the name of the dreaded disease showed just how horrible a diagnosis it was.

"Syphilis, Phin." Lionel faced the problem head on. "It's syphilis. And it's more than just a death sentence."

"But are you certain?" Phin pressed on. "I never was comfortable with that doctor who pronounced the sentence all those years ago."

Lionel barked a laugh. "Pronounced a sentence indeed." He drew in a breath, sitting straighter and shaking some of the tension from his shoulders. "Why should either of us have any reason to doubt the truth?" he asked. "Consider the method of transmission. Consider the men I was in contact with at the time."

His stomach boiled with rage at the memory of that

particular summer. He'd always been painstakingly careful, both in whom he'd chosen to interact with and in how he'd taken care of himself. Illness was entirely avoidable if one knew what one was doing and did it diligently. All it took was a single mistake, a wolf in sheep's clothing, set loose in the sheepfold with the expressed intent of poisoning another member of the flock, for everything to fall apart.

"Have you consulted a physician about this recurrence?" The firm concern in Phin's tone shook Lionel out of his bitter thoughts.

"I've sought the advice of Dr. Sullivan at the club," he answered with a sad sigh. "He is the only physician I trust not to judge me or run off to the authorities and make my life a living hell on the presumption of how I contracted it." In fact, it was nearly impossible for men like him to receive any sort of fair and effective medical treatment, especially for afflictions of a sexual nature, without ending up in trouble with the law. Lionel knew far too many young men who had died in prison after seeking out help on Harley Street.

Phin continued to stare at him for several beats of silence. "I don't like it," he said at last. "I want you to see my physician, if only for a fresh set of eyes viewing the situation."

"Absolutely not." Lionel shook his head, feeling his face heat. "I refuse to have any eyes viewing the situation at all at the moment." He knew it was pure vanity, but it was horrible enough to gaze at his once perfect body in a mirror to see what had become of it, let alone allow someone else to see the damage.

Phin let out a disapproving breath. "I still don't think it's wise—"

"I need you to throw a ball," Lionel cut him off.

Phin pursed his lips, frowning sharply. "You're not going to let me be your brother and solve this problem for you, are you?"

"It cannot be solved," Lionel snapped. "The issue of the ball can be, however."

A brittle moment of silence followed as the two of them stared each other down. Lionel loved Phin with his whole heart, more than he'd loved almost anyone in his life, but there were some burdens he couldn't bear to let even Phin to carry for him.

At last, Phin sighed and shook his head. "Why do you need me to throw a ball?"

Relief that the conversation could finally move away from him and onto important matters of work softened Lionel's stance. "David and I have been charged with the task of hunting down the three noblemen at the center of the recently thwarted kidnapping ring."

"I read all about that," Phin said gravely, steepling his fingers and tapping his lips with a frown.

"We have ample evidence that Eastleigh is hiding somewhere in London," Lionel went on.

"And you think me hosting a ball will draw him out?" Phin's mouth quirked into a grin.

"Of course not. Eastleigh isn't that stupid," Lionel snorted. "His son, George, however, is."

Phin nodded, his grin growing. "You want me, or rather, Lenore, to host a ball that will prove irresistible to George Eastleigh? So that you can get the lout drunk and trick him into divulging his father's whereabouts, I assume."

Lionel smiled freely. "You see? This is why we make such a magnificent team, as brothers and beyond. We think similarly."

"We do." Phin laughed, then shrugged. "I'm sure Lenore would be delighted to host a ball, in spite of being so close to giving birth. In fact, I dare say Lenore would jump at the chance to host a ball *because* she's so vastly pregnant. She loves thumbing her nose at London society."

"Don't we all?" Lionel grinned as he stood. "Do you think she could manage it by Friday?"

Phin jerked to a stop halfway through standing himself, his eyes going wide. "You want Lenore to host a ball worthy of drawing George Eastleigh in just three days?"

"You and I both know that Lenore would revel in the chance to pull off such a feat," Lionel said.

"She would at that," Phin laughed.

"Good. So is it safe to presume that we may proceed with the plan?" Lionel took a step toward the door.

"Provided we are both correct about Lenore's fondness for the unusual and shocking, yes." Phin thumped Lionel's back as they crossed the room together.

Lionel tried not to grimace at the burst of itchy pain the brotherly gesture caused. The sores hadn't affected his shoulders during the original outbreak of his illness. The fact that his whole body was inflamed now was the very worst of signs, as far as he was concerned. The inflammation was a thousand times worse in every spot where his clothing rubbed against his skin.

"Let Lenore know she can consult me with any questions she might have about this grand fete," Lionel said as they stepped into the hallway.

"I will." Phin walked a few steps with him before pausing, forcing Lionel to stop as well. When Lionel turned toward him, Phin asked, "Does David know?"

A wave of unaccountable sorrow washed through Lionel, made even more miserable by the power of the love that drove it. He shook his head. "No. And he's not going to know either."

Phin's look of disapproval was so sharp Lionel was surprised it didn't draw blood. "You can't keep hiding something this important from him."

"I can and I will," Lionel snapped.

"He loves you, and you love him. He'll figure the truth out on his own, and that will only add a sense of betrayal to the misery of loss."

Damn Phin for being so erudite and so right.

"Love is irrelevant," Lionel said through a clenched

jaw. "I've kept my distance for his own good, for his safety."

"And made both of you miserable in the process." Phin crossed his arms, daring Lionel to say he was wrong.

Lionel let out a breath and shook his head. "I would rather make him miserable than make him sick," he said, swallowing the well of unhappiness admitting as much spawned in him.

Phin dropped his arms and shook his head. "I am sorry, Lionel. I can't imagine what this must be like for you."

Lionel sighed and shrugged. "A more fatalistic man would say this is the price of sin."

"But you don't believe sex is a sin." Phin arched an eyebrow at him.

"I don't." Lionel tilted his chin up. "I still don't. But stupidity is. I will be paying for my stupidity for the rest of my life, short though it may be."

"See a physician," Phin implored him.

Lionel didn't want to hear it. He marched on, his heart heavy. "As soon as you can guarantee that doing so won't make things worse than they already are."

Phin looked as though he wanted to argue, but instead, he followed after Lionel, hugging him one last time as they reached the door. "I will always be here if you need me," he said. "For anything. No matter what."

The offer squeezed Lionel's throat tight, not because of its sentimentality, but because he knew just how lucky he was to have a brother who supported him. Most men like him had no one. Which was why he was more determined than ever to bring evil men to justice and to go out of his way to make certain that the things that had happened to him never happened to another soul.

Lionel strode back across Hyde Park, lost in the jumble of his thoughts and emotions. He would have begged Lenore to host her ball that evening if he'd though it were possible. Friday would be soon enough, though. Which meant the mission Lord Clerkenwell had given them was well underway.

That only provided a tiny shred of consolation, though. Catching criminals was simple compared to navigating matters of the heart. Particularly when dire illness meant that absolutely nothing could be done to act on the love that had filled every corner of his being and infused every breath he took for years. Phin had a point about David's right to know, though. Not for the first time, Lionel contemplated getting on with things and just telling him. He didn't even want to think about the consequences, though. He had nightmares about the affection and lust in David's eyes turning to disgust when he looked at him.

Lionel's thoughts were so troubling that he didn't bother hailing a cab to take him halfway across London to the offices of Dandie & Wirth. It didn't matter that it took nearly an hour to cross through the city on foot and left his feet blistered and aching, he needed the time and the exertion to sift through his thoughts. And if he were honest with himself, he needed the pain of abrading the sores that covered his torso as punishment for his long-ago mistakes. Those mistakes weren't entirely his fault, though. He would make the man truly responsible pay.

By the time he reached the office, he was overheated, in agony, and sweating through his clothes. Any other day, he would have been appalled with himself for letting his appearance slip. To make matters worse, David wasn't alone in the office once Lionel stepped through the door. Lord Marshall Scott sat on the sofa facing David, perched tensely on the edge, crushing the brim of his hat as he spoke to David in hushed tones. Lionel fought off the spike of jealousy that came with seeing David speaking so intensely with another man. It was only a matter of time before David abandoned his unrequited feelings for Lionel to run off with someone else. Once that happened, Lionel would welcome the madness that generally went hand in hand with his condition.

"Lionel." David straightened, then leapt to his feet, his eyes lighting first with affection, then with concern as he took in Lionel's appearance. "I wasn't expecting you back here today."

The urge to reply with something flippant and flirty was overwhelming, but the melancholy that seemed lodged in Lionel's soul, like a burr in a saddle, kept him from his usual teasing.

"I only came by to let you know that the ball is on," he said, nodding briefly to Scott. "Phineas has assured me that my darling sister-in-law would relish the opportunity to host a ball on Friday night. Things can proceed as planned."

He nodded, then turned to leave.

"Lionel, wait." David chased after him, stopping him with a hand around Lionel's arm.

The touch was electric. Lionel sucked in a breath, slowly raising his eyes to meet David's. There was so much warmth and concern in David's eyes that it took every ounce of Lionel's willpower not to lean in and kiss him. David's lips were formed for kissing. As many times as he'd dreamed about them, Lionel hadn't touched them once.

"I need to speak with you in private," David went on, his voice hoarse.

For a moment, his hand tightened on Lionel's arm. The heat in his eyes deepened to the point where Lionel felt it in his gut. David's look, combined with his scent, had Lionel's prick stiffening automatically. With a supreme force of will, he tugged his arm out of David's grip and grinned coyly.

"Private?" He infused the single word with innuendo, mostly because he knew that was what David expected.

The increased flush that came to David's cheeks proved he'd hit his mark. David nodded to the door to his office, then started in that direction. "This will only take a moment," he told Scott as he crossed the room.

Lionel followed him. "I'm surprised a man like David

would sell himself short like that," he said to Scott, airy and suggestive.

Scott snorted in response, hiding his laughter with a hand to his mouth.

As soon as David led Lionel into his office and shut the door, Lionel lost his coquettish grin. "What do you have to say?" he asked, stiff in more ways than one.

To Lionel's surprise, David's grin widened instead of falling away. "I feel bad about the way things have been between us for the past few weeks," he said.

A thousand warning bells sounded in Lionel's mind. David was playing some sort of game with him, and David never played games.

"What do you want?" he asked bluntly.

David held perfectly still for a moment, his gaze fixed on the silver pin of Lionel's cravat. Lionel could practically smell the grind of gears as David thought about whatever scheme he was hatching.

"You," David answered at last, swaying forward and fingering the amethyst inset in Lionel's cravat pin. "I want us to be on good terms again."

Lionel let his eyes go wide, but stopped himself from showing any other reaction. David was attempting to seduce him. The signs were all there. It was as laughable as a grammar school student attempting to tutor Isambard Kingdom Brunel in industrial design.

"You do?" he asked, guarding his reaction and playing along to see where David was headed.

"Yes," David said with an inviting smile—a smile that

caused a genuine reaction of longing, in spite of the fact Lionel knew it was a ruse. "I want to make things right between the two of us, especially since we need all of our powers of concentration to track down Eastleigh and the others."

"What do you propose to make things right?" Lionel cursed his voice for turning soft and willing.

David shrugged, brushing lint that Lionel was certain wasn't there from his shoulder, his touch lingering near Lionel's ear. "I'd like to treat you to supper," he said. "Somewhere extravagant and expensive."

Lionel grinned in spite of himself. "My two favorite words."

"I know they are." Mischief filled David's eyes, which, in turn, filled Lionel's gut with butterflies and made his trousers tighter. "How about The Savoy, tomorrow night?"

Lionel's butterflies fluttered harder. The Savoy was not simply a restaurant, it was a hotel. David clearly had more in mind than a meal. The temptation of it sent Lionel's heart racing, even as that same heart threatened to break. He would have given anything to take David up on his offer.

He had to reveal the truth. He'd let things drag on too long as it was. Damn Phineas for being right about every-thing. Perhaps supper at The Savoy was exactly the catalyst Lionel needed to break his silence at last.

"All right," he said, letting out a breath and

wondering if the moment to let go of his secret had come at last. "Supper at The Savoy it is."

David blinked in surprise. His smile widened, as though he was surprised Lionel had given in so easily. "I'll make the arrangements." He took a step back, still smiling. "We can discuss business as well as a few other things."

"Of course, we can." Lionel wanted to burst into laughter. Only David would immediately think of discussing business at what was blatantly supposed to be a romantic rendezvous, particularly a rendezvous he himself had set into motion. It was so poignantly David and so lovely that tears threatened to sting the back of Lionel's eyes. How was he ever supposed to maintain his distance and drive a permanent wedge between himself and David when David was the dearest thing he had ever known in his life?

CHAPTER 5

*D*avid paced the lobby of The Savoy hotel early on Thursday evening, more uncomfortable than he'd ever been in his life. It wasn't the new, tailored suit he'd bought on impulse the day before, although that was certainly tight in places he wasn't used to and made him feel a little too much like a fashion plate. He was attempting to seduce Lionel Mercer, after all—a man who lived and breathed fashion and had probably been a French modiste in a former life. It wasn't the way time ticked by at an alarming pace as he waited either. He pulled the pocket watch out of his waistcoat pocket and checked it again. Lionel would be arriving any moment.

David replaced his watch and drew in a breath, squaring his shoulders and trying to pretend that the elaborately-dressed young woman at the other side of the lobby wasn't studying him as though he were a piece of meat she'd like to devour. If she was what David thought she was, the moment Lionel walked through the door she'd know she had the wrong end of the stick. But her embarrassment would be nothing compared to his own if his plan failed.

He cleared his throat and strode closer to the door, glancing out onto the rainy street to see if he could spot Lionel approaching. He was utterly mad to think supper at The Savoy was a good idea, and even madder to have reserved a private suite for that supper. He was an idiot for thinking that he even had the power to seduce Lionel, let alone that it was a good idea. He'd let Cristofori and Percy talk him into something foolish, he was certain. He shook his head and paced away from the door, deeper into the lobby. When had he become the sort of man who allowed others to influence him and lead him into temptation?

When Everett Jewel had reminded David that Lionel had a past, that was when. Now he had to prove he was better than Jewel, more desirable and a better lover. He could blame Cristofori and Percy for leading him astray all he wanted, but there was no escaping the truth. As humiliating as it was. David checked his watch one more time to keep his shoulders from slumping into sheepishness as jealousy threatened to overwhelm him. Jealousy was an ugly beast and one that got in the way of work. He was a damn fool for giving it so much power over him.

"Don't you look a treat?"

David jumped, sucked in a breath, and whipped

around at the sound of Lionel's voice. He'd been so preoc-
cupied with his thoughts and checking his watch that he
hadn't seen Lionel enter the hotel. He was there now,
though, looking like a dream in a suit of lavender-hued
grey with a blue cravat that matched the color of his eyes.
He shook out the umbrella he'd been carrying, but his
eyes were fixed on David and a mischievous, sultry grin
pulled at the corners of his sensual mouth, as if he knew
more about what David was up to than David himself
did.

David had never wanted any man so much in his life.
The sight of Lionel left him breathless. The coquettish-
ness of Lionel's smile threatened to turn his knees to jelly.
His reaction to the man who had been his friend and
business partner for four years was as potent as if he were
seeing a vision across a crowded room for the first time.
So much so that he couldn't speak.

At least, not until the woman who had been watching
him from across the lobby laughed out loud.

David blinked, the reality of the situation and the
world he had to deal with, whether he wanted to or not,
slammed back into him. "This?" He glanced down at his
impeccable, new suit with a shrug. "It's something I had
in the back of my wardrobe."

Lionel's grin turned downright amused and his eyes
glittered with fondness. He absolutely saw through everything David was doing. But then, he always had, which
was yet another reason David adored him. And if he
didn't gain control of his emotions immediately, Lionel

would run circles around him and never let him live his foolishness down.

As if letting him off easy, Lionel said, "I, for one, am famished. I assume you have a table reserved?" He turned toward the entrance to the hotel's restaurant.

"Actually, I secured us a room." Heat flared up David's neck that must have been visible in his face. His entire body suddenly felt as though it were engulfed in flames. His plan was unforgivably stupid, and stupidity wasn't something he was used to. If he were wise, he would call the whole thing off. He didn't need to prove himself to anyone, least of all Lionel. Fully a dozen emotions flickered through Lionel's expression within the course of a second, from amusement to regret to arousal. None of them did anything to steady David's nerves.

"You reserved a private room?" Lionel arched one eyebrow.

"Of course." David shrugged, feigning insouciance. "We would never be able to discuss the particulars of the mission Lord Clerkenwell has given us in a crowded restaurant."

Lionel's mouth twitched, his eyes smiled, and he tilted his head with a hum. "Yes, of course. Lord Clerkenwell's mission. We certainly couldn't discuss that in public." His soft voice dripped with sarcasm.

He knew, blast him. Lionel knew exactly what David was up to. And yet, he'd agreed to the meeting and he's shown up precisely when he said he would. Knowing that sent a shiver of hope through David. The night might end up horizontal after all.

David cleared his throat and nodded toward the Savoy's elevator. "After you," he said.

Lionel didn't move. His cheeky grin faltered a bit, and the spark in his eyes turned thoughtful as he stared at the elevator. David would have given anything to know what Lionel was thinking, and why a sudden sadness swept over him. Lionel might be able to read him like one of the cheap, erotic novels that his brother wrote, but the man was as much a mystery to David as the secrets of the orient.

At last, Lionel drew in a breath, coming to some sort of a decision. "You're right," he said, as though they were in the middle of a complex argument. "It would be best to have the necessary conversation in private."

He started forward, back stiff and head held high. David followed, catching up to him as they reached the elevator and stepped inside.

"Seventh floor," David told the elevator attendant.

"I'm impressed." Lionel was back to barely containing his amusement with David's plan as the elevator whisked them up to one of the hotel's highest and most luxurious floors. "Quite elaborate for a business meeting."

The elevator attendant peeked covertly at first Lionel, then David, a flush coming to his round face. David swallowed, praying the young man didn't get ideas and alert the hotel manager. Then again, as likely as not, the manager of a hotel like The Savoy saw everything there was to see under the sun.

As soon as the elevator reached their floor, David stepped out, fishing in his pocket for the room key. He walked halfway down the hall, Lionel following him with a smirk as though he were trying not to laugh. That smirk only grew wider when David let them into the room. David had had supper brought up to the suite already. Several covered dishes were set out on a table draped with a white tablecloth and set with silver and china worthy of Buckingham Palace.

"I took the liberty of ordering for you," David said, rushing to the table and covering his nervousness by removing the silver domes from each dish. "I know you dislike heavy meals in the evening, so it's just roast chicken instead of anything fancy." He deliberately avoided looking at Lionel as Lionel strode to the table to survey their feast.

"You always were so kind and considerate toward me," Lionel said in a low purr.

David turned toward him as he set the domes on a side table next to the room's sofa, wondering who was supposed to be seducing whom. "Would you like me to hold your chair out for you?" he asked, attempting to be funny.

"I believe that is how these things are usually done." Lionel moved toward one of the chairs on his own. "But in this case, I think I can be trusted to seat myself."

A grin twitched at the corner of David's mouth. He

was terrible at seduction, but at least he still had the feeling deep in his chest that he and Lionel were friends, and that as clumsy as he was being, they were laughing together.

That warm thought was cut short as David noticed the pinch of pain on Lionel's face as he sat. It was gone as soon as he saw it, but David knew what he'd seen.

"Are you all right?" he asked with concern as he took a seat himself.

"My dear, you know I have never been *all right*." Lionel made a joke out of the question, but there was something deeply serious in his eyes.

"You've always been perfect to me." David knew it was a risk, but he reached across the corner of the table, taking Lionel's hand.

Lionel's face lit with surprise for a moment before falling into sadness. He let out a breath and twined his fingers with David's, but said nothing. David's heart dropped to his stomach, meeting a pool full of butterflies there. The tenderness of Lionel's touch sent one message, but the wistfulness in his lowered eyes sent an entirely different one. He'd played his cards too early and too unskillfully, and it was going to cost him.

"David, there's something I need to—"

"I telegraphed John about helping us search Castleford in Manchester," David spoke at the same time, pulling his hand away and snatching up the cutlery at his place.

Lionel froze as though he'd clapped eyes on Medusa.

Color splotched his porcelain complexion. "You what?" he asked in a strangled whisper.

David recognized the jealousy in Lionel's eyes. It was the same sort he felt in himself every time Jewel was anywhere near Lionel. Recognizing the all too familiar emotion did nothing to make David feel justified in his own jealousy or right about bringing John into a conversation that was supposed to lead to intimacy.

He covered the surge of guilt in his gut by saying, "John has been in Manchester these last four years. He knows the city far better than either of us. If anyone knows where The Silver Serpent brothel is, it will be John. So it was only natural to seek his help."

He cut into his chicken, not daring to look at Lionel to gauge his reaction to the admission. But it was impossible not to note the way Lionel continued to hold stock still for a few more seconds. David could feel Lionel's gaze boring into him.

At last, Lionel moved, picking up his cutlery with stiff movements and carving into his chicken as though it had personally offended him. "And what did your handsome former paramour have to say?"

David swallowed a bite, unsurprised that it seemed to stick on the way down. He reached for the glass of wine he'd poured when the meal had arrived and took a gulp to avoid choking. Once his throat was clear, he said, "John is more than willing to help." Against his better judgment, he added, "And I told you there's been nothing between the two of us for years."

Lionel hummed, unconvinced, and took a small bite.

"He has another lover now anyhow," David went on, uneasy with the awkwardness he felt at the statement.

"Huzzah for him." Lionel didn't look at him as he reached for his wine.

David pursed his lips, wondering how the conversation had veered so off-track so quickly. The tension that crackled between them was as far from the way he wanted to prove to Lionel that he was worthy of trust and intimacy as could be. He took another, long drink of wine, glad he'd ordered an extra bottle, just in case. The only way he was going to be able to get through the evening and stick to his original course was if both of them had considerably more to drink. And seeing as the entire point of the evening was to get on with things and have their way with each other to put the tension behind them, the sooner they were drunk the better.

"I didn't tell John everything," David went on, reaching for the open wine bottle and refilling Lionel's glass once he set it down. Lionel sent him a pointed look, as if he knew why David was refilling his glass. "He only knows that we're hunting for Castleford and that he may be at The Silver Serpent."

"What more is there to tell?" Lionel asked, his tone still clipped. "As I recall, John was a clever chap. He'll put two and two together and come up with four."

"So what if he does? He might be able to neutralize Castleford for us. Then we can focus our efforts on Eastleigh and Chisolm."

Lionel stabbed a vegetable on his plate. "And you would be satisfied with letting your former lover tie up the loose ends of a case the two of us have been working on for months now?"

David sighed, catching the bitter implication of Lionel's words, his appetite all but gone. "I would rather Castleford be brought to justice swiftly so that we can conclude this sorry business once and for all. I'm ready to move on to other things."

He reached across the corner of the table once more, laying a hand on Lionel's forearm. Lionel stiffened, shifting his glance to stare at David's hand. David could feel the tension radiating from Lionel, but he couldn't for the life of him tell if it was anger, jealousy, or desire. The three emotions weren't that far apart.

"Have some more wine," he said when the silence between them grew uncomfortable, reaching for his own glass. "And tell me why you've started using opium."

Lionel huffed an irritable breath through his nose and set his cutlery down with a clatter. "I am not taking opium, David," he snapped. "I never could stand the stuff."

"So you've taken it before?" David frowned over the lip of his wine glass.

"One dabbles in all sorts of amusements when in company with others who enjoy those sorts of things," Lionel answered cagily.

"Lionel." David put down his own cutlery, fixing Lionel with a scolding frown. "Opium is highly addictive. It ruins lives and leaves better men than you useless."

"There are better men than me?" Lionel asked with false offense, teasing, but also genuinely put out.

"You know what I mean." David reached for his hand again. "I saw you purchasing something that looked very much like opium at the club the other day."

Lionel laughed, but all of the color drained from his face. "That wasn't opium," he said, pushing back from the table and standing with a wince. He crossed the room to one of its large windows and looked out across to the Thames.

David stood and followed him. "I'm concerned about you," he said. If outright seduction wouldn't work to get Lionel into bed, then perhaps genuine concern and affection could. "I know you've been unhappy lately."

"Unhappy?" The single word dripped with misery as Lionel twisted to face him. He let out a sharp laugh. "You have no idea, love."

David saw his chance to move in and be the support Lionel needed. It was his chance to break through the wall between them and get what he'd wanted for so long. Maybe one night of passion to get the itch out of his system wasn't what he truly needed. Maybe what he needed was to ignite the fire of something that would last far longer than one night.

"I want to make you happy, Lionel," he said, shifting closer and slipping a hand around Lionel's waist. "I'm tired of us dancing around each other and denying what we both clearly want. It's interfering with work." He brushed his free hand across Lionel's flushed cheek.

Instead of giving into him, Lionel laughed and took a step back. "Oh, yes. We wouldn't want to interfere with work, would we."

David's throat squeezed tight as the echo of John saying those same words in a similar tone swooped down on him like a vulture attacking the carrion of that dead relationship.

"Work doesn't suddenly cease to matter simply because love exists," he said, reaching for Lionel as he tried to march past and holding him to his spot.

"Love?" There was something fragile in the way Lionel spoke the single word and in the vulnerability in his eyes.

"I love you," David blurted before sense kicked in and he stopped himself. He pulled Lionel tighter into his arms. "I have for a long time. And you know it. You knew it before I did." With each statement, he brought his mouth closer to Lionel's.

"Don't do this," Lionel said on a shaky exhale, leaning into David. His gaze dropped to David's lips, just a few inches from his. "Don't you dare do this."

"Why not?" David deftly undid the buttons of Lionel's jacket so that he could slide his hands along the lithe lines of Lionel's slender but decidedly masculine body. "I know you want it. I know you miss it."

"I miss it so much I can hardly sleep at night," Lionel admitted on a passionate sigh that sounded close to tears.

He trembled under David's touch, like lightning in a bottle.

"Then give in. Let me love you, and love me in return," David whispered. "Even if it's just sex. We both need it desperately."

Lionel let out a breath that didn't quite form into words. His body was rigid with emotion, though it felt as though he were trying with every fiber of his being not to let their bodies touch.

David was through with supporting Lionel's resistance. He tugged him close, pressing his body against Lionel's and dropping a hand to his backside to force their hips together, in spite of Lionel's reticence. He slanted his mouth over Lionel's as he did, kissing him with all of the passion he'd stored up over years of longing.

Lionel moaned deep in his throat, breaking with a force that could have knocked David backwards. He slid his arms around David's back and shoulders, working his lips against David's and sliding his tongue into his mouth. The suddenness of his ardor was overwhelming, and in a flash, David went from the aggressor to the helpless receptacle of Lionel's desire. Their tongues tasted each other, and their lips and teeth sought more and more from each other as time ceased to exist. David's whole body was instantly aroused, and he ground his growing erection against Lionel's.

"Bed," he managed to whisper hoarsely between fervent kisses.

Lionel yanked back as though David had spit on him. His blue eyes glowed with lust and misery. "No," he said, taking another step back. His face pinched into a silent sob. "How could you do this to me?" He raised a hand to cover his mouth as tears spilled from his eyes.

"How could *I* do this to *you*?" David knew his question was too loud and too incredulous, but his overwrought senses were reeling.

"You don't know—" Lionel shook his head and darted past David, sprinting for the door.

David rushed after him. "Lionel, wait! Don't run out on me. We have to talk about this. We have to resolve things."

Lionel reached the door, wrenching it open, one hand still held over his mouth as tears streamed down his face. He stepped out into the hall, but immediately lurched back into the room, dropping his hand. His face drained of all color, and his eyes went wide, his lashes wet and clumped.

"I won't let you run out on—"

Lionel jumped toward him, clapping a hand over David's mouth to silence him. David reeled in confusion and attempted to struggle out of Lionel's sudden, wild grip.

Until he heard the voices in the hall.

"—bring itineraries and whatever else you need as soon as I can, but you know Scotland Yard is watching me now too."

David's eyes went as wide as Lionel's. Lionel had left

the door to their room open on purpose. The voice of George Eastleigh was as clear as day in the hotel hallway.

A muffled, male voice answered George. David could have sworn it was Eastleigh himself, but without seeing the man, he couldn't be sure.

"All right," George sighed. "But I'm attending Mercer's ball tomorrow night. It will have to wait until after then."

The other voice grumbled something, then a door shut. George muttered, too low for David to make it out. The sound of footsteps followed, then a bell as the elevator was summoned. A few, long seconds later, the elevator arrived and its doors opened. "Lobby," George said, then was whisked away.

Only when the hallway was silent again did Lionel remove his hand from David's mouth. "Eastleigh is hiding out at The Savoy," he whispered, both shocked and impressed.

"We have to alert Lord Clerkenwell at once," David whispered in return. He marched to the door, intending to close it and continue discussing business with Lionel in private. They had a mountain of things to talk about.

But Lionel pushed past David, striding out into the hall as though intent on escaping before David drew him back into the web of passion he'd barely managed to get out of moments before.

"I'll tell Lord Clerkenwell," he said, keeping his voice low once he was in the hall. "And I'll tell Phineas and Lenore that they don't need to throw their ball after all."

"No." David shook his head. "The ball has to go on. We can't be certain George Eastleigh was here to speak with his father. Neither of us saw who was in that room."

Lionel let out a breath as though he, too, had put together the pieces of the puzzle. "Lord Clerkenwell will need a stronger confession to go on if he is to send officers here to arrest Eastleigh."

"Exactly." David nodded. His stance softened and the whirlwind of desire he'd felt with Lionel in his arms at last returned. "Come back inside," he said with as much heat as he could manage.

"No." Lionel lowered his head, his face pinching as though he might cry again. "I really can't." He glanced up, meeting David's eyes with a level of pleading that left David breathless. "Trust me."

"How can I trust you when you won't—"

Lionel didn't let him finish. He marched away at a swift pace, not even waiting for the elevator to return. He turned into the stairwell at the far end of the hall and disappeared from David's view, leaving him as desperate for answers and relief as ever.

CHAPTER 6

After the torturous mess at The Savoy on Thursday night, Lionel committed the very worst of sins on Friday—cowardice. Instead of going in to work as usual to help David with Lord Clerkenwell's mission and any one of the numerous other cases Dandie & Mercer had on their slate, he stayed home. He told himself that he would spend the day with Phineas and Lenore, helping them prepare for that night's ball and briefing them on the sighting of George Eastleigh at the hotel. Instead, he found himself in an interminable argument with his new laundress about the proper way to starch collars and press suits. The woman didn't seem to know which end of a washboard was up, but he'd had to hire her in a hurry after his previous laundress retired.

Even that was merely an excuse to avoid the truth. Lionel only argued with the dull woman because he needed a way to vent the overwhelming emotions that his interrupted night with David had raised in him. Their kiss was exactly what he'd dreamed it would be for years. David have been aggressive without being a bully, and tender without being a sap. The feel of David's body pressed against his, even with layers of clothing, had ignited every delicious, carnal instinct that Lionel had fought to subdue for years. He would never forget how David tasted—of wine and herbs—or the way David's hands felt on his body as they clasped desperately together.

David would likely never forget the way he'd burst into tears, like a complete ninny. Just thinking of it had Lionel's eyes stinging with frustration and longing as he marched headlong through Kensington toward Phineas's townhouse after lunch. One kiss had come perilously close to destroying the willpower Lionel had built up over the last few, agonizing years. He knew who he was, always had known. He was a man who enjoyed sex and had always partaken of it the way ladies partook of afternoon tea with friends. Boxing up that part of himself and putting it away on a dusty shelf for four years had been hard enough, but to have David, a man he genuinely loved, attempt to unwrap that box and savor its contents was too much.

By the time Phin's butler showed him into the ballroom as Lenore supervised decorations and Phin supervised her, Lionel was trembling with pent-up emotion.

"You look awful," Phin greeted him, leaving his position holding a garland of hothouse roses to cross the room.

"Thank you for your kind words." Lionel smirked. "You always were such a supportive sibling."

"Someone has to keep you from preening like a prize peacock." Phin embraced him.

Lionel's eyes went wide at the affectionate greeting, which was tighter than usual, and his heart soared with maudlin, filial affection, even though Phin pressed a few of Lionel's sores a little too tightly. "Now I'm certain I'm dying," he said, trying to sound cheerful.

"You're not dying." Phin took a step back. "There are loads of men who live long and productive lives while battling...." He finished with a significant look.

Lionel stared flatly at him. "And there are plenty who go mad, have their noses fall off, and die in agony. But let's not discuss this when your charming wife and half the servants are within earshot. I've come to tell you that Lord Eastleigh is very probably hiding out at The Savoy." He danced from subject to subject so fast that Phin would be forced to abandon all inquiries about his health.

As expected, Phin blinked in bafflement, working his jaw for a moment before forming his thoughts into words. "If Eastleigh is at The Savoy, why is my heavily pregnant wife exerting herself to host a ball this evening?"

"It's not an exertion," Lenore called from a table of candlesticks nearby, proving that she was listening in on everything Lionel and Phin said. "I'm delighted to do it."

Lionel gestured to Lenore as though she had made his point for him. "Besides," he went on. "Scotland Yard needs more than a suspicion to go on if they're going to send officers to The Savoy to arrest Eastleigh. We need to extract a full confession from George Eastleigh with enough witnesses overhearing it to allow Lord Clerkenwell to act."

"I see." Phin nodded sagely. "But that doesn't explain why you look like a wet cat trapped in a kitchen grate."

Lionel balked, feigning far more offense than his desperate, aching heart felt. "I do not now, nor have I ever, looked like a cat in a grate. I resent the implication."

"Why are you bothering me and my wife when you should be hard at work with your partner?" Phin asked, crossing his arms.

Phin was just enough of a bounder to mean his double-entendre deliberately. He knew about Lionel's feelings for David better than anyone. And yet, Phin was enough of a kindred spirit that Lionel wanted to spill everything instead of evading the topic.

"He kissed me last night as part of an attempt to seduce me, and it was glorious," he said in a rush. "But there isn't a damn thing I can do about it, as much as I might want to. Now if you will excuse me, Lenore looks as though she could use someone with a far keener eye for style than your housekeeper to organize the flower arrangements."

Lionel marched away without letting Phin share whatever opinion he must have had about the state of his love life. He couldn't bear to think of it anymore himself. Dwelling on David's kiss only reminded him of everything he wanted with a passion but would never be able to have.

The rest of the afternoon passed in a haze of ballroom decorations and assisting Lenore in picking out a suitable gown for the evening's fete. Lionel was a favorite of Lenore's, and she drew him into making decisions about every aspect of the ball. As grateful as he was for the distraction, Lionel knew it was all a ploy. Lenore must have heard every word he'd said to Phin and was empathizing with him in the subtlest way possible. She stayed by his side even after he dashed home to change into a suit worthy of a ball, then returned to greet arriving guests with her. Lord Clerkenwell and his wife had already arrived and taken up a position in the ballroom to monitor the evening, but Lionel and Lenore had been tasked with observing the arrivals.

"There's George Eastleigh," she whispered, spotting the bastard before Lionel did, half an hour after guests began to arrive.

Lionel stood straighter, his expression hardening into a scowl as he glanced to the door as George arrived. The man was alone, dressed in a suit that had been fashionable three years ago, and already half drunk, by the look of it. He stumbled over the top step as he entered the house, then leered at the Duchess of Waterford, whose arm he grabbed to steady himself. The man was an embarrassment, and extracting the necessary confession about his father's whereabouts would be child's play. All

Lionel had to do was corner the man in one of the parlors with enough witnesses on hand to—

His thoughts came to a dead stop as he glanced past George to find David strolling into the house. The sight of him stopped Lionel's breath in his lungs and sent his heart racing. David's expertly-tailored suit was cut to emphasize the broad line of his shoulders and his trim waist, the green cravat he wore with it set off his dark eyes, and his dark hair was combed so that not a strand was out of place. David had already spotted Lionel and looked as though he'd eyed a slice of cake that he was ready to devour. The spark in David's eyes was enough to burn the world down and Lionel with it.

Lionel didn't realize he was holding his breath until David made his way across the foyer to stand in front of him. He let it out in a rush, but was unable to form words.

"Lionel." David nodded to him with an intensity that made Lionel dizzy. "I missed you at work today."

Damn David Wirth and the hints of desperation and sweetness in his soft, tenor voice.

"Lenore needed my help preparing for the ball," he said, his own voice half an octave too high and breathless.

"I don't need you anymore," Lenore said, her expressive mouth pulling to one side in a grin.

Lionel pursed his lips and glared at her, fully aware there was as much affection as annoyance in his expression. He turned back to David. "Apparently, I have been dismissed."

"Then walk with me," David said, issuing it as a command rather than a request.

A burst of weakness shivered through Lionel. He had to admit he liked a lover who would take command.

But no, David was emphatically not his lover and never could be.

No matter how desperately he wanted it.

"George Eastleigh arrived moments before you," Lionel said, hoping to take the upper hand from the start and steer the conversation away from dangerous topics.

"I saw." David nodded ahead of them to where George had just entered the ballroom. "We need to keep him in sight at all times. I've no doubt he'll head straight to the refreshment table. Did Lenore provide strong wine for the night's festivities, as asked?"

"She did." Lionel let out a breath, his shoulders relaxing. The night would be about work after all. "And look, there he goes."

They entered the ballroom side by side just as George made a beeline straight to the table set with food and drink near the French doors that led out to Lenore's courtyard garden. George dodged through a few of Lenore and Phin's guests, knocking a marquess sideways before reaching the table and demanding service from a footman.

"I suppose it's just a matter of time now," Lionel said, nodding to Lord Clerkenwell in acknowledgement that he and David were tailing George.

"It's just a matter of time," David repeated, giving his words an entirely different inflection.

Lionel glanced sideways at him, unsurprised to find David studying him with a look of undisguised wanting. Lionel's gaze dropped to David's lips before he could stop himself. Every sensation their kiss from the night before had awakened in him roared large in his memory. He wasn't going to be able to resist for long, even though he knew he had to. Some fruits were just too juicy not to sink his teeth into, no matter how forbidden they were. Damn Chisolm and his conniving for landing him in this impossible situation.

As if all the ghosts of his past had heard the curse, Everett Jewel strolled up to greet him. Patrick Wrexham was right by his side, looking far more dapper than Lionel had ever seen him—which was clearly Everett's doing—but that didn't stop David from stiffening like a ship's mast in a storm and radiating distrust.

"Jewel," David growled, inching closer to Lionel.

Lionel couldn't decide whether he resented or adored the possessive gesture. "My, my, Officer Wrexham. You're looking quite handsome this evening." Lionel deliberately addressed Wrexham first, only acknowledging Everett with a bare nod.

"Not 'Officer' anymore," Wrexham said, shaking Lionel's hand. "I'm in private employ now." He shot a fond glance toward Everett.

Lionel's heart squeezed with regret in spite of himself. Everett had never been meant for him, and he didn't resent the man for finding happiness, not really. It was merely a bitter pill to swallow to know that the man whom he had once loved but who had abandoned him could find happiness in love when he never would.

"Rumor has it that the two of you have been charged with hunting down Chisolm and the others," Everett said, a fierce light in his eyes.

"Not that it's any of your business," David growled.

Lionel pressed his lips together and forced himself not to snap at David. "Lord Clerkenwell believes there are more tools at the disposal of private citizens in taking care of these sorts of things than would be available to a police officer," he said.

"He's right." Wrexham nodded. "Officers have rules."

"Whereas we all know there are no rules in love and war," Everett said with a wicked grin.

"Why are you here?" David burst out, turning fully toward Everett with a scowl. "It's a Friday night. Don't you have a show to perform?"

Everett's expression hardened. "I am between shows at the moment. I've chosen to take a bit of time off to recover from recent events." He glanced toward Wrexham with a smile.

"Perhaps a few months abroad would do you some good," David continued.

It was all Lionel could do not to roll his eyes. "Stop," he said flatly.

David turned a furious glance on him, but it quickly evaporated into exhaustion. Apparently, Lionel wasn't the only one of them who'd slept poorly the night before. That was no excuse for David to behave like a jealous idiot, though.

"Oh, look," Lionel said in a falsely cheerful voice, grabbing David's arm. "George Eastleigh is on the move."

In fact, George had only moved from the refreshment table to a small circle of painfully arrogant aristocrats that Lionel tried to avoid whenever possible, but Lionel dragged David away from Everett and Patrick all the same.

"Lionel," Everett stopped him, striding a few steps to catch up to them. David glared at the man. Lionel shot Everett an irritated look, warning him to back off and let the whole thing be. But Everett went on with, "When you find Chisolm, give him hell for me."

Lionel met his former lover's eyes with ruthlessness. "Right after I'm finished giving him hell for myself."

Everett's brow knit in confusion, but Lionel had neither the time nor the inclination to stand around explaining his words. He tugged David on, leading him around the outer edge of the increasing crowd of party guests and toward the French doors leading to the court-yard. He dropped David's arm as soon as he was certain David would continue to follow. He might have been friends with enough important members of society to have those who posed a danger to his life and liberty look the other way when he was obvious about his inclina-tions, but it was foolish and pointless to flaunt those incli-nations in public.

That didn't stop David from grabbing him around the waist and pulling him deliciously close once they were outside in the darkness of the courtyard, unseen.

"What the hell are you doing?" Lionel hissed, struggling against David's grip without actually wanting to free himself. "This isn't The Savoy. Any number of people could step out here and catch us at any moment."

"We have unfinished business," David said, backing them farther into the darkness, where several huge, potted palms had been placed beside one of the doors leading into the ballroom.

"Yes," Lionel agreed breathlessly. With David's arms around him, he could feel his resistance slipping fast. "The unfinished business of prying a confession about Lord Eastleigh's whereabouts from his son."

"You know what I'm talking about." David's voice dropped to a deep purr. He backed Lionel against the wall beside one of the doors, leaning into him.

Energy and excitement danced through Lionel. His cock jumped in anticipation as the scent of David enveloped him along with the night-blooming flowers in Lenore's courtyard garden. His knees threatened to give out as David's mouth moved closer to his. But every delicious, sensual sensation pulsing through him, reminding him of pleasure and better days and love, was matched by the pain and irritation of sores that were evidence of why he could never have what he longed for.

"You're only inflamed because you thought Everett was flirting with me," he said with a heavy breath, praying David would find it offensive enough to back off and leave his soul at peace.

"You're right." David nodded. "And I'm not proud of my jealousy. But it's there, so it's pointless to deny it. I wouldn't be jealous if I didn't long for you with every fiber of my being."

"Don't do this, David. Don't—"

Before Lionel could protest any more, David surged into him, covering his mouth with a kiss that turned Lionel's words into a deep moan of aching desire. In an instant, his mind scattered into a million pieces, like the stars visible above the edges of the roof that lined the courtyard. He reached for David, clung to him as though he needed the man to breathe and to live. Because he did. There was no point in living without him.

A moment later, he realized something was wrong. David's kiss held none of the amorous intensity of their kiss the night before. In fact, as soon as their mouths met, David froze. Their bodies were pressed together, but he wasn't moving a muscle. His lips were still against Lionel's, more like he was stopping Lionel from making a sound instead of attempting to kiss him into oblivion.

Then Lionel heard what David must have heard.

"...entrusted me with the family estates and fortune. I can't make heads nor tails of it all, though, which I tell him every day." The slurred voice booming just inside of the ballroom, beyond the French door, was, without a doubt, George Eastleigh's.

"Hang on," whoever George was speaking to said. "You say your father is here? In London?"

"Isn't he wanted by Scotland Yard?" a woman's voice said in a scandalized hush.

"What, that?" George boomed, careless of who might be listening. He snorted. "It's all a bunch of tush and nonsense, if you ask me. I've no idea why anyone would make scurrilous accusations against Father. He's one of the most powerful men in England, you know."

Lionel's body broke out in tingles from head to toe, and not simply because David continued to wrap himself around him as though they were two vines twining with the same tree. At least David shifted his mouth to the side so that both of them could breath. Lionel closed his eyes, digging his fingertips into David's sides, and prayed that one of the guests George was spouting off to would ask the question that would allow them to act, allow him to break free of David and focus on business instead of the pounding in his heart and his cock.

"You don't think your father is guilty of the accusations that have been made against him?" the man asked.

"Of course not." George sniffed. "Child kidnapping indeed. Father doesn't even like children. Why, he's utterly disowned my brother, Maxwell, because Max went and got himself involved in some silly orphanage."

Lionel arched an eyebrow. If that was truly the reason George believed Max Hillsboro had been disowned, then he was a block-headed idiot who got what he deserved.

"I've heard good things about Mr. Siddel's orphanage," the woman said.

"How can you disbelieve accusations against your father when a mountain of evidence was uncovered pointing toward his guilt?" the man asked.

"Please, please," Lionel whispered, eyes still closed, tilting his head back to rest against the wall and praying that Eastleigh would speak what needed to be spoken.

His eyes flew open a moment later as David leaned in to nibble at the stretched line of his neck, his tongue brushing against Lionel's pulse. The sudden movement was so intimate that Lionel gasped and fought to swallow a groan as his prick stiffened even more.

"Stop," he hissed, digging his fingertips into David's sides in a way he hoped hurt, though he doubted it could with the layers of clothing David wore.

"You beg for me one moment then tell me to stop the next?" David asked, leaning back far enough so that Lionel could see the heat and confusion in his eyes as illuminated by the light of the stars and the ballroom.

"I wasn't—" Lionel hissed in irritation, mostly because part of him had, in fact been begging for David. A part of him had been begging for David from the moment they'd met. "Eastleigh," he whispered, glancing toward the ballroom door.

"...will be resolved soon enough." George had gone on with his conversation.

Lionel tensed, praying they hadn't missed the confession they were depending on while distracted.

"But I don't understand," the woman said. "How are you communicating with your father when he is in hiding?"

This time, when Lionel tensed in anticipation, David stiffened as well. The effect pressed them even closer together, but for once, Lionel had something else to think about besides how much better their position would feel without clothing.

"Yes," the man said. "Where is your father?"

"At The Savoy, if you can believe it," George said with a laugh.

"Thank God," Lionel breathed as though bursting into the most magnificent orgasm of his life.

His tone must have been equally as climactic. As David pushed away from him, he made a sound as though it were agony to separate instead of doing whatever it took to make Lionel come in earnest, right then and there. David spared one final, hungry glance for Lionel before stepping into the doorway to surprise George Eastleigh.

"Did you just say your father is hiding at The Savoy hotel?" David asked, blunt and clumsy.

Lionel moved into the doorway as well, searching for Lord Clerkenwell and flagging him down eagerly, as George gaped and stammered.

"Yes, he is," the dolt sputtered. "Has been for a week."

Lionel thanked God for wine and idiocy. He grinned at David. "We've got him."

CHAPTER 7

It was an absolute miracle that David's bumbling interruption of George Eastleigh's conversation actually led to a confession that Lord Clerkenwell and his men could act on. It was a moment of victory, but as David left Phineas Mercer's house, along with Lionel and Lord Clerkenwell, guilt felt like a weight in his gut that he couldn't shake. He'd never behaved so irresponsibly in his life by virtually attacking Lionel in the middle of a public ball, and the shame of losing control of himself was a bitter pill to swallow. It was as if he'd set out to prove everyone who believed men like him were capable of nothing but lust and misbehavior right, and it went against everything he'd worked for in his life. But when it came to Lionel, he lost his head.

"I've had a small contingent of officers standing by near The Savoy," Lord Clerkenwell said as the three of them charged around the side of Mercer's house to the mews, not waiting for a carriage to be prepared and brought around to them. "My man, Smiley, will head straight to Scotland Yard to process the necessary paperwork for the arrest," he went on, referring to the man he'd sent immediately to work after George's confession, even before George was interrogated further.

"It's late," Lionel said in a distracted voice. "What if he isn't able to take everything through the proper channels before we confront Eastleigh?"

Lord Clerkenwell sent a deadly sideways glance to Lionel and David. "Smiley knows how to get things done."

The slightly sinister edge to Lord Clerkenwell's tone made David glad to be on the man's side. There was a reason a man like Jack Craig had risen from being the son of a whore to Assistant Commissioner of Scotland Yard and a newly-minted peer to boot. David was lucky to count him as an ally, and a large part of him was determined to duplicate the man's rise.

As soon as Lord Clerkenwell's carriage was prepared and the three of them were barreling across London toward The Savoy, David's focus of the mission to capture Eastleigh gave way to the sting of everything that had happened with Lionel. That sting wasn't made easier by the silence in the speeding carriage. David had taken a seat beside Lord Clerkenwell on the forward-facing side, which left Lionel sitting directly opposite him in the dark carriage. Every time they passed a streetlight, the ensuing burst of light illuminated Lionel's pale face and piercing eyes staring right at him. David had no idea if the intensity in Lionel's gaze was anger over the way he'd been manhandled or a desire for more. Either way, David couldn't stop staring at Lionel's lips, still flushed from kissing.

He had taken leave of his senses. That was all there was to it. David was convinced he was out of his mind. Taking Cristofori and Percy's suggestion to seduce Lionel had unleashed a carnal force within him that he would have been better off leaving alone. It interfered with work and respectability. But simply thinking that did no good whatsoever, as evidenced by the jolt of excitement that shot through him when his and Lionel's shins bumped as the carriage rattled to a stop in front of The Savoy. He couldn't backtrack and put his wild lust for Lionel back in the bottle where it'd been for years, but he didn't see any way he could move forward without risking the ruination of the one thing, the one man, who meant more to him than anything else.

"McQueen," Lord Clerkenwell called out to a plainly dressed man leaning against the side of a building as he hopped down from the carriage, David and Lionel behind him. "Ready the men. We have the evidence we need."

The man, McQueen, must have planned for the moment when Lord Clerkenwell would arrive to pull the trigger on the operation to capture Eastleigh. He nodded and straightened, seeming to transform from a humble vagrant to a man of command as he whistled and gestured toward a handful of other plainly dressed men along the street.

From there, things moved swiftly. Lord Clerkenwell enlisted the help of the hotel's chief concierge, who accompanied them upstairs. There was nothing David or Lionel could do to add to the mission, so they hung back, letting Lord Clerkenwell and the police officers move in. It was a relief of sorts for David to set aside his tumultuous emotions as he climbed the hotel's stairs by Lionel's side until they reached the seventh floor.

"It was that door," Lionel said, out of breath from exertion, pointing two doors down on the left side.

Lord Clerkenwell nodded, and he and his men moved forward. The hotel concierge fumbled for a ring of keys on his belt, but Lord Clerkenwell gestured for him to stand by and keep quiet. David hung back, Lionel swaying closer to him, both of them rippling with anticipation, as Lord Clerkenwell knocked on the door.

David held his breath, waiting to see if Eastleigh would answer and validate all of their efforts to bring at least one of the evil men responsible for so much misery to justice. The hallway was silent, even though Lord Clerkenwell knocked a second time, but it vibrated with anticipation. Lionel reached for David's hand, squeezing it tightly and sending David's heart soaring.

"Yes, yes, what is it?" Eastleigh's muffled voice sounded from behind the door a second before the fool opened it. From where he stood, David had a brilliant view of Eastleigh's gasp and look of terror as he realized he'd been nabbed.

"Lord Eastleigh," Lord Clerkenwell said in a commanding voice, unable to hide his grin of victory. "By order of Her Majesty and the Metropolitan Police, you are under arrest for the crime of child kidnapping and trafficking."

Lord Clerkenwell stepped boldly into Eastleigh's suite, forcing him backward. McQueen and the other officers moved in with him, and David and Lionel brought up the rear, stopping just inside the suite to watch the final act of Eastleigh's drama. The hotel concierge stood with them, gaping as though he were watching the final act of a drama on stage.

"W-what? No!" Eastleigh backpedaled through his suite, nearly toppling over a chair as he did. "You have no proof. I had nothing to do with it. This is a violation of my privacy."

Lionel snorted derisively by David's side, watching Eastleigh with narrowed eyes. David couldn't blame him one bit for taking vicious satisfaction in Eastleigh's demise. He himself felt a deep sense of satisfaction as Eastleigh—a once-powerful man who had demanded respect from society and provided a commanding presence in the House of Lords, but who earned that position by nothing more than his birth—burst into pathetic weeping and sank into a sofa.

"It wasn't me," he wept, covering his face. "It was

Castleford and Chisolm. They were the real ringleaders. I merely went along with what they said."

Lord Clerkenwell gestured to his men, who surrounded the sofa, looking ready to wrench Eastleigh to his feet by force as soon as Lord Clerkenwell gave the word.

"You know full well what evidence we recovered from Castleford's estate," Lord Clerkenwell told Eastleigh without a shred of sympathy in his tone. "You know how damning it is. Not even your cronies in the House of Lords will acquit you of the crimes we have proof you committed."

Eastleigh only sobbed in reply, crumpling against the arm of the sofa. His movements were so dramatic that David nearly laughed. He'd seen ingénues on the London stage who hadn't fallen into a stupor of misery as eloquently as Eastleigh.

"Come quietly and—" Lord Clerkenwell stopped, his mouth twitching into a bitter grin. "Well, I can't promise you a shred of leniency. But perhaps if you were to cooperate, I—"

Eastleigh jerked his head up. "Cooperate? I can cooperate." He shifted to sit straighter, though it was clear he was trembling from head to toe. "I can tell you where they are, Castleford and Chisolm."

David felt Lionel suck in a breath at his side. He twisted to look at Lionel, who had gone more pale than usual, though sharp splashes of color painted his cheeks.

Lionel's eyes were wide with what David could only describe as fury.

David squeezed his hand. Lionel blinked, his brow dropping into a frown. He shot a sideways glance to David, seemed to realize they were still holding hands, and jerked away, his jaw flexing with tension.

The entire exchange baffled David, but he didn't have time to think about it.

"Castleford is in Manchester," Eastleigh nearly shouted, jumping to his feet. He addressed Lord Clerkenwell for the most part, but shot a quick look in David and Lionel's direction. "He's underground, at a place called The Silver Serpent. You...you may find others that you've been looking for there as well."

David frowned. "What others?" he asked, his mind snapping fully into investigative mode, in spite of his continued awareness of Lionel and his mood right beside him.

Eastleigh turned to David as though he'd found an ally he could appeal to, but Lord Clerkenwell stepped into his path as Eastleigh attempted to approach him.

"You'll tell your story to me, not Mr. Wirth or Mr. Mercer," Lord Clerkenwell said. "And we already know about Castleford, so you'd do best to forget any hope of that paltry information helping your cause."

David shot a sideways glance to Lionel. In spite of Lord Clerkenwell's strong words, having Castleford's exact location confirmed by one of his accomplices was exactly the sort of information they needed to act.

"Chisolm, then," Eastleigh went on, appealing to Lord Clerkenwell. "He's in Hull."

Lionel went ramrod stiff, clenching his hands into fists. His sudden rage was so palpable that David was worried for him.

"He thinks he can escape England through Hull," Eastleigh went on, "either by boarding a ferry that will take him to a larger port in a foreign country or by bribing a fisherman to take him away. That's been his plan all along. He...he used to brag about how he would be the only one of us not caught in the end."

"Give me an address," Lord Clerkenwell demanded, stepping closer to Eastleigh in what looked like an attempt to intimidate the man.

"I don't know." Lord Eastleigh backed away from him, only to smack into McQueen, who had taken up a position behind him. McQueen grabbed Eastleigh's arms to restrain him, which caused Eastleigh to moan and weep all over again. "I don't know," he repeated. "Please let me go. I truly had nothing to do with it. I'm a duke," he wailed. "I've dined at Buckingham Palace. You cannot arrest me like this."

There was no energy in his protest, though. The man knew he'd been caught and that his days were numbered. Lord Clerkenwell nodded to McQueen, who marched Eastleigh out of the suite to the hall, two of the other officers following.

"Search the suite," Lord Clerkenwell told the remaining two officers. "See if there is any further evidence of Eastleigh's guilt or Castleford and Chisolm's whereabouts." The officers nodded and set to work, the concierge rushing to join them. Lord Clerkenwell crossed to David and Lionel. "One down, two to go," he said with a victorious grin.

"We have Castleford cornered," David said, the gears in his mind turning fast. "Eastleigh only confirmed what we already know. As soon as we reach Manchester—"

"We're going after Chisolm," Lionel growled. The intensity of his hatred was so fierce that David did a double-take, whipping to face him.

"We'll go after Chisolm as soon as we can, but we know Castleford's precise location," David argued. "We don't know Chisolm's."

"Chisolm needs to pay for what he's done as soon as possible," Lionel insisted. The fire in his eyes made him appear far more like the powerful man David knew him to be, rather than the boyish fashion plate he pretended to be to the world. The transformation would have been enticing enough in ordinary times, but given the fire that had ignited between them—a fire David couldn't ignore now, no matter how hard he tried to stay focused on business—Lionel's projection of power and masculine strength left David aching.

He stared hard at Lionel for several, long seconds, wondering if it would be worth the risk to drag Lionel aside and kiss him until the viciousness in his face turned to ecstasy, or if a quick, much-needed fuck would calm Lionel enough to see sense in the situation.

Those thoughts were madness, though, proving that David didn't have the situation nearly as well in hand as he needed to.

He turned to Lord Clerkenwell. "If you don't mind, I need to speak to Lionel alone."

Lord Clerkenwell glanced between the two of them, a knowing look in his eyes. He turned to the concierge, who was helping one of the officers sort through a cabinet. "You. Would you be willing to open another room for Mr. Wirth and Mr. Mercer?"

"Yes, my lord." The concierge jumped into motion, taking his ring of keys from his belt. He led David and Lionel across the hall, unlocking the suite directly opposite from Eastleigh's and showing them in.

"Thank you." David nodded to the man, communicating with his expression only for the man to get out.

The concierge nodded and slipped into the hall, shutting the door behind him.

David rounded on Lionel, intending to dress him down for being obstinate when their course of action in going after Castleford first should have been clear, but Lionel beat him to the punch.

"What the hell are you on about?" Lionel demanded.

David balked so severely that he took a step back. "What am *I* on about?" He blinked incredulously at Lionel. "You're the one who can't see the sense in going after Castleford when he's the easier target."

For a moment, Lionel looked stricken and guilty.

"Castleford may be the easier target, but Chisolm is the one who needs to be made to suffer for all he's done."

The venom in Lionel's voice went far beyond the particulars of the kidnapping case. David had an inkling there was something far more personal in Lionel's grudge against Chisolm—something that was, perhaps, connected to Everett Jewel, who had been tortured by Chisolm in his youth—but David hadn't let himself think about that possibility until now.

He took a step closer to Lionel, heart trembling as he considered ways Chisolm might have hurt Lionel as well. He reached for Lionel. "What did the man do to you?" he asked in a tender voice.

"This!" Lionel snapped back, his eyes going wide with frustration as he glared at David. "What the hell is this all about?" He gestured to David's hand, then his whole body. "First you lure me to this hotel last night and throw yourself at me, knowing full well I've taken a vow of celibacy, but also that I wouldn't be able to resist you. Then you kiss me at my brother's house not much more than an hour ago as though you have a right to drive me mad and turn my bones to jelly for your own amusement."

Twin surges of smug pride at the way Lionel admitted to being so affected by him and guilt for his reasons behind making such an ass of himself left David speechless. He floundered for a moment, mouth opening uselessly as heat rose up his neck and flushed his face. "I...you...you know how things have been between the two of us for years now," he stammered, having a hard time meeting Lionel's eyes.

"Yes," Lionel shouted. "I do. That is precisely the point. I *do* know how things have been between us. They have been that way—for years—deliberately. Until you callously crossed the line last night."

"You liked it," David argued, suddenly overcome by the sullen need to be right in the situation. "You're practically begging for it, just as you have been for years now, vow of celibacy or not."

"What I want is beside the point." Lionel began to pace, visibly shaking as he brushed a hand through his hair. "You have no right to cross the boundaries I have erected for myself."

"Interesting choice of words." David crossed his arms, but only to stop himself from reaching for Lionel.

"Don't you start with me." Lionel whipped to face him, fury and something deeper, something very much like pain, in his expression.

"You were the one who started this," David insisted. "You've spent years flirting with me and teasing me, only to leave me high and dry."

"I have my reasons." Lionel looked away, even as he paced closer. "I have my reasons," he repeated in a softer voice once he was only a few feet away from David. "I—"

David waited, but Lionel didn't finish his sentence. Instead, Lionel's expression flashed from fury to frustration to misery, as if he was desperate to say something but couldn't find the words. For one alarming moment, David thought Lionel might burst into tears, as he had the night before. Even that emotion vanished in an instant as he snapped his head up to meet David's eyes.

"Why now?" he demanded. "Why push things now, when we're in the middle of a delicate investigation that could mean bringing some of the evilest men in England to justice?"

For a heartbeat, David fully intended to defend himself as hard as he could. All of his energy to fight drained away as he studied the genuine hurt in Lionel's expression. He let out a weary breath and dropped his arms instead, glancing down at the carpet. "I've been distracted by the lust between us," he admitted, feeling anything but proud of himself. "And I cannot be distracted. Not when I have a business to run and a reputation to maintain. I thought that if I seduced you, if we spent a night together, we could put whatever this is between us aside and focus on work."

Rather than assuaging Lionel's anger, David's admission seemed only to inflame it. "You thought that if you fucked me you would be satisfied enough to dismiss me in favor of your precious work?"

David winced. That was exactly what he'd thought, but hearing it from Lionel's lips made him feel like the worst sort of rake. "Lionel, you know it's more than that," he tried to explain. "You know how deeply I care for you."

"Just because I enjoy fucking doesn't mean that's all I am," Lionel roared. "I'm more than an instrument to be used for whatever cowardly plan you might have to prove to society that a queer boy can rise out of poverty to be a force in business, or finish an important job or bend the world to be the way you'd like it to be."

There was so much truth in Lionel's words and they proved Lionel knew him so well that David glanced up to him in bewilderment. When he saw how tormented Lionel's expression was, that bewilderment turned to deep worry.

"What is it?" he asked, aching to take Lionel into his arms and to soothe with kisses and tenderness whatever inner beast had a hold of him. He stayed rigidly where he was, though. "What is this secret you've been keeping from me all this time? It has to do with this case, doesn't it? Has to do with Chisolm. Did he hurt you the way he hurt Jewel?" If that was the case, David would tear the man limb from limb with his bare hands and light the remains on fire.

"No." Lionel turned away from him, wincing. "Chisolm has never touched me. I've only met him a handful of times, and then only briefly."

David's bafflement grew a hundredfold. "Then why all of this malice toward the man?"

Lionel was silent. His back was bunched with tension, and though David couldn't see his face, he knew Lionel was fighting tears. The air between them crackled, as though lightning would strike. As long as it brought the truth out, David invited it to strike, even if it hurt.

At last, Lionel drew in a deep breath and turned to

face him. His pale face was pink with heat and misery. "I'm going to Hull," he said with absolute determination. "I'm going after Chisolm. You can go to Manchester. Get your old lover to help you find Castleford. I'll find Chisolm alone if I have to."

"You absolutely will not," David insisted. At last, he let himself move toward Lionel, reaching for him. He only let himself go as far as resting his hands on Lionel's brutally-tense shoulders, though. "We know almost precisely where Castleford is. We only have a vague idea about Chisolm. Manchester is the better option, Castleford is the easier target, and you're coming with me. We're leaving tomorrow. I am not letting you go to Hull, or anywhere else, alone right now. You are not alone, no matter how convinced of that you think you are. I am with you. I always have been with you, and I always will be with you."

Lionel's shoulders collapsed, and he let out a heartfelt moan, his face crumpling. "Damn you, David Wirth."

He sagged against David, gripping the lapels of his jacket and slanting his mouth over David's. Given the intensity of Lionel's emotions, David expected the kiss to be much more aggressive. Instead, it felt like a surrender. Lionel's lips molded against his, and his tongue brushed the seam of David's lips. It was an invitation David couldn't resist. He opened his mouth against Lionel's, taking the lead and exploring Lionel's mouth with his tongue and teasing his bottom lip with his teeth. It was sensual and sweet, causing David to forget where they were, to forget everything but the love that filled every part of his body, urging him to be one with Lionel in every way.

But when he paused for breath, inching back to drink in what he hoped was Lionel's expression of ecstasy, tears were streaming down Lionel's face.

"What's wrong, love?" David whispered, brushing his hand across Lionel's cheek to wipe away his tears. "Please tell me. I'll fix it, I swear."

Lionel pulled away from him shakily, letting out a breath that sounded too much like a sob for David's heart to take. "You can't fix this, love," he said, lowering his head and squeezing his eyes until his eyelashes shone with tears. "There is no cure, and so this can never happen."

David's soul rebelled at the idea. There was always a cure, always a solution to every problem, especially when two hearts loved each other as much as he knew his and Lionel's did. That felt like a revelation to David. What use was there in proving to the world that he was a competent solicitor and businessman if he couldn't prove to Lionel that he loved him and would make everything right in his world? Lionel was his purpose. Everything else was secondary.

But before he could find a way to say that and an answer to Lionel's troubles that would make everything better, Lionel lurched into motion, shooting past him and heading for the door. He left before David could stop him, leaving David feeling as lost as ever.

CHAPTER 8

*I*f riding in a carriage with unhealed sores covering his most tender spots was painful for Lionel, riding on a train as it jerked and screeched to a stop in Manchester's central station was agony. Particularly considering all of the other unhealed wounds in his heart and soul that were only exacerbated by sitting in close quarters with David for hours on end.

David had spent the first part of their journey attempting to engage him in light conversation. Lionel sullenly refused to reply to any of the topics David brought up. Once he realized Lionel wouldn't banter with him, David attempted to discuss the mission ahead of them, their prospects in finding The Silver Serpent brothel, and whether Castleford would come quietly. Still, Lionel refused to speak. He couldn't. He knew that the moment he opened his mouth, he would gush forth with a declaration of love that would shame even the angels, or else he would confess the truth of his illness. And a train compartment was not the appropriate place to divulge something so sensitive, particularly when the train journey was taking David right to the doorstep of his former lover.

Hours' worth of silence was finally broken as the train jostled into its platform at the end of the line. Lionel winced at the friction stopping caused, and porters and conductors began shouting orders on the platform.

"Do you need help with your case?" David asked, standing and fetching his own from the rack above his seat.

"No." Lionel rose as gracefully as he could with a large part of his body screaming in protest and turned to reach for his suitcase.

"It's just that you don't look well," David said, his voice equal parts concern and frustration.

"I'm as well as could be expected," Lionel muttered. "But thank you for pointing out that I'm currently hideous and disheveled."

Behind him, David huffed an irritated breath. "It wasn't a comment on your fashion sense, Lionel."

Lionel peeked morosely over his shoulder, catching sight of David's deep frown out of the corner of his eye. "I'm a vain peacock, David. You know that. Any disparaging comment on my appearance is a mortal offense worthy of pistols at dawn."

He concentrated on reaching for his case, hoping David would think he was an arse and would leave him alone. That didn't seem likely to happen, though. Lionel could feel David hovering behind him, ready to help at a moment's notice if he proved too weak to take care of himself.

The irony was, he probably was too weak. As soon as he had his case in his hands and pulled it free of the rack above, his grip fumbled and the case crashed to the floor. Worse still, he and David attempted to reach for it at the same time, and in the process, David kicked the blasted thing right out of the compartment door—which a porter had conveniently opened for them. His suitcase fell into the gap between the train and the platform. The debacle required a young and spritely porter to climb down to fetch it. In the process of leaping down to the tracks, the porter landed on the case. Lionel could have sworn he heard the sickening crunch of the suitcase's contents breaking.

He knew beyond a shadow of a doubt that they'd broken when the porter tossed his case back onto the platform before crawling out. The case smelled of medicine, and spots of damp leaked through its battered side.

"Bloody hell," Lionel muttered, dropping to one knee to open his case right there on the platform. He added a few more colorful curses when he lifted the lid and discovered that every stitch of clothing he'd brought with him to Manchester was stained with the remnants of the tinctures Dr. Sullivan had given him and utterly ruined.

"Bad luck, that," an all-too familiar voice said, ruining Lionel's day even more.

Lionel slammed the lid of his case shut, fastened the clasps, and turned to stand in time to see the devilishly handsome John Dandie striding forward to meet him—or rather, to meet David—on the platform. Dandie was all rakish smile, sun-kissed hair in perfect order, and sparkling green eyes.

"John." David greeted his old lover with a relieved smile, crossing the platform to take Dandie's outstretched hand.

All Lionel could do was stand there, reasonably certain he was dying, as Dandie pulled David into a fond embrace. Some men, like himself, took meticulous care to dress in the finest fashions, choosing colors and textures that complimented their visage and figure, and employing all of the latest cosmetic techniques to look their best. And some men, like John Dandie, were beautiful and desirable without lifting a finger.

"It's so good to see you again," Dandie said, letting David go. "And you as well, Lionel, though it looks as though you've seen better days." He nodded to Lionel's squashed and battered suitcase.

"On the contrary. I'm at my peak," Lionel said with a rakish tilt of his head, his voice managing to be too high and hoarse at the same time.

Damn him, but Dandie stepped away from David, moving to greet Lionel with an embrace similar to the one he'd shared with David. "It's good to see you again, friend," he said quietly.

Guilt roiled through Lionel's already pinched gut.

Dandie had never been anything but kind to him. Hell, Dandie was the one who had listened to his story of wanting to leave his wicked ways—though not the reasons why Lionel wanted out of the game—and had hired him at the law office, in spite of his utter lack of experience. If not for John Dandie, Lionel wasn't sure where he would be. He would never have met David. Though at the moment, Lionel thought perhaps that would have been better for everyone.

"Let me take that from you." Dandie reached for Lionel's case, prying it out of Lionel's hand before he could protest. Dandie sniffed. "Is that sarsaparilla? Or something oriental?"

"Or laudanum?" David muttered, his face darkening to a frown.

"It's not opium," Lionel snapped, glaring at David in return. He glanced to Dandie. "David seems to have it in his head that I'm an opium addict. I'm not. Though I would give my eye teeth for a bit of the strong stuff right now." He snatched his case out of Dandie's hand and charged forward to the end of the platform.

"I'm sure David was just teasing," Dandie called after him, striding on his long legs to catch up. "Weren't you, David?"

Lionel had his back turned to David and didn't hear whatever he mumbled in response. He kept his gaze straight forward as they dodged through the crowd jostling about the train station, making their way to the door and the street beyond. His mind was already spinning with not only the need to buy all new clothes, but to find replacement medicines for the ones that had shattered. Dr. Sullivan's treatments were experimental, but Lionel was loath to stop them altogether until he could get back to London. Anything he could do, any bizarre mixture he could try, gave him that much more hope that his days weren't numbered.

"Lionel, where are you going?" Dandie called, several more yards behind him than Lionel anticipated, once they were outside. "Your hotel is this way."

Lionel stopped, jaw clenched, and turned to face what he was certain he didn't want to see. Sure enough, David and Dandie stood side by side, looking as much as though they belonged together as they ever had. And while Lionel's brain wasn't fool enough to believe that, after everything that had passed between him and David in the last few days, David would toss him over in a snap and fall into Dandie's arms again, his heart still ached with irrational jealousy. David would be better off with hale and healthy John Dandie in any case.

He pursed his lips, let out a frustrated breath through his nose, and changed direction, marching after David and Dandie.

"I received your telegram about The Silver Serpent and Castleford's apparent whereabouts," John said as they walked on. Lionel tried to walk behind David and Dandie, but Dandie slowed his steps until Lionel was forced to walk beside him. "The trouble is, I've never heard of any place called The Silver Serpent."

"I don't suppose you would have," David said. "It doesn't sound like the sort of establishment you would frequent." He glanced around Dandie to check on Lionel.

Lionel pretended to be busy fussing with his case so that he didn't have to acknowledge David's caring or concern, and so that he didn't have to watch the way David looked at Dandie with so much admiration and certainty.

Dandie chuckled. "No, I would never be caught dead in a place like that. Brandon would kill me if I even thought of it."

Lionel snapped his head around, eyes widening a fraction.

"Your new partner," David said, his tone implying that Brandon was more than simply Dandie's new business partner.

Lionel studied David, trying to gauge whether he was bothered that Dandie had a new lover. The only thing he could glean from David's expression was that he already knew about Brandon.

"I'll introduce you when we convene at the office," Dandie said. "If Brandon is there. Lately, he's been...." He let the sentence drop and shook his head before going on. "In the meantime, I've got several sets of eyes on the street keeping a lookout for The Silver Serpent. The problem is, establishments like that tend to only be known by a narrow group of patrons. Which tells me that once we do uncover it, it'll be more like uncovering a nest of vipers than just a hideout for a nobleman in trouble."

David hummed in agreement. "Are you on friendly terms with the Manchester police?"

"Not as friendly as we were with Scotland Yard," Dandie admitted with a sigh.

Lionel swallowed hard, trying not to feel left out by the rapport David and Dandie had. They'd always worked well together. It was why they'd started their law office together. They'd been friends before they were lovers, and apparently they'd remained friends after the fact. That didn't make the pill Lionel had to swallow, along with his pride, any less bitter. He wouldn't have bothered being jealous if he felt like he had any sort of future to offer David. But his future was far from guaranteed.

"Here's your hotel," Dandie announced as they reached a relatively modern looking building only a few blocks from the train station. "And Lionel, that street just across there is loaded with tailor's shops and shops with ready-made suits and sundries. I'm sure you'll adore all the shopping Manchester has to offer as you replace your ruined things."

"I'm sure I will," Lionel agreed without enthusiasm, glancing to the street in question. In spite of his irrational desire to be as difficult as possible with Dandie, he did feel a zip of excitement at the prospect of new clothes.

"You should have the hotel laundry attempt to clean your clothes all the same," Dandie went on, crossing through the hotel's wide front door and into the lobby, Lionel and David behind him, as a porter held the door for them. "I'm sure they have people who can do something."

"I'm sure they do." Lionel tried, for Dandie's sake, to smile, but his heart felt anything but light.

"I can check us in if you want to speak to a concierge about laundry," David said, still looking like he wasn't sure whether he wanted to smack Lionel or kiss him.

"I might just do that," Lionel said, veering away from David and Dandie as they approached the front desk. Anything to take himself out of the presence of his beloved and the man who David should love instead of him.

David watched Lionel stomp over to the smaller desk beside the main one, where he and John headed so that David could check in. Worry made it almost impossible for him to think. Lionel had barely spoken to him throughout the entire, long train journey. That alone would have sounded the alarm. Lionel never passed up an opportunity to banter about everything under the sun or to show off his knowledge and connections by telling stories of his younger years. But after the way the two of them had skated so close to some sort of breakthrough in their relationship for the past few days, the silence wasn't just unbearable, it was terrifying.

Lionel was keeping secrets from him. Of that much,

David had no doubt and never had. It was the nature of those secrets that troubled him. That and how thoroughly Lionel had shut him out. Lionel hadn't even let him carry his suitcase when obviously he needed the help. David felt horrible for being the one to kick that suitcase and cause all the trouble. He wanted to make it up to Lionel, but couldn't. David watched him now as he presented his case to a man who must have been the head of house-keeping and explained the damage to his clothes and other belongings. Lionel was as handsome as ever, as far as David was concerned, and as beautiful a fashion plate as any man could be. But there was a tension that sharp-ened the lines of Lionel's shoulders and made the planes of his face seem harsh instead of regal. And he'd lost weight. David wasn't sure why he was only noticing it now.

Beside him, John cleared his throat. "David?"

David snapped his attention away from Lionel, facing forward. His turn at the front desk had come, but he'd been too distracted with Lionel to notice. He stepped forward. "Reservation under the name of Wirth."

David was well aware of the way John watched him as he completed his business with the concierge and was given two keys to a room on the fourth floor. John knew him better than anyone—except Lionel—and David could tell a lecture of some sort was in the works. He ignored it as best he could as he stepped away from the main desk and approached Lionel.

"Here's your key." He held out one of the keys to Lionel, trying to decide whether to push Lionel into talking about his troubles or to let him be.

Lionel dragged his attention away from the porter who was sorting through the soiled clothes in his suitcase, and stared at David for a moment. Their eyes met, and David had the uncanny feeling that he'd done something wrong. Finally, Lionel sighed and took the offered key.

"Looks like it's room 4-D," he told the porter.

"I'll have it all brought up there when laundry is done with it," the porter said, taking the messy bundle of Lionel's clothes away and leaving him with a mostly empty suitcase.

"I can take the rest of that up to the room," David offered.

"Good," Lionel snapped. "Because evidently, I need to go shopping now, and Dandie has kindly told me exactly where to go."

He spoke as though John had told him to go to hell, abruptly turning and marching out the hotel's front door.

David was left staring at the doorway, baffled by the entire exchange.

"Well. It's nice to see you've brought your domestic tranquility up to Manchester with you," John said in a wry voice, walking up behind David.

David stared at the hotel door for a few more seconds before letting out a defeated breath and turning to John. "I don't know what the hell has been wrong with him these past few days. Especially since things have been...."

He let his words fade as heat rushed to his face. The hotel lobby had too many people wandering about for him to say anything close to what he desperately needed to discuss. "Let me just take our baggage up to the room and then we can head to your office and discuss the case."

"I'll come with you," John offered.

David shot him a wary sideways glance as they started forward to the stairs that would take them to the fourth floor. What had once been between him and John was years in the past, but he still felt a certain closeness to the man. You couldn't go through all the things they'd been through together and not feel a lingering sense of intimacy. Especially since the romantic part of their relationship hadn't ended badly. It had just fizzled.

"I take it the road to love has been a rocky one for the two of you," John said once they were secure inside the hotel room.

"It shouldn't be," David said with a frown, setting his suitcase on one of the room's two beds and Lionel's on the other. "It seemed so obvious how things would go for such a long time. Then, all of a sudden, it was as though Lionel and I were complete strangers."

John crossed his arms, studying David with a frown. "When did things start to go bad?"

David rubbed a hand through his hair, thinking back. "I didn't think they were bad. That is to say, I was mildly annoyed with Lionel's continued fascination with Everett Jewel. The two of them got into a fight at The Chameleon Club a fortnight ago or so. Yes, I was jealous," he admitted when John looked like he would press the issue. "But jealousy is a fairly pointless emotion. Particularly when Jewel is clearly happy with his current lover."

"Lionel is jealous of me, by the way," John pointed out with an amused grin.

David wanted to roll his eyes. "I told him not to be. There's no reason."

"That doesn't change things." John dropped his arms and shook his head. "Even I can tell that's not what's really bothering Lionel, though."

David hesitated before saying, "I really am worried that he's taking opium, in spite of his denials."

"He's not," John answered so fast David blinked.

"How do you know?"

John shrugged. "He doesn't have the signs of an opium addict. He looks to be in good health, he hasn't let his appearance go, and he didn't have any of the ticks or tremors of a man looking for his next fix."

"Then what was it that broke in his suitcase?"

John laughed. That in itself was enough to startle David out of his worry. "Look at you, man," John said. "You're completely besotted."

"I am not," David protested, trying to laugh it off. His insides twisted into knots, though, and he crossed to his bed to open his suitcase so that he'd have something else to do.

"You're drunk on love," John went on, still amused. "And I, for one, think it's about time."

"Don't tease me, John," David sighed.

"I'm not, I swear," John insisted. "You're clearly more in love with him than you ever were with me."

David jerked straight and faced him. "What makes you say that?"

John shook his head. "You never worried about me the way you're worried about Lionel."

"I don't want to be worried about him." He let out a breath. "That's not true. I want his concerns to be my concerns, but I don't like feeling so weak because of it. Something's wrong, though, and he won't tell me."

John held out a hand to David as though he'd just proven a point. "See? You never cared one way or another if I didn't tell you things."

"You told me everything," David said with a frown.

"No, I didn't." John appeared entirely too amused by the conversation for David's liking. "You wouldn't have cared if I'd run naked through the streets of Mayfair with bells tied to my prick. All you cared about were the cases parading through our office."

"Speaking of cases," David stepped away from the bed, beyond relieved to have something else to talk about. "We need to nail down Castleford's location as quickly as possible. It's only a matter of time before word reaches him that Eastleigh has been arrested. Once he finds out, it's likely he'll move, and if we don't swoop down on him, we may lose our one chance."

John laughed out loud.

David scowled at him. "I thought you wanted to help with this investigation."

"I do, believe me, I do. But you just proved the exact point I was attempting to make." When David only stared at him, John went on with, "You were always more concerned with business and legal cases than you were with life. Until Lionel came along. Before him, all you wanted to do was prove how brilliant and capable you were. Nothing else mattered to you but showing off how high a boy from Limehouse could rise. That's why I left, if you must know."

The confession came as such a shock to David that he took a step back. "Is that why?"

"I didn't want to linger in a relationship—or a city, for that matter—where I was as inconsequential as yesterday's roast." John's voice took on a softer tone. "We were good while we lasted, but our bond was never as deep as the bond between lifelong lovers should be. And I'm fine with that." He held up his hands in a conciliatory gesture when David opened his mouth to protest. "We're better as friends anyhow. But you and Lionel—" He shook his head. "You love him far more than you realize, and if you don't pull your head out of your arse and set work aside for two seconds to deal with whatever is between the two of you, you'll lose him. Don't make the same mistake you made with me."

David's heart sank. "That's not it," he insisted. He took a breath, then went on. "I attempted to seduce him a few days ago."

John gaped at him. "Attempted? Why am I not liking the sound of this?"

"Because it was a terrible mistake," David said, moaning and rubbing a hand over his face as the humiliation of the evening returned to him. "Lionel wanted none of it."

John studied him with a flat stare. "Lionel. Lionel Mercer. Wanted nothing to do with seduction?"

"Oh, I think he wanted it," David said, his face heating hotter than a furnace. "But he rejected me. It was awful."

John's brow knit into a frown and he crossed his arms in thought. "You attempted to seduce Lionel...and he rejected you. Even though he wanted it?"

"I may have mentioned to him that I was seducing him so that we could have it out, resolve the tension between us, and move on with the important work of this case."

John threw his head back and burst into laughter. "You really are an idiot, David."

"Yes, I know, thank you," David snapped. He moved back to his suitcase, but there was no point in using it as a distraction anymore. Instead, he sighed, letting his shoulders drop. "I don't know what to do now. Lionel isn't telling me something. He wants me, but he's rejecting me. He loves me, but he's pushing me away."

"And why would a man do that, do you think?" John asked, a sharpness in his eyes that said he could think of a dozen reasons at least.

"I don't know." David pivoted to sit on the bed, all energy leaving him. He rubbed his hands over his face. "I just want things to go back to the way they were between the two of us before that fight with Jewel, before my ham-fisted attempts at seduction, before...."

"Before whatever the thing that Lionel won't tell you about drove a wedge between the two of you?" John finished his thought, one eyebrow arched.

David glanced wearily up at him. "Precisely."

"Then you shouldn't be sitting here moping," John said, crossing to the bed and extending a hand to help David up. "You should be chasing after the man you love and harassing him until he's forced to tell you exactly what's on his mind."

"We have a kidnapper to catch," he reminded John with a stern look. "You can fault me all you want for putting work ahead of my life, but that man—and Chisolm—must be brought to justice."

"I'm not saying they shouldn't or that they won't be," John said. "But even you must admit that the entire investigation will move along much more smoothly if you and Lionel are working well together."

"True," David said.

"And you're only going to work well together once you get out of the morass you've fallen into."

"You're right."

"So what are you waiting for?" John shrugged. "Go after him and wrestle him to the ground, if that's what it takes to get him to confess his secrets."

David stared silently at John, knowing he was right. A small smile twitched across his lips. The romantic part of the love he'd felt for John all those years ago was gone, but he was glad the man was still his friend. And he was right. The only way they were going to be able to find the focus to bring Castleford and Chisolm to justice was if he and Lionel worked out the emotions between them first.

CHAPTER 9

*L*ionel had never been so miserable while shopping for clothing in his life. In fact, shopping for anything—from socks and drawers to tailored suit jackets—had always been his favorite pastime. Well, his favorite vertical pastime. And even though the quality and variety of merchandise available at the high-end shops along the street Dandie had pointed out to him was every bit as fine as the London shops he favored, Lionel felt no joy as he selected silk and linen shirts, trousers and jackets in the latest styles, matching neckties and cravats, and underthings.

"Could you have this sent to The Midland hotel under the name Lionel Mercer?" he asked the sales clerk as he handed over enough cash to make the young man's eyes go wide.

"Yes, sir," the man said, suddenly three times as eager to assist Lionel. "Whatever you'd like, sir."

A grin twitched at the corner of Lionel's mouth in spite of himself. He'd said the same thing more than a few times in his earlier life. The young shop clerk looked to be exactly the sort who uttered the phrase himself after hours.

That in mind, Lionel leaned gracefully against the sales counter, fixing the young man with a look calculated to both entice and intimidate. "You wouldn't happen to know of a particular sort of establishment called The Silver Serpent, would you?" He traced a heart on the countertop with one graceful finger.

The young man's face flushed a deep shade of puce. "No, sir. I've never heard of that particular place." He cleared his throat, glanced across the shop to the older man who had assisted Lionel earlier, a man Lionel assumed was the owner or master tailor, then swayed closer to Lionel. "But if it's entertainment you're looking for during your stay in our fine city, I know of other places, and I'm done for the day in an hour and a half."

Lionel sighed and straightened. A part of him that he sorely missed would have taken the young man up on his offer in a heartbeat. Eager young ones always made for the most entertaining evenings. He should have known. He'd been that eager young man what felt like a lifetime ago.

"I wish I could," he said, treating the young man to a wink. "My heart belongs to another now."

Rather than appear disappointed, the young man beamed as though Lionel had told him a fairytale. Except his was a fairytale without a happy ending. He collected the receipt for his purchases and turned to leave. Everything he'd said to the young man was the truth. His heart did belong to another. It came as something of a surprise to Lionel that, even if he could have indulged in an illicit rendezvous, he wouldn't have. He no longer had a taste for variety and indulgence, only for David.

He shook his head as he walked along the street, searching out the right sort of shop for his second, vital errand. It had always been a simple matter of mental compartmentalization to separate love from sex in the past. One was the province of the body and the other was all about the heart. David had dashed that notion to pieces. It was a shock to Lionel that the two were one and the same to him now. Much good that it did him when he wouldn't dare put David in danger by engaging in any sort of sexual contact with him. But if love and sex were not two entirely separate beasts after all, if he could love and give himself away without putting David in physical harm, perhaps there was a future for them after all.

He rejected the thought outright as he stepped into a tiny chemist's shop on the corner of two quiet back streets. Love was sharing your whole self with someone, and bodies were a part of that. It would be viciously cruel of him to offer his heart to David when his body was as infectious as a plague victim's.

"Can I help you, sir?" The chemist greeted Lionel from behind his counter near the back of the store as soon as he entered the shop. The shelf behind the man was tall, broad, and sectioned into dozens of cubbies, each containing bottles and jars. The bottles and jars were filled with liquid, herbs, powders, and crystals of all sorts, proving to Lionel that he'd come to the right place.

All the same, Lionel approached the man with a twisted feeling of shame in his gut as heat spilled onto his face. Asking a chemist outright for what he needed was a far cry from covertly obtaining what he needed from Dr. Sullivan in the secluded halls of The Chameleon Club. "Yes, I was hoping you could provide me with a few remedies to replace the ones that were ruined by sloppy handling of my luggage by an inept train porter," he said with a grin designed to create a sense of camaraderie with the chemist.

"What remedies might those be?" the chemist asked jovially.

Lionel reached the counter, glancing sideways at the shop's only other customer, a young woman staring intently at a shelf of medicinal teas. She wasn't paying him a bit of attention, but he lowered his voice to a soft whisper all the same. "I'm not certain you would have the particular tincture I'm looking for, as it's a tad experimental, but it involves sarsaparilla root. Or a secondary treatment my physician has recommended of potassium iodine."

The chemist's expression shifted from polite and welcoming to snide and knowing. Lionel had the feeling he'd softened his demeanor too much and hinted at what he was. The chemist turned and fetched a bottle from a high cubby far to one side of the shelf behind him. "Mercury," he said, plunking the bottle on the table. "It's the only effective treatment. At least, as effective as they come. Those others are palliatives more than anything else. Mercury is what you need."

Lionel's back went rigid with a sickening combination of embarrassment and offense. "Do you have the sarsaparilla or the potassium compounds?"

The chemist sighed and turned back to his cubbies. "I can mix the Mercury with sarsaparilla, of you'd like, but it's not going to do any good."

"I would appreciate it," Lionel said, voice hoarse with misery at the turn the conversation had taken. Even worse was the way he had gone from a respectable customer to a pariah in the chemist's eyes. All it ever took was one tiny drop of information or realization for men like him to go from gentleman to worm in most people's eyes. Walking that line of respectability was exhausting on good days and downright spirit-crushing on days like the one he was having.

At the same time, being reduced to dirt in the chemist's eyes did open an opportunity Lionel wasn't certain he'd have otherwise. He waited until he was certain the young woman at the other side of the shop was engaged in her perusing before leaning in toward the chemist and asking, "Have you heard of a place called The Silver Serpent?"

Lionel knew in an instant from the chemist's sly look

of superiority that he had. "Answering their call, are you?" he asked.

Lionel did his best to hide his surprise and curiosity at the comment behind a coy look. "It's a call that cannot be resisted."

The chemist snorted as he continued preparing Lionel's concoction. "You're just the sort Fanny likes to hire," he went on. "You've got the air of a gentleman about you, but it's only skin deep, isn't it?"

Lionel fought not to let his grin turn into a snarl. "I know what my friends want," he said, falling back on old dialogs. "What I don't know is exactly where to find the place."

The chemist was silent for a moment as he finished mixing Lionel's tincture. He took his time stoppering the bottle and presenting it to Lionel. Rather than waiting for the price, Lionel handed the man a five-pound note.

The chemist burst into a smile. "It's on Gartside Street. Look for a grey door with a snake carved into the lower left side."

A thrill of victory coursed through Lionel in spite of how he'd obtained the information. "A thousand thanks, kind sir," he said before snatching up the bottle, sliding it into his pocket, and turning to leave.

Before he was even out the door, his smile turned into a grimace of disgust. He wasn't what the chemist thought him to be. He never had been. His business had always been select and refined. He was not some common rent boy who dropped to his knees for a quid or two. He'd

133

always considered himself a man about town who enjoyed his friends—friends who thanked him financially or with information that would help him advance his own interests. Or at least he had thought of himself that way until Chisolm's nasty scheme had turned him into exactly what the chemist assumed he was. He'd been a rank fool for letting greed blind him to Chisolm's plot and for—

"What is that you've slipped into your pocket?"

Lionel nearly jumped out of his skin at David's sharp accusation. The man had been lurking outside of the chemist's shop and pounced the moment Lionel stepped out. He cursed and whipped to face David.

"What in hell's name are you doing, stalking me through the streets like a cutpurse?" he hissed.

"Is that laudanum?" David growled, falling into step with Lionel as he marched away, heading back to the hotel.

"No, it is not, and for the hundredth time, I am not addicted to narcotics of any kind. For God's sake, David," he snapped.

"Then why did you visit the chemist?" David pressed.

Lionel stopped, whipping to face him with a furious scowl. "What difference does it make to you where I go and how I spend my money?" he barked. "I needed something to settle my stomach. Or I have a rash that needed ointment. Or I have a tickle in my throat and believe I'm coming down with ague. Take your pick of explanations."

"Don't shout at me when I'm only trying to help you." David glared at him. "I care about you."

Lionel's chest and throat squeezed as his earlier thoughts circled back on him. The care David showed him was nearly as potent as a lover's embrace, but he had a hard time believing it would ever be enough. For him or for David.

"Leave me alone," he said sullenly, walking on. "I'm too exhausted to argue with you."

"I don't mean to argue, Lionel, but you have to admit that you've been extraordinarily vexing of late," David said.

"*I've* been vexing of late?" Lionel snorted a laugh.

"I know I'm not entirely innocent," David started.

"And how is your former partner doing this evening?" Lionel interrupted him before he could go on with a topic that was sure to set David off and distract him away from Lionel's mission at the chemist. "Did the two of you have enough time to *become reacquainted?*"

"Would you like me to slap that smug face of yours back to London?" David countered. "Because the way things are now, I'd be more than happy to do it. Why were you visiting a chemist?" he asked as Lionel opened his mouth to argue the previous point.

Lionel snapped his mouth shut, clenching his jaw as he walked on to the end of the street. Because he'd stopped at so many of the shops along the way, it felt as though he'd moved farther from the hotel than he had. In fact, it was only a few blocks away. He crossed the street,

David on his heels, and stepped through into the hotel's lobby.

"If you must know, after purchasing a new wardrobe, I thought to ask a few local business owners if they knew of The Silver Serpent." He kept his voice low as he headed toward the stairs and up to his room.

"Did you find anything out?" David asked, his tone instantly all business.

"Yes, as a matter of fact, I did." Lionel pierced him with a haughty stare as David caught up to his side. "I discovered not only the location of the place, but the fact that they are apparently seeking to hire."

"To hire what?" David asked with a frown as they turned a corner and continued upward.

"Dancing bears," Lionel answered sarcastically. When David scowled at him, he said, "Whores, David. The chemist seemed to think I was looking for work."

"Are you?" David's scowl darkened.

"I'm not going to dignify that with a response," Lionel sniffed as they exited the staircase onto the fourth floor. Lionel fished his key from his pocket and proceeded to the door. As he fit the key into the lock, a flash of inspiration hit him. "Although, that wouldn't be a bad way to infiltrate the place. I could confirm Castleford's presence there without alarming him, and we could send for Lord Clerkenwell and his men to perform the arrest instead of relying on Manchester police."

He pushed open the door to the room, then stopped

dead at the sight of two beds, David's suitcase resting on one and his own, ruined suitcase on the other.

"So you want to waltz into a brothel to ask for employment?" David marched into the room with him, shutting the door and locking it. "I'm sure you'd enjoy that. So much for this supposed vow of celibacy you've taken."

"You booked one room for the both of us?" Lionel twisted to face him, only half listening to David's childish rant.

David blinked at him as though Lionel were the childish one. "Two beds," he said by way of argument. "Although I don't suppose you'll be needing one if you're going to work at a brothel. Silver Serpent indeed."

"I *have* taken a vow of celibacy." Lionel spotted several boxes from the tailor's shop he'd been to in the corner of the room and crossed to unpack his purchases. "A fact that you seem to have forgotten."

"Oh, believe me, I haven't forgotten it." David paced in agitation behind him, shoving a hand through his hair. "It's all I can think about, night and day."

"Then kindly respect my vow and stop trying to seduce me simply so that you can get me out of your system," Lionel shot over his shoulder, opening a box that contained underthings and a nightshirt.

"That wasn't truly what I meant by my attempts at The Savoy at all," David insisted. "I'm sorry for making such a mess of that. But you leave me at an utter loss for how to love you."

"Don't." Lionel carried the box over to the bureau that sat opposite the beds, wrenching one door open and dumping the contents of his box into it.

"Don't what?" David snapped.

"Love me," Lionel said, then went on before he could stop himself with, "I'm not worth it."

He jerked straight as soon as the words were out of his mouth, shocked at himself. Of course, the thought had always lingered in the back of his head that he wasn't worthy. It had since he was a boy playing second fiddle to Phineas in a family with a modest title but no money to back it up. And as he advanced his own interests and paid his way through university on the "generosity" of his "friends" when he failed to win a scholarship. But he'd never let those things influence the way he thought about himself. Not until the first sores appeared on his body all those years ago.

"You are worth it," David said, the tone of his voice transformed from frustration to tenderness. He stepped up behind Lionel, gripping his arms and leaning his head close to Lionel's. "Believe me, love, you are."

Lionel drew in a long breath that only made his body more rigid. The heat of David's body against his was so devilishly tempting. The scent of him was perfection. It would have been so easy to sink against him and revel in David's embrace for as long as he could. But David's right hand was clamped hard over a particularly painful sore on his arm, and the pain of that was a vivid reminder of all the reasons they had to keep their distance.

"I misspoke," he said, writhing out of David's grasp and stepping to the side. "I am fabulous, and I am brilliant. Which is how I was able to come up with such a brilliant plan." He overemphasized his arrogance in the hope that David would go back to being annoyed with him and leave him alone. "I'll go to The Silver Serpent and inquire after employment. It's the best way we have of finding Castleford and keeping him in our sights until the authorities can arrest him."

David scrubbed a hand over his face, practically shaking with irritation. "And what if your prospective new employer requires you to demonstrate your skills?"

Lionel hadn't thought of that. He'd never worked for anyone other than himself before, but it made sense that some sort of proof of talent would be required. All the same, he shrugged. "I have a sliver tongue to match the Silver Serpent's. I'm certain I could talk my way out of whatever they ask of me."

"Like you talk your way out of being with me?" David arched one eyebrow at Lionel in challenge.

There was something heartbreaking about the need that lay underneath David's wry comment. In so many ways, if circumstances had been different, he and David would have been a perfect match. Neither of them let the other get away with the unique kinds of arrogance they were each inclined toward. The physical attraction was there to a degree that made them both miserable. And they cared for each other as only partners in business and in life could. Which only made the entire situation all the more depressing.

Lionel squeezed his eyes shut and pressed his hands to his temples, trying to think of a way out of the situation that didn't involve him spewing the ugly truth about how diseased and disgusting he was and sacrificing what little pride he had left. He needed that pride if he was going to continue operating in such close quarters with David. "Darling, this impasse between us has to end," he said. "It has both of us behaving like children when we need to be at our peak performance to catch Castleford and Chisolm."

"Agreed," David said, stepping closer to him. The frustration in his eyes had shifted back to calculation, and from there to desire. "Which now has me considering the point of my original seduction all over again."

"Bloody hell, David," Lionel huffed. He wasn't fast enough to slip away from David before he pinned him against the bureau, though. Lionel was forced to lean against the edge as David planted his feet on either side of Lionel's, bringing their hips into close contact.

"I'm beginning to think my mistake the other night was not in what I attempted to do, but in how I went about it. I should have been honest with you from the start instead of trying to seduce you on the sly."

"You shouldn't have done any of it," Lionel said, far more breathless and aroused by David's encompassing presence than he should have been. "You shouldn't be doing this now." But, oh, how Lionel wanted it. Every bit of it. His cock betrayed his thoughts by hardening between them as David leaned into him, though there was as much pain as pleasure in the excitement.

"We need to go to bed together, Lionel," David said resting his hands on either side of Lionel's face. "We need to give in to the tension between us. We need to release it together. Otherwise, neither of us will have the presence of mind to do the work that needs to be done. We need to do this, or else neither of us will be of any good to anyone."

Lionel found it strangely charming that David didn't or couldn't crudely say "We need to fuck." What he didn't say spoke even more than what he did.

"We can't," Lionel said, resting his forehead against David's. He gripped the edge of the bureau to stop from sliding his arms around David and exploring his body.

"We need to," David murmured, soft and seductive, his lips so close to Lionel's.

"It won't be just once, and you know it," Lionel argued.

"So? We've known this is where we've been headed for years now."

Lionel let out a frustrated sigh, closing his eyes and telling himself he needed to move away as soon as possible. His mind knew it, but his heart and his body wanted to stay right where they were.

"I'm sick, David," he whispered at last.

"No, you're not," David argued. "You're sensual and free. You enjoy yourself and others freely. Yes, it drives me mad with jealousy to think about your past lovers. But just because you may have enjoyed many men in a variety of ways doesn't make you sick."

Lionel didn't know whether to laugh or cry at David's sweetness, or his faith in him. Of course, he would think he meant "sick" metaphorically.

"No," he said, his heart breaking. "I mean, I'm—"

David stopped his words with a kiss, his mouth fully covering Lionel's. It was tender and amorous, and it sent Lionel's senses reeling. David's arms slid around him, not in demand, but as a lover who wanted nothing more than to comfort his beloved. Their tongues danced together as David fully explored his mouth, filling him with the warmth of promise and the ache of desire. It was so good that Lionel moaned deeply, squeezing his eyes shut as tears threatened, and dreaming of all the things that could have been if Chisolm hadn't used him.

"Come to bed with me," David whispered at last, following up their deep kiss with smaller, softer ones. "I swear, I'll be an absolute dream. I'll make you forget every other man you've been with."

Lionel's heart felt as though it would shatter at the slightest touch. He'd never known love so all-encompassing, or so painful. He placed shaking hands on David's chest and pushed him back.

"You already have made me forget them, love," he said, voice high and trembling. "But if I forget myself, we'll both pay the price." He wriggled away from David, stumbling toward the door.

"I don't understand." David pressed a hand to his temple, visibly frustrated.

Lionel snatched his room key from the small table by the door where he'd tossed it earlier. "Think about what I've said and you will understand," he said, unlocking the door and turning the handle. "I'm going for a walk."

He left the room before David could protest, and before he could put the facts together and realize what he'd confessed earlier. David was wrong about the two of them making love to ease the boiling tension between them. That tension would only resolve when David knew the truth, but Lionel didn't want to be there when that truth finally dawned on him.

CHAPTER 10

*D*avid didn't sleep a wink that night, and not
because he knew the following day would bring
them one step closer to catching Castleford and bringing the
leaders of the kidnapping ring to justice. He paced the hotel
room like a tiger after Lionel left, tempted to kick the furniture and tear the drapes from the windows in frustration. He
didn't understand why Lionel wouldn't acknowledge what
they both knew was between them, why he was being so
arrogant and stubborn. What was worse, now that he'd had a
glimpse of how little Lionel actually thought of himself, in
spite of playing the intimidating peacock whenever possible,
David wanted to hold him close more than ever.

But Lionel didn't want him to. It was as simple as
that. He stormed around the room, putting away his
things in the bureau beside Lionel's new purchases, then
unpacked the rest of those purchases on Lionel's behalf,

hanging the new suits in the wardrobe alongside his own. The new clothes didn't smell like Lionel, which irritated David to an irrational degree. It was just one more way the whole situation felt wrong.

Lionel didn't return for supper, or for hours afterwards. David waited up as long as he could, but exhaustion and the knowledge that he would need to be at least partially rested the next day drove him to bed eventually. He managed to doze off at some point, and when he awoke with the first rays of dawn the next day, Lionel was asleep in the bed next to his. David shifted to his side and watched the rise and fall of Lionel's chest in the scant, dawn light as he slept. Lionel was peaceful in sleep, which was such a contrast to the way he'd been for the last few weeks that it made David's chest tight with emotion.

He got up to use the chamber pot, grumbling about Manchester facilities being woefully behind those in London, then lit a lamp and moved to the bureau to select his clothes for the day. Something about Lionel caught his eye, though, and he turned away from the bureau to creep silently toward Lionel's bed. Lionel's bedcovers were rumpled and pushed askew, as though Lionel had been too hot in the night. The new nightshirt he'd purchased to replace his ruined one was too large and hung off one of his shoulders. The sight of Lionel's skin, even if it was just his shoulder, neck, and a small part of his chest, stirred inconvenient lust in David. He hadn't seen Lionel anything but buttoned up to the hilt in the latest fashions for weeks.

The urge to brush his fingers across Lionel's skin and to reveal more of his body was almost too much for David to bear. But then something else caught his eye. In the dim light, he could just make out the redness of Lionel's skin and what looked like a rash across his chest. Curious, he fetched the lamp from the bureau and brought it to the table that sat between the two beds to get a better look.

It was more than just a rash. Lionel's skin was badly irritated, and David could see two particularly painful-looking sores near Lionel's armpit and lower. Aching concern filled him, and he sat carefully on the edge of Lionel's bed. Desperate not to wake Lionel, he undid the top few buttons of Lionel's nightshirt and pushed it aside to reveal more of his chest. There were more sores, more irritated skin. They were bad enough that David's heart thumped faster against his ribs. They must have been extraordinarily painful. He reached a shaking hand to rest on Lionel's chest, his curiosity turning into soul-deep worry.

Lionel awoke with a start, sucking in a breath and snapping his eyes open. Sleep left him quickly, and he jerked away from David's touch so fast that he tumbled off the side of the bed.

"What are you doing?" he demanded, struggling to his feet and backing away from David. He clutched his nightshirt tightly around himself as he did.

"What's wrong with your skin?" David asked, standing. Pieces of a puzzle started to fit together in his mind, but he didn't have the entire picture yet. "Is that what the medicine was for? A skin irritation?"

"You have no right to manhandle me while I'm asleep." Lionel ignored his questions. He looked charmingly disheveled in the dawn light and as far from the carefully constructed image he presented to the world every day that David reacted physically to the intimate image, in spite of the tension in the air.

"I'm concerned," David insisted. "Some of those sores look painful."

"They're extremely painful," Lionel hissed, backing away farther as David rounded the bed and attempted to approach him.

"I'm sorry," David said. "I didn't know. You could have told me. Let me see." He stepped purposefully toward Lionel.

"No!" Lionel's protest was too loud, too anxious, and he clutched his nightshirt tighter, looking comically like a modest old biddy, which couldn't have been further from his true personality.

David sent him a lopsided grin. "You've never been shy about showing your body before. I can't even count the number of times in past years when you've deliberately shown me enough to heat my blood without ever following through on those promises."

"What I did in the past is not an excuse for you to take liberties now." Lionel continued to keep his distance, edging around David and heading for the bureau. He yanked it open and took out underthings and a new shirt. "Kindly turn away so I can wash and dress."

"Lionel." David adopted a firm tone, trying to reason with him. "Just let me see. Perhaps there's something I can do to help."

"There's nothing you can do to help, so just—"

A knock at the door cut their argument short. David let out an irritated breath and fetched his robe from the chair where he'd draped it before going to bed. As he put it on, Lionel disappeared behind the privacy screen.

"Yes?" David asked the young porter once he answered the door.

"Telegraph came for you, sir," the young man said, handing over a slip of paper. "It's urgent. From Scotland Yard."

"Thank you." David nodded to the man, then shut the door and opened the slip of paper. It was a simple note from Lord Clerkenwell, stating that he and a handful of officers were taking the first train they could catch to Manchester and that he expected to be there that afternoon.

The sense of satisfaction and impending victory that the telegraph gave David was quickly drowned by continued frustration as Lionel stepped out from behind the screen, washed and partially dressed. He headed for the wardrobe to select one of his new suits without saying anything.

"Lord Clerkenwell is on his way," David told him, walking to the bureau and setting the note down before selecting his own clothes. "We'll have Castleford by the end of the day."

"If we all play our parts," Lionel said, stepping into his new trousers.

David turned to lean against the bureau as he watched him finish dressing. Whatever faults of sullenness and stubbornness Lionel possessed, he had an uncanny sense for fashion. As soon as his trousers and waistcoat were fastened and smoothed, he stood straighter, once again the elegant fashion plate. David continued to watch as Lionel tied his necktie and donned his jacket, then brushed his hair into a style that wasn't technically fashionable, but that suited his face perfectly.

"You watch me dress the way some men watch others undress," Lionel commented with a wary, sideways look.

"It's because you do it so well," David admitted. "And well-wrapped packages are always more enjoyable to unwrap."

Lionel's sideways look turned miserable. "Well, you won't be unwrapping this package anytime soon, so stop leering." He snatched his pocket watch and wallet from the bureau, tucking them into his waistcoat and jacket.

David crossed his arms. "Because of the rash?"

"Because of a lot of things." Lionel didn't look at him as he headed toward the door.

"Where are you going?" David stood.

Lionel turned back to him as he reached the door. "To seek employment as the whore you clearly think me to be."

"I never said—"

"The Silver Serpent is on Gartside Street. Look for a door with a snake carved into the bottom left corner."

"Lionel—"

Arguing was pointless. Lionel marched out the door, shutting it far too noisily for early morning. David could only huff an irritated breath and shake his head. Lionel would be the death of him one day, that much was certain.

Disheartened, he finished selecting his clothes for the day, washed and dressed. As much as it infuriated him, Lionel was on to something with his plan to infiltrate the brothel quietly to make certain Castleford was there. As far as David knew, in spite of Lionel knowing most of the nobility in one way or another, he'd never met Castleford face to face. That gave them a chance of speaking to the blackguard before he realized who Lionel was.

Though he hadn't had a chance to consult with Lionel about it, David's plan was to go to the brothel pretending to be a client to see what he could discover. He didn't have much hope of being ushered into a room with Castleford straight off and being introduced to the man by name, but then again, he'd never visited a brothel before and had no idea what to expect.

All the same, he waited—impatiently—through the morning. He'd said he would visit John to discuss the case, but doing so without Lionel felt akin to cheating, which he wouldn't do. Instead, he bided his time seeing a few sites and making a few small purchases in order to look like a holiday-maker, before seeking out Gartside Street. He assumed most patrons of brothels didn't seek out their entertainments first thing in the morning, and the longer he gave Lionel to carry out his part of the plan, the better.

That didn't stop him from being more anxious than he anticipated as he knocked on the door with a snake carved into it shortly after lunch. He didn't expect much, and was surprised when the door was opened by a cheery young woman in a gown that was just stylish enough to distract from how revealing it was.

"Can I help you?" the young thing asked, all smiles and welcoming.

David cleared his throat, feeling decidedly awkward. "Yes, a friend recommended this establishment to me as a place where I might relax for the afternoon."

He was certain he sounded ridiculous and as transparent as glass, but the young woman reached out to grab his hand, dragging him into the well-appointed hallway and shutting the door behind her.

"And which lovely friend was this?" she asked, clinging to his arm as she walked him slowly along the hall.

David thought fast, scrambling for anything that might help. "Mr. Jeffers, the chemist," he said, remembering the name of the shop Lionel had come out of the day before.

"Oh, yes," the young woman said. "Mr. Jeffers is ever

151

so vigilant about sending friends our way. Come right this way and I'll introduce you to Matron."

David would have sighed in relief if he hadn't thought it would make him look as guilty as sin. Though the more he looked around the colorfully decorated premises, particularly the parlor that the young woman showed him to, the more he saw sin painted in every detail.

"Wait right here and I'll fetch Matron," the young woman said.

She left David alone to glance around the room. There were so many lewd paintings and decorations that they all seemed to blur into one. The vast majority were of the sort that would arouse men unlike him, but there were a few pieces more suited to his tastes tucked in between the rest, proving that the brothel catered to all sorts. It wasn't the art that caught his attention, though. He could hear voices from a room adjacent to the parlor where he waited, male voices. They were laughing and chattering animatedly. The sound had a ribald edge to it. One laugh in particular stood out to him. He would know the sound of Lionel laughing anywhere.

Without waiting for the Matron, David marched toward the door separating his parlor from whatever fun was being had in the next room. He braced himself for what he might find on the other side and pushed the door open.

The second parlor was decorated similarly to the one where David was supposed to be waiting, but instead of being empty, it appeared as though a party of sorts were underway. Half a dozen gentlemen lounged on Baroque furnishings, in various states of undress. A few were smoking from oriental hookahs that filled the room with an acrid scent, and had the glazed eyes of opium addicts. Several women, most of them partially or completely undressed, lounged with them, draping themselves across the gentlemen as though they were silk scarves. A naked woman sat at an upright piano in the corner, playing a popular tune with questionable skill.

But what caught David's attention and wouldn't let it go was the sight of Lionel sitting casually across an older gentleman's lap. He was still fully dressed, but the way he was positioned, with one foot propped up on the arm of the man's chair in such a way that allowed the gentlemen to rest his hand at the very top of Lionel's thigh sent fury pulsing through David. Worse still, Lionel was playing with the gentleman's hair with one hand while holding a glass of wine in the other.

"And so I said to the duke, if you're going to plan a supper party while balls-deep in my arse, at least let me choose the place settings for you," Lionel said in a merry tone, as if finishing a story.

The rest of the party roared with laughter. One of the undressed whores giggled so hard she slipped off of her gentleman's lap and onto the floor, where she continued to laugh, obviously inebriated. The gentleman on whose lap Lionel sat laughed loudest of all, red in the face, and shifted his hand to cup the bulge in Lionel's trousers.

David wanted to leap across the room and yank Lionel from the man's arms. The only thing that stopped him was the sudden wince of pain on Lionel's face. Once he saw that, David realized Lionel was sweating far more than usual. That, coupled with remembering the rash that must cover Lionel's entire body, convinced David that Lionel wasn't actually enjoying his ruse. Perhaps far from it.

"Monsieur, there you are." An older woman walked into the room behind David, startling him. The gentlemen and whores of the party seemed to notice him and shifted or sat straighter. Lionel remained where he was, but David could have sworn he caught a flash of relief in Lionel's eyes. "Customarily, new friends wait in the parlor to be introduced."

"I heard a party underway and I couldn't resist," David said, doing his best imitation of Lionel at a party.

He must have been at least slightly successful at his ruse, because Lionel let a laugh slip out before he could stop himself. "The more the merrier," he said, shifting the way he sat on the older gentleman's lap so that he straddled one of the man's legs and faced David. "And what a delicious specimen this one is."

"Oh. No, thank you, sir," David said, his mind spinning as fast as it could. He glanced to the whore nearest him—a dark-haired girl who couldn't have been more than fifteen—and pretended the sort of interest he would never have for her. If he was going to dive fully into the scheme, he needed to get as far outside of himself as he could. "Hello." He grinned at the girl. "And what is your name?"

"That's Lily," Matron said with a tight sigh. "She's pleasant to look at, sir, but perhaps a bit feisty."

Indeed, Lily looked as though she would just as soon tear David's head off as behave the way a whore usually did. It didn't matter to David, though. A thousand bells went off in his mind. He glanced to Lionel as subtly as he could. Lionel pretended to be flirting with Matron, but he managed to meet David's eyes for a split second and nod.

David's heart raced at their unexpected good luck. He remembered Eastleigh's cryptic words as he'd attempted to convince Lord Clerkenwell to let him go. The Silver Serpent held more of the people they were looking for than just Castleford.

"Lily," David repeated, sidling over to Lily's side and scooping an arm around her waist. Lily attempted to wriggle away from him before David leaned close to her ear, pretending to nibble it, and whispering, "Lily Logan. I know your brother. I'm like him."

Lily went dead still in his arms. When David pulled back, keeping what he hoped passed for a lascivious smile in place, she stared up at him with wide eyes. Wide, trusting eyes. She bit her lip and glanced past him to Matron, then back at David. "You'll really give me that if I...."

"Absolutely." David winked at her. "You can trust me."

Lily hugged his arm with sudden desperation.

"Well, isn't that something," Matron said with a laugh. "Whatever did you offer her, sir? Our Lily hasn't taken to any man as quickly as she's taken to you."

"That's between the fair Lily and I," David said, again imitating Lionel's coy superiority as he smiled at Lily.

"It must have been something spectacular," one of the other gentlemen said.

"Let me show the two of you to a room, then," Matron said, stepping closer to David.

"If it's all the same." David turned to her, then glanced at the others. "I do love a good party. What is this story about a duke and a supper party?" David asked Lionel.

"I was regaling the assembly with tales of my wicked youth," Lionel said without missing a beat. "Castleford, what was I saying two stories ago? About the Indian raja and his elephant?"

"Elephant cock, you mean," a dark, rather oily man who was so consumed with opium and the young, blond woman draped over him that he seemed partially melted into the sofa said.

David's heart beat in double time. Every bit of the information they'd been given about The Silver Serpent was correct. Either they'd stumbled on a bit of amazing luck, or Castleford and the Matron had grown so sloppy with opium that they'd let their guard down. The more he observed the inhabitants of the room, the more he thought the latter was entirely possible.

"Please," Lionel said, looking at David and gesturing toward the empty end of a chaise lounge where one of the more cogent gentlemen sat fondling a red-headed whore's breast. "I brought enough treats for everyone to share. Enjoy." He nodded to one of the hookahs.

David drew Lily to the end of the chaise and sat with her on his lap, pretending to be more interested in her than the opium. If Lionel had indeed provided the party with high-quality opium, then that explained everyone's laxity. And it was exactly like Lionel to know the quickest way to loosen tongues and discover hidden identities. Even Matron had a seat to take a few puffs from a hookah as she oversaw her guests. David wasn't sure if he loved the man more for his cunning or if it inspired a deeper degree of fear in him. Probably both.

"As I was saying about the raja and his elephant penis," Lionel said, snuggling back into the older gentleman's arms. David tensed, clenching his teeth so hard he thought they might shatter. "No!" Lionel blurted, sitting straight again. "I have an even better story for you."

"I love a better story," a red-faced gentleman said, then snorted into the ample bosom of the whore straddling him.

"This one is priceless," Lionel said, holding his arms out and giggling for a moment. He twisted to look at the gentleman whose lap he sat in. "You're going to love it, darling. It's a story of greed and betrayal. Very bloody, utterly sinful."

"Those are the best kind," the gentleman said, grabbing Lionel in places that made David see red and burying his porky face against Lionel's neck.

If that was the sort of behavior Lionel regularly engaged in in his past life.... But no, David knew Lionel well enough to see the stress that being manhandled was causing him. David kept a sharp eye on Lionel, wishing he'd arrived at the brothel to protect Lionel from his own plan sooner.

"So there was a particular gentleman of my acquaintance years ago," Lionel said, addressing the party as though he had taken the stage and held them all in thrall. "Lord Chisolm. Do you know him?"

Most of the others shook their heads and hummed in a haze of opium. One man nodded and said something indistinct.

"I know the bastard well," Castleford said, sitting up straighter. The whore in his lap slipped to the side. "He nearly cost me my life."

"You don't say." Lionel's eyes took on a sharp shine, even though he smiled as though he and Castleford were the closest of friends. "He nearly cost me mine as well. His treachery still might kill me at that."

"Ha! You don't know the half of it." Castleford slumped against the back of his sofa. "What'd he do to you?"

"He used me as a weapon," Lionel said with exaggerated excitement for Castleford, but a different level of intensity when he glanced to David.

"What, did he affix a blade to your cock and get you to fuck someone to death?" one of the gentlemen laughed.

"No, he was far more insidious than that," Lionel went on, lowering his voice and leaning forward in a way that drew the entire room in. "He used me as a Trojan horse."

"Yes, well, after the stories you've told us today, I wouldn't be surprised that you'd had a hundred men inside you," the inebriated gentleman laughed.

The others laughed with him, but Lionel's face turned grim. "Chisolm has a particular enemy," he went on in a hush. "A man he once controlled. A man whom he hates more than the devil for getting away from him. Chisolm knew he couldn't hurt that man directly, he was out of his reach. But he also knew that that man was a particularly close acquaintance of mine."

He met David's eyes. David sucked in a breath, his stomach twisting in dread about what he might hear next. Lionel was talking about Jewel, he was certain. He hid his fear by playing with a strand of Lily's hair, though Lily watched Lionel with as much wariness as David felt.

"So, Chisolm used you to get revenge on this old friend of his?" the red-faced gentleman asked. "How?"

"By putting a snake in my bed," Lionel said, his eyes glassy with hate.

"This story makes no sense," the inebriated gentleman snorted.

"That's because he's telling it in allegory, you dolt," Castleford said. He turned to Lionel. "You're talking about Jewel, aren't you?"

Lionel nodded.

"Who was the snake, then?" Castleford asked, more understanding in his expression than anyone else's in the room, including David.

"One Horace Cleaver," Lionel said.

"Good God." Castleford screwed up his face in disgust. "Who in their right mind would dally with that pestilential boob?"

"Someone whose pride got the better of him," Lionel said, lowering his head. "Someone without a choice, who needed money to make a change in his life, and who was ignorant of the circumstances."

"Has your prick fallen off yet?" Castleford laughed.

"It hasn't," the older gentleman with Lionel said, grabbing the front of Lionel's trousers.

Lionel yelped in pain, but managed to make it sound like a groan of desire. David wasn't fooled, though, and from the look of things, neither was Castleford.

"Chisolm is a bastard who deserves what he gets," Castleford said.

"I'd give it to him, if I knew where to find him." Lionel stared hard at Castleford.

"Would you now?" Castleford's eyes gleamed with a

desire for revenge, at least, as much as a man consumed with opium's eyes could gleam.

"I know of as many ways to make men suffer for their crimes as I do to reward them for good behavior," Lionel simpered to the old roué, tapping his nose. The buffoon laughed.

"After the way he made a mess of the escape plan we'd had in place for months, and all because of that actor, I would gladly see Chisolm burn," Castleford went on.

"I could arrange to light the torch." Lionel dragged his attention back to Castleford. "If I had the first clue where the man was."

Castleford snorted. "He's hiding, like a dog that's been whipped too many times, in a seaside cottage belonging to his old butler, near Hull."

David's pulse shot up so fast that the corners of his vision darkened. Castleford's information confirmed Lord Clerkenwell's intelligence. They knew where Chisolm was.

Lily whimpered and threw her arms around David's neck. "You have to get him," she whispered.

"We will," David murmured in return, stroking her hair and kissing her cheek, as though he were interested in other things.

Something else had grabbed hold of him and wouldn't let go, though. Lionel's story had him shaking with horror as even more of the pieces of the puzzle fell together. Their conversation from the night before slammed back into him. How could he have been such a blind dunce? Lionel was *sick*. He'd tried to tell him, and, idiot that he was, David had mistaken his words, failed to take them as the literal admission they were. Lionel had contracted something from Horace Cleaver, whoever he was. Something Chisolm had intended he carry on to Jewel.

"I have to go," he said, standing so suddenly he had to pick Lily up as he did.

"No." Lily clung to him as he tried to put her down.

"But the party has just started," Matron said, getting clumsily to her feet in a haze of opium smoke.

"I...I've got to meet someone," David said. "I cannot believe I forgot about it until just now. But I will bring him back with me later this evening." He stared deep into Lily's eyes as he spoke.

Lily loosened her grip on him, the trust in her eyes tested. But it was the bitter pain in Lionel's eyes when David glanced to him—the sort of pain that came with understanding David had figured out the truth—that wounded David's heart. Damn him, Lionel must think he was making a runner the moment he'd put two and two together.

"I will be back, love," he told Lily, meaning his words for Lionel. "Believe me, I would never abandon you in your hour of need like this."

"She needs something, all right," the red-faced gentleman snorted.

David ignored him, peeking at Lionel to see if he'd

understood the message. But Lionel had gone back to playing with the older gentleman's hair, seeming not to have a care in the world.

"I will return," he repeated as he escorted Lily to the other side of the room. He reached into his jacket, taking out a pound note from his wallet. "See that this one is ready for me," he told Matron, hoping his demand would earn Lily the time she needed to gather her things and prepare for rescue.

"Of course, sir," Matron said, winking at him.

The entire blasted situation was hopelessly muddled. David didn't have a clue where things stood with anyone anymore. All he knew was that he had to meet Lord Clerkenwell at the train station as soon as possible and bring him and his men straight to The Silver Serpent, then pack up and head on to Hull and Chisolm.

CHAPTER 11

*H*aving Chisolm's exact location confirmed brought Lionel no sense of joy whatsoever, only a smoldering determination to find the man and make him pay. Castleford's information set his brain to work thinking of all the ways he and David could rush to Hull and find the man before he had a chance to flee.

But his usually energetic mind flopped into a depressed stupor within minutes of the burst of energy Castleford's information gave him. David had figured things out. Lionel's story had done exactly what he'd intended it to do, and he'd never been more miserable. The pain was made a hundred times worse as David rushed to leave The Silver Serpent, as though spending any more time in proximity with him were a death sentence.

Of course, he knew full well that wasn't why David

left. Lord Clerkenwell was on his way, and now that they had proof of both Castleford's and Chisolm's whereabouts, the faster David brought Lord Clerkenwell to the brothel, the faster they'd be able to put the whole mess behind them. David had seen what he needed to see at The Silver Serpent and had no reason to linger. Neither did he.

"Darling, I have a few pressing matters to take care of myself before I take up my new *position* here at The Silver Serpent," he said with a wiggle of one eyebrow, kissing the miserably old roué whose lap he was sprawled across lightly on his thin, dry lips.

The roué made a pitiful sound of disappointment. "I was so hoping we might become better acquainted sooner rather than later." He fondled the front of Lionel's trousers. The gesture was obviously intended to bring Lionel pleasure, but with the current state of his sores, so much pain coursed through Lionel that it was all he could do not to scream with it. The nasty old man probably would have enjoyed that.

Lionel turned his yelp of discomfort into a laugh as he slipped off of the man's lap. "Believe me, darling," he flirted, running his fingers through the man's hair. "You will be so much happier if you wait until I gather a few particular items from my old abode and bring them here."

"Oh?" The roué lit up, licking his lips and raking Lionel's body with a glance. "What items might those be?"

"I will leave that up to your imagination, sweeting." Lionel rested his hands on the back of the chair and leaned in to kiss the man one last time. He pulled away with a wink, then turned to go, his expression sagging into disgust.

He only let his true feelings show for half a second. Matron was enough of a woman of the world to know what whores actually thought of their clients and wouldn't hold it against him, but he didn't want the others in the room, especially Castleford, to suspect he was anything other than what he pretended to be.

"Enjoy my gift to you, gentlemen," Lionel said, nodding to one of the hookahs as he crossed the room.

"It's the finest stuff I've had in ages," Castleford sighed and leaned back against his sofa. "It'll make my interminable stay here that much more bearable."

"Don't worry, love," Lionel told him as he reached the far end of the room. "Everything comes to an end eventually. Usually sooner than we suspect."

Castleford laughed, then reached for the whore that was apparently passed out from opium beside him.

Lionel continued out of the room, but Matron jumped up from her chair and followed him into the outer parlor.

"You are going to accept my offer, aren't you, Mr. Glasscock?" she asked, catching his arm and swaying slightly.

"Of course, my dear," Lionel lied, leaning in to kiss

her forehead. "Prepare your finest room for me, for I am about to earn you a small fortune."

Matron laughed low in her throat, her eyes alight with avarice. At least, alight as much as they could be after smoking so much opium.

Lionel rushed on and out of the brothel. He took a deep breath to clear his head once he was in the street. Even though he hadn't smoked himself, the fumes in the room had been enough to leave his head spinning far more than he cared for it to be. But he knew full well that wasn't the true cause of the uneasiness that twisted his stomach and had his heart beating in his throat as he made his way through the city to the hotel. David had figured things out, which meant the time had finally come to spill the whole truth instead of just apocryphal stories.

He half hoped David wouldn't be at the hotel by the time he strolled into the lobby, but of course he was. Lord Clerkenwell and a handful of officers in Metropolitan Police uniforms were there as well, drawing curious stares from the hotel guests.

"Speaking of," Lord Clerkenwell said the moment he spotted Lionel. He and David crossed the lobby to meet Lionel. Once he grew near, Lord Clerkenwell sniffed and wrinkled his nose. "You smell like an opium den."

"Hazzard of the job," Lionel answered as charmingly as possible, not feeling as well as he wanted to when faced with Lord Clerkenwell. "I assume David has informed you of today's adventure and the information it has provided?"

Lionel glanced to David. Where he expected to see David's usual, solemn expression of business he instead found a look of anxiety and compassion. It was utterly disconcerting. Nothing had ever snapped David out of the seriousness of business when their work had reached such a crucial moment. Things had changed, and Lionel wasn't sure he liked it.

"He has informed me," Lord Clerkenwell said, glancing between them. The man wasn't stupid. He had to have known there was something deeply personal going on between the two of them. But unlike David, he was focused on business. "Plying them all with opium was a stroke of genius," Lord Clerkenwell went on. "They'll all be in a stupor when we arrive, which will make the whole operation easier."

"It was the least I could do," Lionel said with an unsteady bow, pretending modesty. In fact, offering opium to neutralize the enemy was exactly his aim when he'd purchased the stuff late the night before. He only wished he hadn't had inhaled so much of it. While it had relaxed his body, he hated the muddled feeling it gave him.

"We should get on with things as swiftly as possible," Lord Clerkenwell said. "I've already telegraphed the Manchester police to let them know what we're about. Officer Morton here will be on hand to take care of the brothel as soon as we've extracted Castleford." He turned and gestured to a man in a Manchester policeman's uniform.

"I've got several more men coming, if you can wait a few more minutes," Officer Morton said.

Lord Clerkenwell nodded to him.

"I need to change into something a little less...." Lionel hesitated, picking at the fabric of his suit jacket. "Odiferous," he said at last. "If you will excuse me." He started toward the stairs.

As expected, David leapt after him. "I'll come with you."

Lionel said nothing. He only sighed as he began to climb the stairs to the fourth floor. There was no point in delaying things further. The time for truth had come.

All the same, he kept silent, even after they reached their room, shedding his opium smoke infused clothes slowly as he fetched clean ones from the new clothing he'd bought the day before.

"About that story you told at the brothel," David said at last.

"I thought it was fairly clear," Lionel muttered without turning to look at him.

David was silent for a few more seconds before saying, "When you said you were sick last night, you meant it literally."

Lionel sighed, stepping out of his trousers and tossing them on the room's empty chair, then turning to David at last. "Yes, I meant it literally," he said, eyes downcast.

David looked as uncomfortable as Lionel had ever

seen him. His usually certain expression was pinched with trepidation. "Chisolm set you up to get sick in the hopes that you would infect Jewel?"

"Yes." Lionel looked away, bending to remove his socks, then straightening and starting on the buttons of his shirt. "One has to admit, it was a very clever form of revenge."

"It was diabolical," David hissed.

"So is Chisolm," Lionel grumbled, turning away from him as he worked loose the buttons of his cuffs.

"You implied you needed money in your story, that that's why you did it," David went on. "I thought you made a fine living carrying on the way you did."

"Fine if I wanted to continue that life forever," Lionel said over his shoulder. "But as much as I enjoyed the sex, I didn't enjoy the pressure. Chisolm's offer represented a grand prize that would have enabled me enough of a nest egg to find a profession to support myself that could remain separate from my nocturnal hobbies. In short, I was greedy and ungrateful to the friends I had."

"No one would ever call you ungrateful," David said.

Lionel didn't answer. It was lovely for David to think so highly of him, but that good opinion was misplaced.

"What is it, then?" David asked after a pause, lowering his voice to a tone so tender that tears stung at the back of Lionel's eyes. "Gonorrhea? Chlamydia?"

Lionel turned to him and fixed him with a flat stare. "You know what it is, love," he said in a tone as sweet as David's. There didn't seem to be any point hiding his feelings anymore, since there was no possible way David would return those feelings now or attempt to act on them.

David frowned and stepped closer to Lionel. His concern was as deep as ever, but the repulsion Lionel expected to see wasn't there. "Let me see," he said, nodding to Lionel's shirt.

"You really don't want to see it," Lionel sighed.

"Yes, I do," David insisted.

Lionel studied him with a long, regretful stare until David stopped looking at his body and glanced up to meet his eyes. David's expression was nothing but genuine, so Lionel shrugged and tugged his shirt up over his head. He kept his eyes closed as he tossed it to the bed and stood before David in nothing but his drawers.

A moment later, Lionel's eyes snapped open and he sucked in a hard breath as David's fingertips rested on his chest.

"What are you doing, man?" He jerked away from David's touch. "The sores are infectious. You could contract it from touching them."

David's frown deepened. "To be honest, they don't look that bad."

Lionel's brow shot up in shock. "Don't look that bad?" he repeated, then glanced down at himself. His torso was littered with painful sores and red skin.

"Nothing is bleeding or oozing," David said, sending the heat of embarrassment straight up Lionel's neck to his face as David ogled him. "There isn't an odor."

"Are you suddenly a physician now?" Lionel snapped at him.

David's eyes jumped up to meet his. "I don't need to be a physician to see you've been in pain for weeks, Lionel," he said. "You're brilliant at hiding your true feelings, but not that brilliant. And I could see how much it pained you when that man handled your—" He finished by going bright red and waving a hand at Lionel's drawers. "Come on. Let's give it a look."

"I am not dropping my drawers so that you can gape at my genitals," Lionel growled. He marched past David to the bureau, throwing it open and taking out a new pair of drawers and a clean shirt. "It's bad enough that my cock and balls hurt, but I don't want my pride wounded as well."

"And you know for a fact that it's...." David went silent.

"Syphilis," Lionel snapped, turning back to face him and slamming the bureau drawer shut. "Syphilis, David. God, you're as squeamish as Phineas."

David's face went bright red, and misery filled his eyes. "Do you know for certain?" he asked, barely above a whisper.

"What else would it be?" Lionel shot over his shoulder as he moved behind the privacy screen to change his drawers. "You heard what Castleford said. Horace Cleaver was no better than a plague carrier. He died years ago, so infected with it that the morticians tossed him in a furnace rather than giving him a proper burial. And Chisolm knew the man was riddled with it. That's why he introduced us and paid me a small fortune to entertain the man for a fortnight at his country estate."

Anger for everything that had happened and his rank foolishness in being tricked into the tryst made Lionel clumsy as he stepped into his fresh drawers. He tipped sideways, slamming into the wall and groaning as the sores on his arms rubbed the wrong way.

"Are you all right?" David stepped behind the screen to help him.

Lionel batted his help away and continued dressing. "No," he snapped. "I'm infected with a deadly disease that will eventually kill me or drive me mad, a disease that prevents me from all of the enjoyments of life I once had and forbids me from giving my heart away, lest I kill the object of my affection in the process."

He stepped out from behind the screen, throwing his shirt on and feeling miserable for blurting too much too fast.

David walked slowly behind him, understanding dawning in his expression. "You figured out what Chisolm did quickly, didn't you?" he asked.

Once Lionel's clean shirt was in place and buttoned, Lionel sighed, shoulders dropping. "I knew before the end of that blasted house party. The whole thing was an elaborate ruse to infect me so that I would return to London and infect Everett. But one of Chisolm's other guests informed me of the plot and Cleaver's predicament after ten days. I left immediately, of course, praying that it wasn't true, that everything would be all right. But it was ten days—or rather ten nights—too late. In short order I developed unmistakable signs of the disease. I sought out the services of a physician who would be discreet, but no one on Harley Street would see me."

"What?" David barked, suddenly angry. "They wouldn't see you?"

Lionel stared flatly at him once again. "Don't be naïve, darling. You may be able to hide what you are, but I have never been able to. I'm too effeminate. I'm lucky that none of those physicians called the police to have me carted away."

"What if you'd been seriously ill?" David insisted. "What if you'd been bleeding or worse?"

Lionel laughed. "They would have left me to bleed out in the street rather than touch me. You know as well as I do how impossible it is for men like us to receive medical treatment."

"But then how did you receive a diagnosis?" David asked, shaking his head, outrage battling with hurt on Lionel's behalf in his expression.

"I kept trying until I found a doctor willing to treat me," Lionel said with a shrug. "Nowadays, I consult with Dr. Sullivan. He's the only one I trust at this point, thanks to his connections to The Brotherhood. He agrees with my assessment, based on my history, that my original diagnosis is probably correct."

"Probably? Has Dr. Sullivan examined you? What were the original doctor's qualifications?" David stepped closer to him. "How did he come to his diagnosis? Could he have been wrong? You should be reexamined at once."

"No, David," Lionel shouted. He pressed a hand to his temple and squeezed his eyes shut for a moment. He had to take a breath before going on. "I can see where your thoughts are heading, but there's no point. It's syphilis. I had sex with a man who was infected, several times. I developed the initial symptoms within the proper time frame. Yes, it went into remission, as syphilis does, but as you can see, it has returned in its second phase." He held his arms out to his sides. "And we all know what happens as the phases progress. There is nothing to be done, and I am far too vain to undergo the humiliation of further, intimate examinations."

"I won't accept that." David tried to step toward him again, a new phase of anger and misery entering his expression. "There has to be something we can do."

"There is nothing," Lionel said, all of the energy leaving his voice as he snatched up his clean trousers from the bed and put them on.

"You have to see another physician. There are several doctors who are members of The Brotherhood. I'm sure any one of them would—"

"David, stop. For the love of God, stop." Lionel stomped into his trousers and fastened them, glaring at David. "There's no point in doubting. I am sick. I am dying. I could be going mad as well. It might not take me tomorrow, but it will eventually. There is no cure, and frankly, the treatments are gruesome."

"That was the medicine you got from Dr. Sullivan, the bottle that broke in your suitcase, why you went to that chemist," David said.

Lionel smirked at him. "Oh, you are a clever boy, aren't you?"

"Don't be smart with me when all I want to do is help you," David snapped, moving in on Lionel as he tucked his shirt into his trousers and reached for his clean waistcoat. He paused only a few feet from Lionel. "That's why you broke things off with Jewel, isn't it?"

Lionel was too tired to continue the argument, or to pretend things were anything other than what they were. "Yes," he said, turning to sit carefully on his bed. "Granted, things had run their course between us anyhow, but I ended them abruptly because I didn't want Chisolm's plan to succeed. I didn't want Everett to get it." He paused for a moment, letting the memory wash over him. "But the bastard bloody well could have noticed that I was hurting and at the very least asked me what was wrong before running away to Scotland."

"You needed him and he wasn't there for you." David pushed a hand through his hair, staring off into space, likely remembering what Lionel had said during his argument with Everett at The Chameleon Club. His expression shifted, and he stared hard at Lionel. "I will be here for you," he said, surging forward. He dropped to his knees, startling Lionel as he knelt between his legs and took his hands. "I will be here for you no matter what happens," he pledged. "I love you, Lionel."

Lionel laughed, even as his heart overflowed with affection. "There's no point in loving me, sweetheart." He tried to pull his hands out of David's grasp, but David wouldn't let them go. "Loving me is a death sentence. Prolonged contact, particularly sexual contact, with the sores of an infected person spreads the disease. The very best I can offer you is a frustrated, sexless existence as I degenerate into a disgusting madman."

"We'll find you another physician," David insisted, shaking his head. "A competent one. There have to be newer, better treatments. Frankly, that rash on your chest and shoulder looks a good deal better than it did this morning. Perhaps there is another answer."

"David, I love you, but if you don't stop acting like a ridiculous fool, I am going to slap you into next Sunday," Lionel said, brimming with affection in spite of himself. He managed to free his hands from David's grip and rested them on either side of David's face. "I have a deadly, contagious disease that is spread through the act of love, therefore, loving me is a pointless exercise in futility. You'd be far better off patching things up with Dandie and living out the rest of your days with him."

"Is that why you're so jealous of John, no matter how many times I tell you I'm not in love with him anymore?" David pulled back, standing.

Lionel dragged himself to his feet, reaching for his jacket and throwing it over his shoulders. "Of course it is, love. John Dandie is handsome and whole, brilliantly intelligent, industrious, and caring, and no matter how much you deny it, you love him."

"Yes, I love him. As a friend. As someone I once shared a part of my life with," David said, following Lionel to the bureau as he fetched a clean necktie and put it on. "I never loved him the way I love you."

Lionel pursed his lips and stared sharply at David through the mirror as he fastened his tie. It baffled him how he could feel so desperately in love and so annoyed at the same time. "You're a fool, David Wirth," he said, his heart heavy. "I love you for it, but you're a fool. And there can never be anything more than frustration between us."

"I don't believe that," David said stubbornly.

Lionel finished with his tie and turned to face him. "What do you propose to do about it? Bully the disease into leaving my body? Willfully infect and condemn yourself for a fuck?" He shook his head. "It's best to leave well enough alone." He started for the door.

"But it's not well enough," David insisted, following him. "And I refuse to leave it alone."

Lionel was tired of arguing. He said nothing as he wrenched the door open and stepped out into the hall, David on his heels. It was almost a relief to find Dandie himself striding down the hall from the stairs as if he was on his way to fetch them. At the same time, it was the bitterest end Lionel could think of to the entire, sorry argument.

"There you are," Dandie said with an excited smile.

"The Manchester police are here and Lord Clerkenwell is eager to move."

"And so are we," Lionel said, striding past Dandie on his way to the stairs. He turned in time to see David step up to Dandie's side. The two looked perfect together, like they were a couple that was always meant to be. "I'm ready to move on, and so should you be," he called back to David before turning away.

CHAPTER 12

"Wurmured as David fell into step with him, following Lionel to the stairway.

David sighed and rubbed a hand over his face. "I wouldn't know how to explain even if there were time."

They started down the stairs, quickly losing sight of Lionel as he charged down and around the corner.

"You took my advice, didn't you?" John went on. "You spoke to him about how you feel instead of burying it all under work?"

David huffed a laugh, sending John a wary, sideways look. "Remind me to never take your advice again."

John hummed in sympathy as they rounded the last corner and stepped out into the lobby. "So I was wrong, then? He doesn't love you the way you love him?"

"Oh, he loves me, all right," David said gingerly, then

left things at that as Lord Clerkenwell stepped forward to greet them.

"Gentlemen." Lord Clerkenwell nodded. "Let's take care of this business as swiftly as possible." He turned to Lionel, who was already near the door, bristling with impatience. "Lead the way."

Their group made quite a spectacle as they marched through the streets of Manchester toward Gartside Street. David was certain it was a mistake for them to appear so obvious as they closed in on the brothel. Surely, someone would see them coming and warn Matron, giving everyone time to escape. Then again, if Lionel's opium did the trick, even if a clarion was sounded in their ears, the inhabitants of the brothel wouldn't have the presence of mind to run.

Lionel. David watched him like a hawk as they paraded on. Lionel was by far one of the cleverest men David had ever known. And the most stubborn. And the dearest. He had to be wrong about his diagnosis. There had to be some sort of treatment that none of the doctors he had consulted so far had considered. There had to be a way to—

"If you don't stop staring at me like that I'll demand that Lord Clerkenwell tie you to a lamppost to keep you from taking part in this raid," Lionel growled as he fell back to walk beside David, shocking him out of his thoughts.

"I was just—"

"I know what you were just," Lionel stopped him

again. "I never thought the day would come when I would say this, but for God's sake, David, focus on work and leave your personal feelings for later."

Lionel strode forward to join Lord Clerkenwell again. John, who had witnessed the entire exchange, stared at David with wide eyes, then burst into laughter.

"I can assure you, there is nothing here that is a laughing matter," David grumbled.

"Perhaps not." John shrugged as they reached the door with the serpent carved into it. "I cannot help but take a certain amount of giddy satisfaction in watching you be put in your place for not focusing on work. I never thought I'd see the day."

David darted an acid look at John, certain that if he knew the truth, he wouldn't be teasing. There wasn't time to debate the point, though.

Lionel stepped up to the door and knocked as though they were all there to pay a pleasant call. After a short pause, the door was opened by the same young woman who had greeted David earlier.

"Oh! Mr. Glasscock, you're back," she said, all smiles for Lionel.

David blinked at the name she used, but things moved too fast for him to dwell on it.

"Yes, darling." Lionel stepped into the doorway, pushing the young whore back with his presence and allowing space for Lord Clerkenwell and his small army of police officers to enter the establishment. "This is a raid, I'm afraid. If you will just stay calm and assist these kind officers, I'm certain whatever penalties you will incur will be light."

The young woman blanched and stumbled back against the wall as the police officers surged through the place, some heading upstairs and others to the back of the house.

"Have a care," Lionel told them, turning to Lord Clerkenwell. "Some of the young ladies and boys working here are not here of their own volition. Lily Logan is among them."

"Lily Logan?" Lord Clerkenwell's brow shot up for a moment before his expression turned downright victorious. "Gather all of the whores in this parlor," he ordered his men. "We'll sort them out as best we can."

What followed was a burst of pandemonium that left David as startled as he was relieved to bring the whole thing to an end. Officers invaded the back parlor, where many of the gentlemen who had been there earlier were passed out or in a stupor from the opium. Castleford had gone upstairs, but was dragged down, barely dressed, to join the other men as the Manchester police arrested them and prepared to drag them off to a local prison.

"This cannot be happening," Castleford whined, still high from the opium. "How did you find me? I was assured this place was a foolproof spot to hide."

No one bothered to answer his tearful pleas.

"Lord Castleford, you are under arrest, charged with abducting and trafficking children, along with soliciting minors," Lord Clerkenwell informed Castleford as one of his men shackled his hands as he sprawled in an over-stuffed chair. Lord Clerkenwell sneered and gave up informing him of what few rights he had left.

"By whose authority?" Castleford continued to protest. "You cannot do this. I am an earl. My brother is the bloody Duke of Selby."

"Your brother cooperated with Lord Clerkenwell here to locate you and bring you to justice," Lionel informed the man with a self-satisfied smile.

"Oh." Castleford merely blinked and sank into his chair in a daze. "That was bloody unsporting of Blake."

David had half a mind to rail at Castleford for all of the misery he'd caused. He wouldn't have minded kicking the bastard repeatedly in the balls for good measure, but before he could make his way across the room to the lout, Lily Logan burst into the room and ran to him, throwing her arms around his shoulders.

"You came back for me." She burst into tears, weeping against his shoulder. "You came back."

"I promised you I would." David was so startled by the strength of her reaction that all he could do was hug her and offer what little comfort he felt capable of.

Apparently, what he gave was enough. "Thank you," Lily wept. "Thank you so much."

In a flash, Lionel was by their side. "Come away, Lily," he said in his sweetest and most soothing voice. "Let's get you tidied up and ready to return to London. Your brother has been searching tirelessly for you since you first went missing, and he will be overjoyed to have you returned to him." He motioned for David to take Lily across the hall to a smaller parlor, where one of Lord Clerkenwell's men had gathered a group of children who were far, far too young to be in a brothel.

"No!" Lily surprised them by jerking to a stop and yanking out of David's arms. Her eyes were wide as she hugged herself. "No, I can't go back to London. I...I can't go back to Joe." Her face crumpled into tears.

"Of course, you can," David said, brow knitting in confusion.

Lionel sent him a disapproving look and shook his head slightly, as if David had committed a cardinal sin. He stepped between them, sliding an arm around Lily's shoulders and leading her to the stairs, where he sat with her. "Why can't you go back to Joe, love?" he asked.

Lily crumpled into a ball as soon as she was seated, hiding her face in her hands. "You don't know what I've done, sir," she wailed. "You don't know what they've made me do."

Lionel continued to rub her back. "Believe me, love, I do," he said. "I can guarantee I've done worse than you have. But that's all in the past now."

Lily shook her head, lowering her hands and staring at Lionel with large, vacant eyes. "I won't ever be able to forget those things."

"No one said you would." Lionel used his free hand to brush the tears from her pink cheeks. "I remember every horrid thing that has ever happened to me, but I don't let those things own me anymore."

"You don't?" The emotion in Lily's eyes turned to admiration.

"Of course not." Lionel shrugged. "No one ever makes it through life without horrid things happening now and then. It's part of being alive. The trick is not to hold onto those things and not to let others hold onto them for you." He glanced subtly up to David. "We can't change what's already been done, we can only move on."

"But how?" Lily sobbed, drawing Lionel's attention back to her as she sagged against his side. "How, when the things I've done make me a wicked person? Joe will never forgive me."

"Joe is your brother," Lionel insisted. "And brothers understand when we've done things because we were forced into them. My brother does, at least."

"You have a brother?" Lily glanced hopefully up at him.

"I do." Lionel smiled. "And he's the very best of men. He takes me for who I am, blemishes and all. And I'm certain your brother will do the same. He's been mad with worry this past year as he's searched for you. All he wants is to have you home."

Lily's face lit for a moment before falling again. "I can't go back to Leeds."

"Neither can your brother," Lionel said, sending David a brief look of knowing and camaraderie that took him by surprise. Even in a moment like that, Lionel could still find a way to make David feel as though the two of them were on the same side. "Joe is living in London now with a lovely man named Alistair Bevan, whom I am certain you will adore as much as he does."

Lily only looked confused for a moment before her mouth dropped open and she blinked. "Oh." She paused, blinked again, then repeated, "Oh," drawing the syllable out. "I don't suppose he *could* go home again either."

"And now you see why you have nothing in the slightest to worry about in reuniting with your dear brother," Lionel said, then kissed her forehead.

Lily stayed lost in her thoughts for a few more seconds before letting out a breath of relief. "Thank you." She threw her arms around Lionel's neck. "I knew I could trust you as soon as I saw you. And I didn't think I would trust anyone ever again. I certainly won't trust men ever again."

"Darling," Lionel laughed, standing and taking Lily with him. "Let's not throw the babies out with the bathwater."

"All right," Lily said, her spirits visibly improved to the point that warmth filled David's chest. Though that could easily have been his pride in Lionel. "But I will never lay with another man the way I've been forced to ever again," Lily vowed.

"You won't ever have to," David said, stepping forward and resting a comforting hand on her shoulder. "And believe me, you have friends who will keep you safe for the rest of your life."

He glanced to Lionel, letting him know that the same went for him. Lionel arched one eyebrow, acknowledging that he understood David's meaning, but that he wasn't going to do a bloody thing about it.

"We're nearly finished here," John said as he stepped into the hall from the main parlor. "I'm going to go with Officer Morton to help process the local gentlemen. Lord Clerkenwell wants to speak to the two of you about Castleford."

David and Lionel exchanged a look, then marched back into the parlor. Lily grabbed hold of Lionel's hand and went with them.

"It was you who gave us away." Matron launched herself toward Lily as soon as they entered the room. One of Lord Clerkenwell's men held her back, but she was furious all the same.

"It wasn't me," Lily said, standing straighter, but holding fast to Lionel's hand. "But it would have been. I would have brought an army of avenging angels down on this place if I could have." She turned to Lord Clerkenwell. "You don't know the things she made us do. She's an evil one, Matron is."

"I'm certain the court will be more than happy to hear your story," Lord Clerkenwell said, trying to appear confident for Lily's sake, but clearly ready to move on with things, if David judged his look correctly.

"The court won't listen to the likes of me," Lily said with far more seriousness than someone her age should have possessed. "They think we're worms. You take any of us into a court, and we'll be the ones who end up in prison, not the ones who really belong there."

David's heart sank. Lily was right. He glanced to Lionel, who seemed to know it too, then at Lord Clerkenwell. "Is there a way to quietly take the innocent victims of this whole thing away without the law interfering?"

"There most certainly is." Lord Clerkenwell nodded to one of his men. "Zink, please take Miss Lily and the other children to the hotel. Quietly. Find them some decent clothes, and book train fare to take them all to London, to Stephen Siddel's orphanage, as soon as possible."

"Yes, my lord." The man, Zink, nodded and gestured for Lily to come with him.

Lily gasped and cowered against Lionel's side, shifting from indignant and powerful to fearful in a moment.

"It's all right, love," Lionel assured her. "You'll be safe with Lord Clerkenwell's men. Go with Officer Zink, and I promise I'll come visit you once you're safe with your brother."

Lily seemed reluctant to go, but stepped away from Lionel all the same. She left the room with Zink, glaring at Matron as she did. Once she was gone, activity resumed in the parlor as the Manchester police began escorting people out of the building.

"All in all, I'd say that went well," Lord Clerkenwell said, forming a circle with David, Lionel, and John. "Plying them with opium was a stroke of genius."

"One would almost think you've been in a situation

to entertain a bunch of reprobates before," John said with a lopsided grin and a conspiratorial wink for Lionel.

If John expected Lionel to respond with equal teasing, he was disappointed. "I don't have time for your jests, Dandie." Lionel pulled himself up to his full height, sending John a scathing look that David was certain was fueled by jealousy. "We've caught two of the bloody demons, but Chisolm is still out there, and I want him captured."

"You'll have to act fast, then," Castleford spoke up from his chair.

They all turned to him. David was surprised the man was still there and alert, though he wore a grin as though he were still floating in a cloud of opium.

"What do you mean?" Lord Clerkenwell asked, marching to tower over him.

Castleford cowered as though seeing the very devil. "Only that Chisolm has plans to escape by sea before any of you know where he is."

"He's in Hull," David said, crossing his arms and glaring at Castleford. The man was lower than swine, as far as he was concerned, and had already given them all the information they needed. "All we need to do—"

"You'll never reach him in time," Castleford interrupted.

They all stared at him again.

"What do you mean?" Lord Clerkenwell asked.

Castleford shrugged as though he enjoyed being the center of attention. "He has friends, you know. Friends who are willing to smuggle him out of the country. For a price, of course." Castleford's expression took on a dreamy look. "Though can one call those friends, if money needs to be exchanged to maintain the friendship?"

"Who are his friends?" David asked, joining Lord Clerkenwell in standing over the man.

Castleford seemed to notice them for the first time and shuddered in fear all over again. "I don't know. Truly, I don't. But before he left, he said he would be gone by the fifteenth."

"The fifteenth of what?" Lord Clerkenwell asked. "It's been a fortnight already since he fled your estate."

"Today is the thirteenth," Lionel said, a fierce light in his eyes. "If we're going to catch Chisolm before he escapes, we have to be in Hull immediately."

"If this rat is telling the truth," John argued.

"I never lie," Castleford said with the most disingenuous look David thought it was possible for a man to have.

"Whether he's telling the truth or not," David said, "we cannot take the risk. Lionel is right." He shifted to meet Lionel's eyes, feeling as though he'd finally found a way to truly be of help to the man he loved. "We need to leave for Hull immediately."

CHAPTER 13

Standard wisdom said that old habits were hard to break, but as David returned to the hotel with Lionel and John, he could barely remember his old habit of focusing on work to the detriment of everything else.

"Are you certain you don't need any help shopping for more clothing?" he asked Lionel as they rushed about their room, packing their things. "John can purchase tickets for our journey while I help you."

Lionel slammed shut the lid of his battered and stained suitcase, which he'd just finished packing with his new clothes, gave John a brief, bitter glance, then frowned at David. "When have you ever known me to need assistance shopping?"

David shrugged, his back and shoulders itching with the need to do something, anything, to help the man he loved. Nothing else mattered, not even catching Chisolm.

"I could go back down to the laundry to see if the concierge is wrong and if they're finished cleaning your old things."

Lionel huffed in irritation, pursed his lips and stared hard at David for a moment, then said, "The laundry isn't finished with my old things. You saw the look on the head housekeeper's face when I asked about them. The woman knows what I am, and frankly, I would be surprised if I ever saw those things again." He wrenched his suitcase off the bed and carried it to the table where David was packing his own things. "I've left them a forwarding address all the same. There's nothing for it but to purchase a few more essentials that I'm far more likely to find here than in Hull. So if you will excuse me, I'll be about my business."

"Lionel." David reached for him, grabbing Lionel's arm before he could escape to the door. Lionel didn't flinch the way David expected him to, but he glared as though David had committed a mortal offense. After holding his gaze for several seconds without knowing how to put the wealth of emotions he felt into words, David let out a breath. "We need to talk about things."

Lionel's jaw hardened. He turned his glance to John, reminding David that they weren't alone. "There's nothing to say," he murmured, shaking out of David's grasp. "I'll meet you at the train station in an hour."

David could only stand helplessly by as Lionel fled the room, shutting the door loudly behind him. As soon as Lionel was gone, David let out a breath, his shoulders sagging helplessly.

"He'll come around." John strode toward him, thumping David's shoulder. "Whatever you've done to put his nose out of joint, he'll come around."

A split-second of irritation deep in David's gut gave way to a deeper melancholy. "I haven't done anything to offend him." He crossed back to the bureau to take the last of his things from the drawer to his suitcase.

"Really?" John seemed cautiously amused. "You used to offend me all the time."

David shot a wary, sideways glance at John as he placed his things in the suitcase. "I know you only want to help, John, but none of this is a laughing matter."

John must have seen the misery in David's expression. His usually jovial spirits grew serious. "I take it you discovered what's at the heart of the problems between you two."

"Lionel is sick," David admitted, barely above a whisper. He shut the lid of his suitcase, then turned to lean against the table. He rested one hand on Lionel's battered suitcase. "He's been keeping the truth from me all this time, but he's sick."

John crossed his arms, his brow knitting into a frown. "How sick?"

David dragged his eyes up to meet John's. If it were anyone else, he would have made up a story to protect Lionel, but he trusted John. "He says it's syphilis."

The shock in John's eyes melted into sympathy. "I'm

sorry, David." He paused, his brow pinching. "What do you mean he *says* it's syphilis? Do you think he's lying?"

David shook his head and sighed, then rubbed a hand over his face. "I asked a few questions when he told me, and I'm not convinced he received proper medical care when he was initially diagnosed."

"A lot of us don't," John admitted, though by the gravity in his expression, David could tell John wasn't convinced hope was possible in the situation.

"Apparently, Chisolm set him up with a man he knew was sick with it so that Lionel would become infected and carry it on to Everett Jewel," David went on.

John flinched, grimacing. "That strikes me as an overelaborate plan for revenge."

"Does it?" David shrugged. "This is Chisolm we're talking about. If he's capable of spearheading a child kidnapping ring and torturing Jewel throughout his youth, I can certainly see him making Lionel into a Trojan Horse simply for revenge."

John opened his mouth to make some reply, but thought better of it and shook his head instead. "Whatever Chisolm's motivations and madness, it sounds like what's done is done. If Lionel says he's sick, who are we to doubt him?"

"He can't be sick," David said with sudden passion, pushing away from the table and taking a step toward John. "I've waited my whole life for a man I could love as much as I love my work. I've waited interminably for someone to give me a reason to glance up from my books and cases and to make me enjoy my life, not just live it."

"Thank you for that glowing endorsement," John said with a wry twitch of his lips.

"You know full well that I care about you," David said with a frown. "I cared about you when we were together and I always will, but—"

"I was never your soulmate," John finished for him with a nod, clapping a hand on David's shoulder. "I know. I knew back then too. Which is why I left."

"Lionel was like a breath of fresh air right from the start," David went on. "He was the most beautiful thing I'd ever seen. He makes me laugh, and he keeps my head from swelling."

"While making your other head swell constantly, I'm sure," John said with a grin.

"God, I have wanted him so badly for so long," David said with passion, proving John right. He broke away, pacing restlessly across the room. "But that's impossible now."

"Is it?" John asked, following David with his gaze but not impeding his pacing.

"Syphilis is highly contagious," David said, miserable to his core. "Lionel has rebuffed every attempt I've made to seduce him, recently and through the years."

Now that he knew the truth, a thousand tiny interactions the two of them had had made complete sense. The wealth of flirtatious glances and suggestive touches they'd shared over the years would have turned into the most torrid of love affairs, if Lionel hadn't taken his vow of celibacy. That vow made all the sense in the world now. It wasn't a vow to punish himself for the profligate ways of his youth, as David had always assumed, it was Lionel's way of keeping the men he loved safe. Lionel had a far bigger heart and was a far better man than David knew him to be.

"You know," John said slowly, breaking into David's aching thoughts, "there are ways to make love to someone who is ill like that which can reduce the possibility of passing the disease along."

"Lionel won't want to risk it," David grumbled.

"But there are ways," John repeated. "Preventatives and the like."

David winced at the clinical sound of the word, though he knew the devices John was talking about. They were popular with prostitutes for the prevention of disease.

"And if the two of you truly love each other, as anyone with eyes can see you do," John went on, "it is entirely possible to enjoy a long, loving relationship without sex."

David's heart and gut rejected the notion, but guilt immediately followed the rejection. What kind of a man did it make him if he shrank away from love because it came without the possibility of intimacy?

"I can hardly think about the future right now," he said, pausing his pacing to return to his suitcase, shutting the lid. "I can't think about anything but making sure Lionel is safe and cared for."

John let out a gentle laugh. "You truly have grown a tender heart, then."

"I know." David turned to him, haunted by how true it was. "I don't even know who I am anymore."

"You're a man with something more important than his case load to worry about," John said, crossing to wrap him in an embrace of support. "It warms my heart to see it."

David remained stiff in his embrace. "I don't know how to be this way," he muttered, pulling away. "I'm not sure I like it."

"Change is never comfortable," John admitted with a shrug. "But trust me, you're going to be happier with this change than you would have been otherwise."

David sent him a wary look before gathering his suitcase and Lionel's and starting for the door.

"One more thing before we go." John stopped him. He marched forward, reaching for the door handle, but not opening the door yet. His face pinched slightly. "I'm thinking of moving back to London."

"You are?" David blinked. "What about your law practice up here? What about your partner?"

John winced. "It's not working out," he admitted. "With the practice or with Brandon."

David's brow shot up. "Professionally or personally?"

"Both," John admitted. "It hasn't been working for a while. Brandon knows it as much as I do, though we haven't formally called things off yet. I wanted to let you know before I simply showed up in London and upset whatever apple cart you have."

David frowned. "You mean, you don't want to get in the way of me and Lionel."

"I would rather die," John said with his usual teasing, though there was enough seriousness in his eyes to tell David he meant it. "I won't return to London if you think it would interfere with you and Lionel," John went on. "I can always go abroad."

"Don't stay away from London on my account," David said, walking through the door once John finally opened it. "Your life is your own."

"True, but you and I both know—even more now that you've told me what's going on—that if I move to London before things between you and Lionel are sorted, Lionel would see it as a direct threat."

David let out a breath, feeling as though a whole new weight had descended on him. "You're right. God knows just how much Lionel would read into your return. He'd probably take out a lease on a flat for you and I and lock us inside until we 'sorted out our differences' so that he could claim not to be jealous."

"And we both know that Lionel eats his heart out with jealousy any time the two of us are in the same room together," John said with a grin.

"Because you're hale and healthy and he thinks he's going to die or go mad," David said without a hint of amusement. So many things made perfect sense now that he knew the truth.

They reached the bottom of the stairs, and John turned to take the suitcases from David. "Go on," he said. "Go find Lionel and tell him how you feel. I'll take care of your tickets and meet you at the station. I'll even check out of the hotel for you."

"Are you certain?" David's chest throbbed with the need to find Lionel and say all the things he didn't know how to say.

"Absolutely certain."

David nodded to John, then headed for the door, full of energy. Perhaps John was right and it didn't matter whether Lionel was sick. David truly had waited his entire life for someone who he could love and be loved by, someone who would make everything else worthwhile. Even if they couldn't make that love physical, it didn't mean it wasn't love.

His enthusiasm began to crack as he strode up and down the street containing all of the tailor's shops without finding Lionel. What if Lionel didn't want him? Lionel prided himself on his intelligence and on his appearance. What if he didn't want David around to witness what could very well be an ugly decline? Was it better to respect Lionel's wishes on the matter, if those were indeed his wishes, or to force Lionel to let David care for him?

David stopped at the far end of the street, shoving a hand through his hair and glancing around at the unfamiliar buildings. He didn't know where he was, in reality or in the tangle of his life. The reason he'd put so much focus and energy into his work over the years was because it was infinitely easier to focus on something concrete, something with immediate solutions, where people could be helped in definitive ways, than it was to navigate the twists and turns of love. He could track kidnappers, locate safe housing for the men of The Brotherhood, and fight the injustice of discrimination men like them were so often faced with, but he had no idea how to convince Lionel that he was loved, no matter what.

Time was running out either way. He started back down the street, hoping he was traveling toward the train station. On a whim, he ducked inside a chemist's shop—thankfully not the one where Lionel had gotten his information about The Silver Serpent before—to ask for directions.

"You're only two blocks away, sir," The wizened old man behind the counter told him with a smile. "You've plenty of time to catch your train."

"Thank you." David was about to turn and leave when an idea struck him. "Do you have any sort of ointments to treat irritated skin?"

"Irritated with a rash?" the chemist asked, pushing his spectacles farther up his nose.

David nodded. "Or, perhaps, painful sores?"

"Ah." The man nodded, held up a finger, and turned to the shelves behind him. He selected a green glass jar and brought it to the counter. "I mix this myself. It's mostly calendula with a few special things imported from India, but it works miracles."

"It sounds perfect." David reached into his pocket for his wallet as a second idea struck him. He cleared his throat and glanced furtively at the chemist as heat rose to his face. "You wouldn't, er, have any French letters for sale, would you?" he asked, certain he was blushing up a storm.

The chemist grinned knowingly and bent to retrieve a small, flat packet from under his counter without a word.

David paid for his purchases, slipping the ointment into one pocket and the French letter into the pocket of his waistcoat before thanking the man one last time and heading out the door. Lionel would probably kick up all sorts of fuss if David even brought up the subject of intimacy with preparation, but he would cross that bridge when he came to it.

"There you are," John called to him as though he had been waiting impatiently once David reached the train station. Lionel was already there with him, looking as closed up and guarded with his expression as a statue. "I was about to send someone out to look for you. You're in luck. I managed to purchase tickets for a train departing in about fifteen minutes."

"Then we'd better run." David picked up his pace, meeting John and then continuing on with him and Lionel toward the numbered platforms.

"Telegraph me when you reach Hull to let me know

how things are proceeding," John said as they waited in line at the barrier. "I'll let Lord Clerkenwell know you two were able to leave immediately."

"Thank you." David rested a hand on John's arm as Lionel juggled his suitcase, a tied parcel from a tailor's shop, and the two tickets he held awkwardly in one hand, presenting them to the porter at the barrier. "I only regret we didn't have more time to catch up."

"We'll have all the time in the world to catch up soon," John assured him, handing David's suitcase over and thumping his shoulder. "Remember everything I said."

"How could I forget?" David sent him a wry grin, then hurried on after Lionel onto the platform.

As they rushed toward the first-class compartments of the train that stood steaming and ready to leave, Lionel asked, "What does John mean that you'll have all the time in the world to catch up soon?"

David glanced sideways at him. The last thing he wanted to do right then was open the can of worms John's revelation about returning to London represented. "Once we bring Chisolm to justice," he said, hoping Lionel would be satisfied with the answer.

Whether he was or not, they had to hurry to make it to their compartment as a conductor called for all remaining passengers to board the train. They made it in the nick of time. The train started to roll forward before they were finished stowing their cases and Lionel's new purchases on the racks above their seats.

"With any luck, we'll nab Chisolm before he knows we've arrived in Hull, then we can go home and put this whole thing behind us," David said, sinking into his seat, feeling far wearier than he should have, even though it had been a momentous day. The journey would continue through the night, but he wasn't counting on sleeping for much of it.

As he shifted, attempting to find a comfortable way to sit, Lionel nodded to David's jacket pocket. "What do you have there?" he asked.

David glanced at his pocket, then reached for the jar. "I bought something for you." He took out the jar, handing it across the compartment to Lionel as the train picked up speed, its whistle sounding.

Lionel studied the jar with one eyebrow raised dubiously.

"It's for your rash and sores," David admitted, no idea why he suddenly felt sheepish about his offering. Perhaps it was the intimacy of purchasing something meant to be applied to the skin with the purpose of soothing the flesh.

"I don't need you to take care of me, David," Lionel said, as though he could see right through the gesture. "I've done quite all right taking care of myself these last few years."

"I want to take care of you," David insisted. "I don't care if you're sick or what the future might hold, I love you and—"

"I don't want to talk about this right now." Lionel

nearly shouted over him, shrinking back into his seat and hugging himself, the jar of ointment still in one hand.

"Lionel, I—"

"So far today, I have been awakened by a man inspecting my person without my permission, been fondled by a malodorous oaf in a way that caused more pain than I want to admit to, nearly ended up whoring myself out for the sake of an investigation, participated in a raid on a brothel, rescued a beautiful and unfortunate young woman whose brother wants her back, confessed my darkest secrets to someone whose opinion means the world to me, had my pride utterly decimated, and watched said someone flirt with his former lover. All without stopping for a proper meal. I simply cannot deal with one more thing today."

David snapped his mouth shut, swallowing all the things he wanted to say. "You're right," he mumbled. "It can wait."

"Thank you," Lionel said breathily, closing his eyes. He turned to sit with his back wedged into the corner of his seat, swung his legs up onto the seat with him, and hugged himself. "Now, if you will excuse me, I am going to attempt to sleep. Wake me if someone comes around with a tea cart."

David pressed his lips tight and watched as Lionel shut in on himself and turned his face away. Lionel's posture was so defeated that it was all David could do not to pull him across the cramped compartment and into his embrace so that Lionel could sleep in the shelter of his arms. He couldn't imagine the sort of distress Lionel must have been in, but he sure as hell wasn't going to let him go through it alone. He vowed to try to stay awake so that Lionel could finally rest. If he couldn't hold Lionel, at least he could hold vigil over him and protect him from afar.

CHAPTER 14

$\mathcal{L}$ ionel expected to spend the night jostling about the train carriage, writing in pain. It shocked him to wake up to the sound of the train's shrill whistle as dawn light filtered in around the corner of the blinds David must have pulled down over their compartment's windows during the night. He'd slept most of the way to Hull. What was odder still was the relative relief of standing and stretching once he woke up. The pain he expected to feel at the simple gesture was negligible.

He hadn't fully stretched for weeks, so as soon as he was certain David was still asleep, curled up on his seat with his arms crossed and a frown on his handsome face, Lionel removed his jacket—which still smelled of fresh cotton from the tailor's shop—and lifted his arms above his head to stretch more thoroughly. It felt so good, and so strange, that he couldn't conceal a sigh of pleasure as his muscles and skin moved without irritation.

As soon as David popped one eye open, Lionel snapped to stand straight, feeling as though he'd been caught doing something dirty. He glanced around for a way to hide, or at least regain his dignity, and ended up reaching for his suitcase on the rack above his seat.

"It seems you slept well," David said groggily, pushing himself to sit and rubbing his face. He was a disheveled mess. His clothes were rumpled and creased from sleeping on the train, his dark hair stuck up at odd angles and was in need of a wash, and stubble covered his strong jaw. All in all, he looked like the very picture of vulnerability.

Lionel's heart pounded against his ribs at the sight, in spite of his efforts to concentrate on taking down his suitcase, opening it, and searching for his toiletries. He couldn't take his eyes off the lock of David's hair that slanted across his forehead or the softness of his lips. It took all of his powers of resistance not to slip across to David's seat so that he could stroke his hair into submission and kiss him until they were both in a state entirely inappropriate for a train approaching its destination.

"I know. I look a fright," David grumbled, then yawned as he pushed a hand through his hair.

Lionel started, realizing he'd paused what he was doing simply to look at David. He cursed himself for being a clumsy, obvious mess and found the leather case within his suitcase that contained his hairbrush and other things. Ogling David was a pointless endeavor, especially now. There wasn't a damned thing he could do about his raging attraction, and the only thing he could do about his all-consuming love was to nobly sacrifice what he wanted for the sake of David's health.

But it hurt. More than any of the sores that covered Lionel's body. His heart ached pitifully as he held a small mirror in one hand as he brushed his hair with the other. David watched him, his expression veiled. That could only mean one thing. David was reconsidering everything he thought he felt now that he knew the truth.

"Can I borrow that?" David held out his hand, nodding to Lionel's brush, once Lionel had made himself reasonably presentable.

Lionel stared at him as though he'd asked for a limb. "Don't you have a brush of your own?"

David shrugged and glanced up to his suitcase in the rack above him. "It's in there."

"Then retrieve it." Lionel hugged his brush close. "I do not share grooming implements with anyone."

David let out a sleepy laugh. "It's just a brush, Lionel."

"I would have you know that I ordered this brush from Germany. It cost more than your entire suit."

That only made David laugh harder. "Who orders a hairbrush from Germany?"

"Someone with discerning tastes who takes great pride in his appearance," Lionel answered, sitting straighter and attempting to look as dignified as possible in the clothes he'd slept in.

David shook his head and arched one eyebrow.

"You're not afraid to let me use it because you believe it's contaminated, are you?"

Heat flooded Lionel's face. He tried to look indignant, but David had hit the mark with painful precision. "One cannot be too careful," he muttered.

David huffed a breath and held out his hand again. "Give me the damn brush, Lionel." The train whistle screeched, and he went on with, "It appears we're about to arrive, and I would rather risk illness than frighten any small children that might be at the station by looking like a werewolf."

"You do not look like a werewolf," Lionel sighed, handing over his brush. A sudden burst of coyness hit him as he went on with, "You look ruggedly handsome."

David's brow shot up as he brushed his hair. "And you like the ruggedly handsome look, do you?"

"There is a certain amount of...appeal to that sort of raw, masculine power," Lionel admitted breathlessly, a quiver in his gut.

David finished brushing his hair with a devilish grin, then handed the brush back to Lionel. "I'll keep that in mind," he said with a wink.

Lionel cleared his throat to fight off the wave of lust that threatened to make a mess of him. It was bad enough that he wanted something he couldn't have, but the scintillating buzz of hope that David's flirting gave him was too much for his crushed spirits to handle. David couldn't be serious. He knew just how disgusting he was now, how much of a risk even touching him presented.

Lionel's gloomy assessment of the situation seemed to prove itself true when they arrived in Hull and found a hotel that would accommodate them.

"Two rooms, please," David told the young woman behind the counter at the humble, seaside inn they'd found with vacancies.

Lionel's heart sank. Of course, David wouldn't want to share a room with him this time, knowing what he knew now.

"I've got the two attic rooms free," the woman said. "If you want to stay on the same floor. They're the only two up there, and if you open all the windows, they get a nice sea breeze and aren't too hot."

David studied Lionel for a moment, something that was either compassion or pity in his eyes. "Yes," he told the woman. "That would be fine."

The attic rooms turned out to be at the top of a harrowingly narrow staircase. They were both tiny, with slanted ceilings and a faint smell of damp. Lionel silently parted ways with David as he entered his room. He tossed his suitcase on the tiny table that stood next to the door and narrowed his eyes at the bed. It was barely big enough for one, let alone....

He sighed and rubbed a hand over his face. How could he even think things like that anymore? Aside from the fact that every fiber of his body wanted to twine itself with David's. He considered himself a maudlin fool for wanting nothing more than to have David hold him while he lamented his sorry fate.

"This is ridiculous," he whispered to himself, crossing the room to throw open the wardrobe wedged into the corner where he would store his things. "No more bemoaning your fate, Lionel Mercer. You got yourself into this mess, and now you'll face the consequences. Finding Chisolm should be your only priority."

As soon as the words were past his lips, he laughed at himself. David was the one perpetually consumed with business to the point of excluding his personal life, not him. "Though I suppose it's true what they say about turning into someone you spend your life with," he went on muttering as he crossed back to his suitcase to unpack.

"Are you talking to yourself?" David asked from his own room. With both of their doors open and the hallway between them barely larger than the width of the doors themselves, it was almost as though they were in the same room.

"I'm so sorry to have disturbed you," Lionel snapped, stepping toward the door, intent on shutting it.

"Leave it open," David said. "We can talk this way."

Lionel let out a heavy sign, pressing his fingertips to his forehead. "Why obtain separate rooms if all you want to do is talk?"

David shrugged, dipping temporarily out of sight as he hung his clothes in the wardrobe in his room. "I thought you would be more comfortable with your own room."

"You thought *you* would be more comfortable, you mean," Lionel muttered.

"No," David said with deliberate patience, "I did it for you. Because you were so furious with me for getting just one room in Manchester."

"And it doesn't have anything at all to do with the fact that I have a dread disease that you're not afraid of catching," Lionel said sullenly, moving to hang his newly purchased suits in his wardrobe.

"Don't be tetchy, Lionel," David called across the space between them. "You're insufferable enough when you're merely being arrogant, but when you add martyrdom to the mix, you're a pill."

Lionel froze in the middle of hanging a suit. David was being deliberately difficult, but for some ungodly reason, it made Lionel want to smile. It was the sort of banter they'd enjoyed day after day for years, when everything was normal and the threat of illness was dormant.

"You adore it when I'm difficult," he called back, allowing himself to indulge in the illusion that nothing had changed for just one moment. "You consider it a challenge."

"You certainly are a challenge," David said with a wry laugh.

Lionel brushed the suit he'd just hung in the vain hope it would unwrinkle itself, then turned to unpack more things. He nearly jumped out of his skin when he found David standing in the doorway with his arms crossed, watching him as though he'd been there for ages instead of seconds. For the space of a few heartbeats, the sight of David—still looking rough and appealing—thrilled Lionel's heart. Until he saw the deep sorrow in David's eyes.

"Don't look at me like that," Lionel mumbled, going back to his suitcase. "I can't stand pity."

"It's not pity," David insisted, taking a step into the room. He glanced around. "Where is that ointment I bought you?"

"I told you, I don't need you to take care of me," Lionel snapped, eyes darting straight to the shelf in the wardrobe where he'd put the jar. His heart whispered something entirely different from his words, though.

"Can I at least see how the rash is doing today?" David asked.

"No," Lionel said definitively, eyes wide in offense. His chest squeezed in disappointment. Their banter had been an illusion. Things weren't normal. Far from it. "Go away, David. I cannot stand your pity."

"You think what I feel is pity?" David asked, his tone offended.

"Yes, I do. And I want none of it." Lionel continued unpacking his things without looking at him.

David let out a long-suffering breath. "I regret everything that has happened to you," he said, "but if you think I pity you, then you understand nothing."

"I understand that we are here to catch Chisolm before he gets wind that we're after him," Lionel said. "So if you will excuse me, I'd like to wash and change clothes before venturing out in search of the man."

David was silent for several long seconds, studying Lionel as he finished unpacking, deliberately not meeting his eyes. "All right," David said at last. "I'll wash and change as well, and we'll look for him together."

Half an hour later, they each emerged from their rooms looking considerably more presentable. Though Lionel found himself regretting that David had shaved. He didn't usually care for a man with an unkempt appearance, but David was the exception. David was the exception to just about everything, including his determination to keep a stiff upper lip and not care what people thought of him. It was infinitely worse having David fuss over him as if stubbing his toe would cause him to expire on the spot as they explored the streets of Hull, looking for the address of Chisolm's former butler, than it was to have the man attempting to seduce him at every turn.

"Shouldn't we alert the Hull police to this investigation before we knock on Chisolm's door and shout 'surprise'?" Lionel asked as they made their way down a steep street to a row of cottages that bordered a rocky cove.

"We're not going to leap out and surprise anyone," David told him, adding, "Careful, the pavement is wet there."

"Yes, I still have eyes," Lionel hissed. "You told Dandie you would telegraph him as soon as we arrived."

"He probably hasn't gotten out of bed yet," David reasoned. "We'll just slip down to the cottage where Chisolm is hiding to see if we can spot him. Then we'll find a telegraph office and let John know that we've arrived. And we'll telegraph Lord Clerkenwell with what we've discovered as well."

Lionel made a doubtful noise, but before he could say anything, David rounded on him.

"You're the one who wanted to come out in search of Chisolm first thing after settling in the hotel," he growled.

Lionel clenched his jaw. There was no way he would admit that his eagerness to search for Chisolm was mostly so that he could avoid being in a confined space with David for a second longer than he needed to be. The closer he stayed to David, the harder it was to resist what he knew was right for David's own good.

"I'm impatient to bring Chisolm to justice," Lionel said through clenched teeth. "He has so much to answer for."

"Believe me, Lionel." David took a step toward him, resting a hand on Lionel's arm with a look that was so compassionate it made Lionel's skin crawl. "No one wants to bring Chisolm to justice more than I do."

Lionel laughed. "I highly doubt that."

"I now have a very personal grudge against the man," David said, his expression darkening.

Lionel was about to say more, but the upstairs window of the cottage they stood in front of swung open, and a round, red-faced woman popped her head and shoulders out.

"Who out there is talking about Chisolm?" the woman said.

Lionel's blood seemed to freeze in his body. He exchanged a look with David before they both glanced up at the woman.

"Do you know the man?" David asked the woman.

The woman let out a wry laugh. "Do I ever. Right royal pain in the arse that one was. Strutting about the place as if he owned us all."

"Is he here?" Lionel took a step closer to the window, his heart suddenly racing.

The woman sniffed. "He's around here somewhere, the snake."

"Where?" Lionel and David asked at the same time.

"Who knows?" The woman shrugged. "He was staying at Culver's cottage up until three days ago."

Lionel sucked in a breath, counting back through the eventful days they'd just had. A sinking feeling formed in the pit of his stomach.

"What happened three days ago?" David asked, though Lionel had a feeling he already knew the answer.

"He got a telegram from London," the woman said. "I know because my niece, Flora, was keeping house for him and saw him trying to burn it in the stove. She pulled it out of the fire before the whole thing burned. Some bloke named George warned him the coppers were on to him."

Lionel swore under his breath and shot an angry glance to David. "I told you we should have come after Chisolm first."

David returned his look with a wary one that might just have been agreement. "What's done is done," he

217

sighed. "Do you know if he's still in the area?" he asked the woman.

The woman shrugged again. "How should I know? Except, if he's wanted by the law, where else could he go when he's made such a nuisance of himself that we all know what he looks like?"

Lionel tilted his head to the side. It was a fair enough point. And Castleford's information seemed to be that Chisolm didn't have a definitive way out of Hull until the next day at least. "I think we've found out what we need to know," he told David. "Many thanks," he told the woman in the window, then turned to march up the street.

"Lionel, wait. Where are you going?" David called after him.

"To telegraph Lord Clerkenwell as we should have done when we first arrived," he said. "And after that, to find the bloody bastard myself."

CHAPTER 15

*D*avid jogged to catch up with Lionel, frowning at himself for not following Lionel's advice in the first place. He'd made the decision to go after Castleford first with his head instead of heeding the impulse of Lionel's heart to secure Chisolm while they could. The decision had been bloody typical of him, but the entire journey had taught him nothing if not that his heart was just as important as his head.

"If Chisolm knows we're after him, knows it enough to abandon the safety of the cottage where he's been hiding, then it's likely he has ways of knowing we've arrived in Hull," he reasoned aloud once he caught up to Lionel.

Lionel glanced sideways at him without breaking his stride. "We've probably just announced our presence to him as effectively as if we'd marched through town blasting trumpets."

"Then time is of the essence," David went on. "You find a telegraph office and send word to Lord Clerkenwell and John. I'll take myself to Hull's central police station to inform them of the situation. We'll meet back at the hotel in an hour and decide what to do from there."

They reached a crossroads at the edge of the town and moved in different directions. Before walking on, David turned back.

"Lionel," he called. When Lionel paused and turned to him, David went on with, "Be careful. I...I don't know what I would do if anything happened to you."

Lionel's expression flickered from surprise to a brief pinch of annoyance to something tender and conciliatory. His shoulders dropped, and for a moment, David caught a rare look of vulnerability in Lionel's eyes. "I'll be careful, love," he said before marching on.

David couldn't shake the feeling that his heart walked away with Lionel. He had a mission ahead of him, an important task related to the business that had occupied his life for the past several months. He should have focused on it with single-minded determination, but as he located Hull's central police station, introduced himself to the chief of police, explained the search for Chisolm and presented his credentials as part of the search, his thoughts were scattered. As important as finding Chisolm and bringing him to justice was, there was something more important, something that was a deeper part of his soul. Lionel needed him.

David didn't breathe easy until he met up with Lionel at the hotel.

"Well, the telegrams have been sent," Lionel greeted him with the sort of smile David hadn't seen in days as David approached the terrace in front of the inn. Lionel had a rough sack slung over one shoulder. "Assuming Lord Clerkenwell has reached London and locked Castleford up tight, he'll receive our message and be on the next train up here."

"I look forward to the day when we can all stop shunting off around England as though we are migratory birds," David said, acknowledging Lionel's information with a nod. "The Hull police are aware of the situation. They're sending out patrols to look for Chisolm, but they don't have the manpower of Scotland Yard."

"Then we'll have to continue the search ourselves," Lionel said with a shrug.

"If you're sure you're up for it," David said.

Lionel fixed him with a flat stare, all of his fledgling joviality vanishing. "Darling, if you continue to say things like that, you will end up deceased long before I do, because I will have murdered you myself." He adjusted the sack over his arm.

David held up his hands in surrender, the point taken. "If you want to search for Chisolm, we'll search for Chisolm." And he would stay right by Lionel's side to make certain he didn't wear himself out.

Not that he was certain syphilis caused a man to tire quickly. And as they headed away from the hotel, journeying closer to the ocean and the coastline, Lionel seemed to have more energy than he had in weeks. He walked with less tension—an observation that made David realize Lionel had been in pain for weeks and he hadn't noticed—and he seemed to breathe easier. The sack he carried didn't seem to be chafing or irritating his shoulder at all, even though it was slung tightly over his arm. David was tempted to ascribe the change to the fresh, sea air, but Lionel had only been in that air for a matter of hours.

"I was thinking," David began cautiously as they reached a small road that seemed to wind out of town toward rocky cliffs and coves. "Once this whole matter is concluded and Chisolm and the others are charged for their crimes, we should take a holiday."

Lionel turned an incredulous expression to David, his blue eyes wide. "What is this I'm hearing? The indomitable David Wirth, tireless solicitor and champion of the downtrodden, constantly attempting to prove how competent he is to those who would doubt him, is actually considering abandoning his post for something as trivial as a *holiday*?"

"I've taken a holiday before," David snapped back, stung by Lionel's sarcasm, but also enjoying the banter they fell into.

"When?" Lionel asked with a wry look.

"Just last year," David said. "I went to Blackpool."

"Because you were searching for Roger Miniver's sister after he passed away so that you could inform her of her inheritance," Lionel argued. "In all the time I've known you, you have never taken a pure holiday, without work on the side, simply for your enjoyment."

"And you have?" David teased him.

They reached a wooden staircase that had been built at the beginning of a slope that turned into a cliff as it bordered the sea. Lionel shot David a haughty look as they descended so that they could continue their search along the beach. Though at the moment, it felt more as though the two of them were enjoying a stroll along Hull's rugged coastline instead of searching for a fugitive.

"The only reason I haven't taken a holiday in the past few years is because your business would crumble to dust without me to administrate it."

David barked a laugh. "A likely story."

"It's true," Lionel said with a sniff. "You wouldn't know what to do with yourself if I wasn't there to pay the rent on the office, purchase coal for the fire, and undertake all of the background investigative work that your cases entail."

"I did perfectly fine before you came along," David teased him, "and I could do quite well without you." Which was an utter lie no matter which way he meant it.

Lionel's mouth quirked up into a wry grin as he stepped ahead of David. He seemed to know where he was going as the beach turned rocky. The tide was out, and the closer they drew to the crags and escarpments at the base of the cliffs, the more David found himself thinking they would have made perfect smuggler's coves.

And if smugglers could hide out in coves like that, so could Chisolm.

"You had Dandie before you had me," Lionel said, his humor fading.

David's gut felt as though he had missed a step. "Lionel, you know you don't have to be jealous of John."

Lionel tilted his head up enough for David to see he'd hit a sore spot. "I have a thousand reasons to be jealous of John Dandie," he said, his voice taking on a brittle edge. He didn't look at David as he continued with, "Dandie comes from a well-off family that could afford to send him to university. He didn't have to resort to the methods I did in order to pay his way. Dandie is handsome as the devil and charming beyond measure. He makes friends easily."

"You're far handsomer than him, and you have scores of friends," David said, concentrating on climbing over a boulder as they drew near the base of the cliffs.

Lionel shot him a sideways look, his cheeks flushed with exertion and emotion. "I don't have friends, I have contacts," he said.

"Of course, you have friends," David argued, hoisting himself over another boulder, this one covered in seaweed. He reached back, offering Lionel a hand as he struggled to mount the slippery rock. "You've got—" He paused, thinking about all of their acquaintances. Lionel was on friendly terms with all of them—from Alistair Bevan to Niall Cristofori—but David couldn't recall

Lionel spending leisure time with any of them in the past few years.

Lionel reached the top of the rock, shifting the sack over his arm and crowding close to David, since there wasn't much space atop the thing, and stared hard at David. "I've got?"

"Everyone at the club appreciates your company," David said, rushing down the other side of the rock to hide his sudden embarrassment at realizing Lionel didn't, in fact, have real friends.

"Who doesn't appreciate the company of a man with gossip about three-quarters of the nobility?" Lionel shrugged and followed David down. "That doesn't make them friends, and you know it. You can't hide the fact that you know it either. I just saw the realization dawn in your precious eyes."

David let out a breath, sending Lionel a guilty look, then turning to the base of the cliff in front of them. They'd reached what looked like the mouth of a cave. It was hidden from sight on land. He could only see it now that it gaped in front of him. Which made it the perfect place for smugglers, or Chisolm, to hide.

"Do you think he could be in there?" David asked, avoiding the conversation by nodding to the mouth of the cave.

"Why else do you think I would scuff my Italian leather boots on these dreadful rocks if I didn't think Chisolm could be here?" He shrugged the sack he'd been carrying off his shoulder and opened it, taking out two prepared torches and a tinderbox.

"You bloody devil," David said, shaking his head as he took the torches so Lionel could light them. "You knew why we were coming out here right from the start."

"Once I returned from telegraphing Lord Clerkenwell, that lovely young woman at the inn regaled me with stories of smuggler's coves and how she and her young friends sneak out here for illicit rendezvous," Lionel said with a wink. "She even loaned me the torches so we could search."

David laughed. "And you think you don't have friends. You make friends wherever you go."

"I would argue that point," Lionel said between attempts to light the torches with the tinderbox, "but there doesn't seem to be much reason to."

With a few more attempts, Lionel managed to light the torches then tucked the tinderbox back into the sack and slung it over his shoulder. David handed him a torch, and the two of them made their way gingerly into the mouth of the cave.

"No wonder smugglers secreted themselves away in caves like this," Lionel said as the fresh sea air gave way to heavier, damper air. His voice echoed on the cave walls as the sound of the ocean became muffled. "It looks as though this goes on for miles."

"I doubt it's miles," David said, his feet squishing into the damp sand as they walked on. Although, once they reached a shelf of rocks and climbed onto that, peering into what looked like endless darkness, he wondered. "Who knows what we might find in here?"

"As long as we find Chisolm, I'll be happy," Lionel grumbled.

David was fairly certain that if Chisolm were hiding in the cave somewhere, he could likely hear the two of them talking, as their voices echoed in the cavern. He didn't dare speak that thought aloud, though, for fear that Lionel would clam up. The two of them were talking freely for the first time in weeks, and he wouldn't have given that up for anything.

"Would you be happy?" he asked, glancing over his shoulder at Lionel. "Catching Chisolm and bringing him to justice."

"Of course," Lionel said with a shrug.

David paused and stared at him. "Truly? You would be happy?"

Lionel's expression shifted to wistfulness as he caught the full meaning of David's question. "It would make me as happy as I'm capable of being these days," he said with a sigh. "But I fear my days of bliss are behind me."

He moved on, holding his torch ahead of him and casting as much light as he could into the far reaches of the cave. David followed him, a gnawing feeling in his stomach that had nothing to do with their eerie surroundings.

"Just because you're sick doesn't mean you cannot live a happy life," David said cautiously after searching for several minutes, certain Lionel would find some way to take offense at the comment.

Sure enough, Lionel let out an irritated breath. "I suppose you are going to instruct me in all the ways I can be perfectly happy as my body and mind fall apart?" His words echoed in the darkness as he explored a branch of the cave.

"We could take that holiday I mentioned," David said, feeling utterly out of his depth. "Rest cures are all the rage these days."

Lionel laughed. "You wouldn't be any happier with a rest cure than I would be."

David tilted his head to the side. That much was true. Just because his heart was making itself known now didn't mean he could ignore his head entirely. And he loved his work, even if he had given himself too much of it.

"We could consult a different physician," David went on after they'd explored one section of the cave and found nothing but a dead end, then circled back to explore another. "Find someone who specializes in difficult diseases, someone who might recommend how to live with things."

Lionel laughed again, shaking his head. They came to a second dead end along the new branch they'd started down fairly quickly, and he turned to face David. "Your optimism is endearing, even if it is hopeless and misplaced."

"Dammit, Lionel," David huffed. "Stop writing yourself off. You're not dead yet, and as far as I can see, you're still in good health."

"But for how long? There isn't any way to tell," Lionel argued, marching past David into the main section of the cave. "I refuse to live on false hope."

"And I refuse to let you give up on yourself simply because of a few sores." David marched after him.

Lionel snorted as he chose a third branch of the cave to explore. "You are the most endearing creature in the world, David, but please do not also be the stupidest."

"Stupid?" David caught up to Lionel, walking ahead of him as they turned down a particularly winding section of the cave. "Because I choose to hope? Because I question a diagnosis given years ago by God knows what sort of physician?"

Lionel stopped, resting his weight on one hip, and pursing his lips. "You weren't there, David. You don't know what it was like for me at that time."

David gave up searching and turned back to him. "Then tell me. What was it like? Why are you so intent on condemning yourself to a grisly death when you admitted yourself that you had trouble finding a physician who would treat you because of who you are?"

Lionel stared at him for a moment before sighing and lowering his head. The section of the cave they were searching had outcroppings in the walls that were at the right height to act as benches. Indeed, several empty bottles and other debris were scattered here and there, as if that were the spot where the young woman from the inn and her friends conducted their clandestine meet-ings. Lionel moved to sit on one of the rocks. David followed him.

"When you have seen the sort of things I've seen, you come to know what you are looking at," Lionel said, annoyingly cryptic.

"I'm not an ignorant boob, Lionel. I've seen things too," David argued.

"Then if someone handed you a waterfowl with webbed feet and a flat bill, one that swam and quacked, you would not think it an eagle," Lionel went on. "You would know a duck when you saw one."

David scowled. "I would have thought you'd use a Bird of Paradise to describe yourself rather than a garden variety duck."

Lionel's mouth twitched into a tense grin. "I'm a duck. Always have been, whether I'm wearing exotic feathers or not. Denying the truth is not going to change my duckness."

"You are ridiculous, you know," David said with far more fondness than he'd intended. "And I love you." He rested his free hand on Lionel's leg, squeezing it.

"Oh, David," Lionel sighed, his voice soft and shaky. "I love you too. But don't."

Instead of heeding him, David inched closer. "If you can face the possibility of being sick, then you will damn well face my love for you," he said with a burst of strength. "I'm not letting you push me away anymore."

Lionel's brow shot up in surprise. "This is a different sort of passion than I'm used to from you."

"Well, get used to it. As far as I'm concerned, from here on out, you are my primary concern. Not the office, not the cases we're charged with solving or the people we're asked to help, not even Chisolm. All I care about is you."

"Who are you and what have you done with David Wirth?" Lionel asked in a flat voice.

David responded by leaning in and slanting his mouth over Lionel's. The kiss took him by surprise as much as it startled Lionel, though with a torch in one hand, sitting on a damp rock in the dark, David wasn't able to embrace Lionel and deepen their kiss the way he wanted to. It was the kiss he needed, though, even if it wasn't half as passionate as he wanted.

For a few, glorious seconds, Lionel leaned into it, making a sound of acceptance deep in his chest. That sound and the kiss stopped abruptly, though. "No," he said, standing and stepping away from David. "I'm not going to let you lead me down this primrose path. Every time I let my guard down and allow you to kiss me, it gets harder to resist. And you know as well as I do that we have to resist."

"No, we don't." David charged after him, following Lionel deeper down the branch of the cave. "There are ways that the two of us can be together, even if you are sick."

Lionel laughed humorlessly. "I am not going to

condemn you to a sexless life of caring for an invalid in the name of love."

"That's not what I meant," David insisted. They were both speaking louder than before. The echoes of their voices hinted that they were nearing the end of that branch of the cave before the light from their torches proved as much. Lionel was forced to stop at a dead end and face David. "I spoke with John about it, and he informed me that there are all manner of ways the two of us could be intimate, as long as we're careful."

Lionel's eyes went wide in the torchlight, shining bright with offense. "You spoke to John Dandie about me being sick and about intimate relations between the two of us?"

David winced, wishing he'd kept his mouth shut. "There are ways—"

"Then by all means, go enjoy them with your former lover, since the two of you are clearly on good terms again." He pushed past David, storming back down the sloping cave.

He stumbled slightly as he went, causing David to jump after him with a gasp. "Are you all right?" David reached for him.

"No, I am not all right," Lionel snapped and kept going. "My life has been cut short by a vindictive bastard who used me, the way scores of other men have used me. And as horrible as it is that I can no longer engage in an activity that I used to adore for fear of infecting anyone who touches me, it is especially bitter that I cannot share that with someone I actually love instead of merely for fun. And though you profess love and care for me now, we both know that it is only a matter of time before you regret that decision and leave me worse off than I was before."

"Never," David insisted, trying to catch up with Lionel so that he could grab his arm and stop him. Lionel was too damned agile as he made his way back to the cave's entrance to let him catch up, though.

"Never is a very short time," Lionel snapped. "I would rather suffer unrequited love than be utterly ended by letting you love me and leave me, as you inevitably will."

"How dare you suggest that I would be so shallow as to leave you simply because you are sick?" David shouted. At last, Lionel stopped and spun to face him. The rolling sound of the ocean could be heard again at the far end of the cave. "How dare you belittle the love I feel for you because you are bitter?"

"Because I know human nature," Lionel said. "I was never just an empty-headed pretty-boy sucking cock because I didn't know any better. I studied people more than I ever studied the law or the classics at university. People are shallow, self-interested animals."

"And that's what you think of me?" David asked, going stiff with indignation himself. "You think I'm just like every other roué who's ever dandled you on their knee in exchange for money or secrets?" Lionel jerked back at the question, but David rushed on with, "You're not the only one capable of jealousy."

"I haven't been with anyone since meeting you," Lionel fired back. "Can you say the same?"

He wanted to be able to say he hadn't been, but even after John, there had been a night or two when the itch had taken him and he'd turned to a friend to satisfy it. He was only human, after all. Shallow and self-interested.

Lionel's face went stony, and he nodded as though David had answered him aloud. "Don't insult me by pretending you're not a man," he said in a low, wounded voice. "Spare me the pain of watching you grow to resent me and leave by making a clean break from me now." He turned and charged away toward the mouth of the cave.

"I *am* a man," David admitted, chasing after him. "So are you. Don't try to pretend celibacy hasn't taken its toll on you. My argument is that we can be together. We don't have to suffer through self-denial. We love each other, and if we stay committed to each other, this whole argument is moot. There are ways we can—"

He stopped dead when he reached the cave's entrance, where Lionel stood, gaping at what had been sand around the mouth of the cave. David hadn't thought they'd taken that long exploring the cave, but apparently time had moved by swiftly and the tide had come in. Instead of a clear way out of the cave, there was nothing but water.

CHAPTER 16

*I*t was a metaphor for his life. He and David had gotten into a predicament where their way was blocked with no way out except to get wet. It was such an apt comparison to the muddle they'd trapped themselves in with their emotions that he couldn't help but laugh aloud.

"It's not funny," David growled, his brow knit in deep concern.

Lionel glanced to him, barely able to keep his laughter inside, mouth quivering with mirth. When David shot a scowl his way, he burst into what effectively amounted to a giggle.

"It's not funny," David repeated, with more indignation.

"Oh, darling, it's hilarious," Lionel beamed. "We got ourselves into this mess, and there's no way out but under."

"What are you talking about?" David's anxious frown turned confused.

Lionel glanced back to the pool that had taken over the mouth of the cave. It hadn't reached all the way to the top of the cave's mouth yet—though by the look of things, it would once the tide had come in completely—so there was still a fair amount of sunlight streaming in from across the ocean. As far as Lionel could tell, the water might only be three or four feet deep around the mouth of the cave.

He glanced down at his new suit, sighing over his about-to-be-ruined boots. "There's no way out but under," he repeated. "Underwater, in over our heads, swept away by the tide. We're either stuck in this cave for good or we have to take the plunge."

Still, David frowned at him. "Or we could wait until the tide goes out again."

Lionel sent him a look that was almost sympathetic. The poor dear thought he was talking about the cave. "My whole life, I have refused to live in a cave, darling. I refuse to live in one now."

David still hadn't caught on to what he was saying, but Lionel was fairly certain he knew that he wasn't talking about a smuggler's cave near Hull. He turned back to the water, shook his head, then leapt off the shelf of rocks where they stood and into the surging tidewater.

"Lionel!" David shouted after him, his voice echoing in the cavern.

As Lionel suspected, the water was only waist-deep,

but the current was strong. His torch was doused when he took the plunge, so he tossed it away, adjusting the sack over his shoulder to make certain it was secure. "I'm fine," he called back, pushing forward toward the mouth of the cave to see if the water was deeper or the current stronger there. "Jump in," he ordered David over his shoulder. "The sooner we swim out of here, the safer we'll be. I can't guarantee how deep the water gets once the tide is in."

A few seconds passed, but Lionel didn't hear the splash he expected to. He made it nearly to the mouth of the cave before turning back. David stood on the ledge of rocks, staring at the water as though it were his mortal enemy.

"Dearest, you are familiar with that old adage, 'time and tide wait for no man', aren't you?" Lionel nodded to the water. "This is what it means. Don't worry about ruining those clothes. They aren't worth salvaging anyhow," he added in a sly undertone.

He moved on toward the cave's entrance in the sunlight, but David's call of, "I can't swim," stopped him.

Lionel paused, turned back to David, and let out a long-suffering moan. "You cannot be serious."

"I'm serious," David said, grim-faced.

Lionel pursed his lips and would have crossed his arms if he didn't need them to keep himself steady in the increasingly powerful current. "Every boy learns to swim before he's out of the schoolroom. Paddling naked in the pond on Lord Hayward's estate with all the other boys was how I discovered I liked them and not the girls." He tilted his head to the side, mouth twitching into a coy grin. "It's how I learned I liked other things as well."

"I grew up in London," David reminded him with a growl. "I didn't see a pond until I was fifteen years old."

Lionel blinked in astonishment. "Oh, you poor dear. That settles it, then." He slogged back through the seawater toward the rocks where David perched anxiously. "When we go on holiday, we're going somewhere with copious bodies of water, and I will teach you to swim." He paused. "Mostly so that I can keep you naked for the entire holiday."

David blinked in utter astonishment. "Are you saying you'll go away with me? That you'll—"

"I'm trying to get your stubborn arse into the water by promising you whatever I think will work as bait, love," Lionel cut him off. The idea of splashing around a pond or lake with David on holiday was a potent one, but it didn't change the facts of medical science. At the same time, he'd been far more affected by David's suggestion that there were ways for the two of them to safely be together than he wanted to admit.

All of that was a long way off, though, and would continue to be if David didn't get in the water.

"Look," Lionel said, standing and demonstrating that the water was just above waist-deep at the edge of the rocks. "You don't even have to swim. Just get in and walk through it."

"The torch," David argued.

Lionel signed impatiently. "Give it to me, you lily-livered Nancy."

"I am neither lily-livered nor a Nancy," David protested, scooting to the edge of the rocks and sitting so that he could slip into the water instead of jumping. He handed Lionel his torch.

"I'm sure John Dandie and countless others will argue that you are, indeed, a Nancy," Lionel said. "I have more than enough proof of that myself."

David sent him a scathing look before sucking in a breath and plunging into the water. "It's cold," he gasped, holding out his arms to steady himself before wading closer to Lionel, who had deliberately backed away.

"Sissy," Lionel muttered, his mouth twitching into a grin. "Nelly boy."

"Stop it, Lionel," David muttered.

"Margerie."

Lionel backed farther and farther toward the cave's entrance, keeping David's torch out of his reach, even though he swiped at it. He couldn't contain his giggles as David pushed after him, looking more like an irritated sea monster with each step he took.

"Come on, poofer," he laughed. "It's just a few more feet."

"Will you please stop insulting me to get me to move? I'm already moving," David huffed.

"But it's so much fun." The cave's entrance was only a few yards away, so Lionel shifted to his back, swimming the last few feet. "Besides, only queens never learned to swim when they were little girls."

"For the love of God, Lionel, stop," David shouted. He reached the mouth of the cave and grabbed the rock wall with one hand, reaching for Lionel's foot as he kicked above the water with the other.

Lionel purposely submerged once he was caught, causing David's torch to go out. David let go of his foot before Lionel could poke his head above water again, but he could feel David flailing and reaching for him. As soon as he was above the water, David snagged him around the waist and yanked him close.

"Don't you ever, ever do that again," David said, hoarse and panicky, eyes wide.

"Unlike you, you silly sod, I know how to swim."

David ignored him. He heaved Lionel around to press his back against the cave's entrance, then brought his mouth crashing down over Lionel's. The kiss took Lionel utterly by surprise, both in terms of its timing and its intensity. For one, blissful moment, he forgot himself. The teasing he'd directed at David turned into passion as he clung desperately to David's soaked jacket, groaning low in his throat as their mouths and tongues twined. A thousand beautiful memories crashed back into him as David pressed his body into his, practically melding the two of them together. His cock ached in spite of the cold water, and even though he was certain it was his imagination, there wasn't a lick of pain to go along with the pleasure.

"Don't you ever do that again," David hissed, breaking their kiss at length.

"If it earns me a kiss like that, I plan to drown myself far more often," Lionel flirted before he could think better of it.

David growled in frustration. "You are impossible." He surged into Lionel again, stealing another kiss that left Lionel feeling as though he were floating and in danger of being pulled under by a current that had nothing to do with the ocean around them. He'd waited so long for a moment like that, and illness or not, his heart was suddenly so light that he just wanted to enjoy it.

Before he could grasp David closer and perhaps figure out a way to unfasten the man's trousers underwater, David pulled away.

"The water is getting deeper, and I still can't swim," he said, face red and eyes glittering with lust.

"Then by all means, let's get to dry land as quickly as possible."

Lionel pushed away from the cave's wall and swam out into the sunlight. David followed, wading through the shifting sand and swelling tide. It was a wise decision not to linger in the cave as the geography of the area meant the tide rolled in with amazing speed. By the time Lionel found a way back to the beach, the water had already reached as high as David's chest. It was beyond fortunate that they left the cave when they did, or else their silliness and dallying would have turned serious in a heartbeat.

All the same, making the trek back to the inn soaked

in seawater, boots squishing, heart pounding with unsat-
isfied and ill-advised desire, was an exercise in
discomfort.

"I'm never exploring caves with you again," David
grumbled after they returned to the inn, gave the young
woman at the desk her sack with the tinderbox back,
apologized for losing the torches, gathered armfuls of
extra towels, and headed up to their rooms. "That was a
singularly miserable experience, and we didn't even
locate Chisolm."

"Come now, it wasn't that bad of an experience,"
Lionel said with a teasing look as they parted ways at the
top of the stairs, heading into their own rooms. They left
their doors open, though.

"It was bad enough," David said.

Lionel paused in his doorway, watching David peel
his soaked and ruined jacket and waistcoat off and toss
them across the small, wooden chair in his room. He
sucked in a breath at the way David's wet shirt clung to
the lines of his chest and shoulders. His body responded
eagerly to the sight, but it was his heart that thrummed
the hardest. In another life, if things had worked out
differently, in spite of who he'd been and what he
enjoyed, Lionel was certain beyond a shadow of a doubt
that he would have given up his profligate ways and been
as faithful and true to David as any man had ever been.
That thought filled him with a wistful sentimentality, and
he leaned against his door frame, letting out a sigh.

David heard him and turned. The spark of lust was

still in his eyes, which only made Lionel's heart pound harder. It made other things harder too. He was still floating, still drifting and in danger of drowning. He was as far from ignorant as it was possible to be, but he caught himself wanting to ask David about the ways he thought they could be together safely again just to watch David blush and stammer his way through an explanation of things Lionel knew far better than him.

"You look happier than I've seen you in ages," David said in a soft voice, unbuttoning his shirt.

A thousand witty replies jumped to Lionel's mind, but he ignored all of them in favor of continuing to stare at David as he removed his wet shirt. Damn the man, but he was deliberately playing with Lionel's control, seducing him far more expertly than he had at The Savoy, or any other time in their lives together.

"The sea air suits you," David went on. "Or perhaps it's the sea water." He paused. "I bet it's improved the state of your rash as well."

Lionel arched one eyebrow, but still said nothing. David was subtly ordering him to take his clothes off. Prickles broke out across Lionel's skin, and a tremor started in his belly. He straightened, working free the buttons of his jacket, then shrugging it aside. His waistcoat and boots came off next.

He was halfway through removing his shirt when David stepped quietly out of his own room, shutting the door behind him, and invaded Lionel's room. He shut and locked Lionel's door as well. Lionel sucked in a breath that was more excitement than alarm. A weak voice in the back of his head shouted at him to put a stop to the madness before it was too late, but the rest of him had waited far, far too long for what was about to happen. It was already too late.

"You can't touch me directly," he said backing toward his bed and tossing his wet shirt carelessly aside.

"Not even with this?" David held up a small, square packet that he must have taken from his room before crossing over.

Lionel knew exactly what it was and held his breath, brimming with excitement. "They're not foolproof, you know." His heart slammed against his ribs as hope and possibility blossomed within him.

"I'll be careful," David insisted, coming nearer still. The back of Lionel's legs hit the bed. There was nowhere else he could escape to. David slipped an arm around his waist and tugged him close before slanting his mouth over Lionel's.

The kiss melted Lionel in an instant. He hadn't been so close to any man in years, but to feel the heat of his skin against David's, to taste him to the fullest as their tongues brushed, was so heavenly that he wasn't sure he cared if it was also dangerous.

"I'm not certain that I want you to be careful with me," he sighed as David moved from his mouth to his jaw to kiss and nip at his neck.

"I'm not sure I want to be careful with you either,"

David murmured between kisses that had Lionel spinning wildly out of control.

It was all too wonderful, too perfect. Lionel tipped his head back, giving David greater access to his neck and shoulder. He closed his eyes with the bliss of it, brushing his hands across David's sides to dig his fingertips into his back. The salt from the sea that covered them was only half as tempting as the salt of David's skin. Lionel ached to experience David in every way, as deeply as possible. It was sheer madness, and Lionel was certain they would both regret it once the heat of passion subsided, but he'd passed the point of being able to stop.

David, however, pulled away from him suddenly. A thoughtful frown replaced the desire in his eyes. For a moment, panic threatened to buckle Lionel's knees.

"Lionel," David said slowly. The way he chewed his lip for a moment did nothing to quench the fire that continued to rage inside of Lionel. "Have you used that ointment I bought for you in Manchester?"

The question seemed utterly out of the blue. Lionel blinked and shook his head. "No."

"It's just that your rash is gone. Your body is exquisite." The heat returned to David's grin as he glanced down at Lionel's chest.

Lionel opened his mouth to make a smart reply, but nothing came to mind. He glanced down to see what David was looking at. An odd feeling formed in the pit of his stomach. It wasn't as though he hadn't noticed the lessening of the pain that had hounded him night and day for weeks, but with everything they'd been through in the last few days, he hadn't stopped to consider that his skin was no longer in a state of constant irritation. The worst of his sores were still there, but they had faded to minor annoyances.

He pulled away from David, turning his back to him and loosening his trousers.

"Now you decide to be modest around me?" David asked wryly, taking a step away from him.

Lionel didn't answer. He buzzed with curiosity as he pushed his sodden trousers down, peeling them off and kicking them aside, then studying himself. The horrors he expected to see simply weren't there. He certainly wasn't one to believe in miracles, but seeing and feeling were believing.

In the middle of his perplexity, David stepped toward him once more, sliding one hand across Lionel's side to spread across his belly, tugging Lionel's back tight against his chest. The hot, thick spear of David's cock pressed into Lionel's backside. David had finished undressing as he inspected himself. Lionel sucked in a breath, then moaned at how absolutely perfectly they fit together.

David didn't stop there, his free hand held the French letter, already removed from its paper. He fit it over the head of Lionel's cock, then rolled it into place, igniting every inch of Lionel as he went.

"Dear God, that feels incredible," Lionel sighed, sagging back into David.

"Yes, it does," David agreed, stroking his hands across

Lionel's hips, belly, and sides, as if sculpting him. He only barely brushed against Lionel's balls and his sheathed cock, and Lionel teetered on the edge of orgasm. He held on as best he could, debating whether it might be better to give in to the pleasure and come just so that David could work him back into a frenzy all over again. It wouldn't take long.

He twisted in David's arms, pressing their chests together and curling his arms around David's back. The moment was too good and he'd waited too long for it not to take full advantage of the situation. He slammed his mouth over David's, taking everything he'd ever wanted from the man and more. It was folly to pursue the pleasure he desperately needed to share with David, but every voice of reason within him had been silenced by need. He needed more than just David's body, he needed all of him, heart and soul.

He wasn't sure how they ended up sprawled across the bed, David heavy atop him. The sounds they made as they kissed and touched were wicked and delicious. David nudged his legs apart, stroking his inner thigh and putting every last bit of Lionel's patience to the test. Not even the protective sheath was enough to dull the glorious sensation of David stroking him and learning his shape and size.

"You are the most beautiful creature in the entire world," David hummed against Lionel's lips. "I have waited so long for this."

"So have I," Lionel confessed. He was so undone that

all he was capable of was honesty. "I don't think I could ever get enough of you."

David kissed him with particular passion, sliding his tongue along Lionel's before sucking on it. If Lionel had been standing, his knees would have given out. He felt as though he were floating in the sea of David's love, and if he wasn't careful, the current would carry him away forever.

"This is a terrible idea," he sighed, arching his neck so that David could kiss and lick it, driving him wild.

"It most certainly is not," David argued, kissing his way to Lionel's shoulder and chest. His hands explored Lionel's body, and Lionel had the feeling he would feel David's hands on him for the rest of his life.

David pulled up, catching his breath and studying Lionel's splayed and helpless body as though it were a treat he was about to devour. Lionel prayed that he would do exactly that. "You are perfect," David said, though there was a hint of confusion in his eyes as he spoke.

"Try not to look so surprised," Lionel said with pretend self-satisfaction.

"No, I mean it." David stroked his hands across Lionel's chest and lower. Lionel held his breath as David gently caressed his cock, fully expecting David to work him until he burst apart. But David continued to study him with a slight frown. "Don't take this the wrong way, love, but didn't you say you hired a new laundress several weeks ago?"

"Darling. That wretched laundress is the very last thing I want to think about right now," Lionel panted.

David ignored him. "Are you absolutely certain that your rash and those sores weren't caused by a reaction to laundry soap?"

Lionel stared flatly up at him, lips pursed in annoyance in spite of the fact that his senses were on fire and he still lingered on the edge of explosion. "Wishing something away is not considered effective medical treatment, love."

"It's just that I've seen what a bad reaction to certain detergents can do to the skin," David pressed on. "It occurs to me that perhaps the problem is with your laundry, not with your body." His mouth twitched into a lusty grin. "Because there is absolutely nothing wrong with your body."

"David," Lionel began scoldingly.

"And for the last several days, you've been wearing new clothing. Clothing that your new laundress has never seen, let alone washed," David went on. "Isn't it possible that you aren't really sick at all, that this has all just been some sort of bitter misunderstanding and—"

"Are you going to fuck me or not?" Lionel interrupted him, his heart even closer to exploding with love for the daft fool and the hope shining in his eyes than his cock was to bursting with lust. When David blinked at the interruption, Lionel went on with, "After all, you've gone through all this trouble to sheathe me for your own protection. It would be a shame to waste such a delightful preventative." He paused. "Unless you bought more."

"I only have the one." The heat returned to David's eyes and the tension to his body as he dipped closer to Lionel.

"If you don't have one for yourself, you can't actually fuck me, you know," Lionel said, surprised at how disappointed he was by the truth. He would have given just about anything right then to have David's cock balls deep inside of him.

David seemed to be thinking the same thing. His momentary flicker of disappointment was replaced by a devilish grin. He leaned closer to Lionel, bringing their bodies into intimate contact. "I'll just have to find another way to satisfy both of us," he rumbled, then captured Lionel's mouth in a searing kiss.

Lionel hummed and shivered, wrapping his arms around David and lifting one knee in order to open himself further and bring their hips into closer contact. As far as he was concerned, he could get off a thousand times over just holding David like that and kissing him until they were both breathless. The urge to move against David, causing enough friction to climax, was enough to drive Lionel mad, but he paced himself, not wanting the moment to end. Ever.

David had far bolder ideas. He left Lionel's mouth to rain kisses over his shoulders and chest again, continuing lower still. Lionel knew exactly what he intended, and for a few, blissful seconds, he moaned with anticipation as David's mouth slipped lower and lower across his belly.

Only when David gently took hold of the base of his cock and lifted him so that he could kiss and caress his tip with his lips—something Lionel felt intensely, in spite of the thin layer sheath covering him—did he snap to his senses.

"Don't, David," he warned, barely able to form the words, he was breathing so hard with pleasure. "It's too dangerous. Even with—"

His words disappeared into a groan as David bore down on him, taking him far deeper than Lionel ever would have imagined stoic and businesslike David Wirth could take a man. And Lionel wasn't exactly petite. There was a reason he had so many friends that went beyond his charming personality and clever stories. But David swallowed him thoroughly all the same. Expertly. He had Lionel sweating and overwhelmed in no time. There was no possible way he could hang on with David's mouth around him, and he came with a deep cry of satisfaction.

David echoed the wild sound he made, drawing his pleasure out as long as it could possibly go and then some. When he lifted his head, he wore a look of surprise. "That's different," he panted.

"What are you talking about, you insane man?" Lionel sighed, disjointed, post-orgasmic bliss turning him to jelly.

"Nothing to swallow." David grinned, sliding his body along Lionel's until their mouths met and entwined.

Lionel laughed, wrapping his arms and legs around David with what little energy he had left. David was still full of fire, and kissed him with abandon. It was the most delightful juxtaposition of satiety and need Lionel had ever experienced, especially as David thrust impatiently against the inside of his hip, seeking his own release.

"My turn," Lionel said, trying to gather enough strength to flip David to his back and return the glorious favor David had just done him.

"No time," David grunted between kisses, smiling wider and wider as he moved.

"No time?" Lionel scoffed, already feeling the fire reignite in his belly.

"Give me your hand," David panted, reaching for Lionel's hand himself when Lionel didn't move fast enough.

He drew Lionel's hand between them, closing it around his cock, then jerking harder. It was ridiculous. Two green schoolboys could have managed things better. But Lionel couldn't stop grinning as he stroked David in coordination with his thrusts until David's body bristled with tension and the sounds coming from him bubbled over. David spilled against him, head thrown back in a powerful orgasm. Lionel's eyes went wide at the revelation of the man he loved losing himself to pleasure. He loved every single thing about David climaxing, from the sounds he made to the way his face pinched with pleasure to the warm gush that spread between them. He wanted to experience it again and again in every possible way. He wanted to spend the rest of his life giving the man who sighed and collapsed at his side, drawing their bodies together in a tender embrace, all the pleasure he could handle and more.

Wanted to, but knew he couldn't. Not without killing him.

The fire of lust gave way to sinking dread as David collapsed to the narrow bed by Lionel's side. In spite of the smile on David's face and the way he fell so swiftly into post-coital slumber, panic rushed in on Lionel. They'd done far more than they should have, been careless in their enthusiasm. If that was how they started, how would they proceed?

His heart ached ten times more than it had before, even though his body was satisfied. All he wanted in the cruel, mad world he lived in was David. It was a crime that their life together was destined to be so short. As wonderful as it was for them to finally be together, it was bittersweet. They'd taken more risks than they should have. If they were taking risks now, how much more careless would they get with each night, each kiss? If the pleasure was so sweet now, how long would it be until they lost their heads and pretended that was all that mattered? How many chances did they take before their luck ran out entirely?

CHAPTER 17

It all made sense now. Everything in the vast, spinning world suddenly felt as though it made sense to David as he dozed in and out of sleep, tangled in Lionel's sheets, surrounded by his scent. His life wasn't about proving everyone who said he'd never amount to much wrong. It wasn't even about helping his fellow man by fighting for justice on their behalf. It was about love. It was about taking care of a vain, stubborn, infuriating prima donna with a colorful past, in spite of the fact that Lionel insisted he didn't want to be taken care of.

It was a lie. David had felt it in every inch of Lionel's body and heard it in every wild sound the man made as they melded together the night before. David didn't care how much of a risk it was to love Lionel, and he certainly didn't listen to the adorably frustrating fool when he tried to banish him back to his own room after their passion was spent the first time. He'd gotten up to wash the salt of the sea and sex off, found them some supper, fed it to Lionel in spite of his protests, then took him back to bed for another sinfully long bout of lovemaking.

The memory of Lionel's combination of protest and surrender had David grinning from ear to ear before he was fully awake. Somehow, his sleepy mind grasped onto the thought that they would have to buy a great many more French letters as he turned and reached for Lionel.

He snapped his eyes open when he came up empty. The bed wasn't that large to begin with, so David knew instantly that Lionel wasn't there. He sat up abruptly, glancing around the tiny room with a frown. The window was open in the sloped ceiling above the bed, letting in a salty sea breeze and the sound of gulls over the ocean. Everything else in the room was in perfect order. Lionel must have picked their clothes up off the floor. David's trousers and drawers were draped over the room's single, wooden chair. Lionel's clothes were nowhere to be found, though. Worse still, his battered suitcase was gone as well.

David threw back the bedclothes and jumped to his feet. "You wouldn't dare, you bastard," he growled, lunging for the wardrobe and throwing it open.

Sure enough, the wardrobe was empty. Fury and panic pulsed through David. He shoved a hand through his tousled hair and headed for the door. He charged across the hall, checking on his own room, but it was exactly as he'd left it the evening before. His heart hammered against his ribs as he crossed back into Lionel's room, looking for clues about where the sweet idiot had gone.

He spotted a small envelope on the washstand near the window and rushed to snatch it up, hands shaking.

"Forget, syphilis," he grumbled. "I'm going to kill him myself."

The letter contained exactly what he expected it would.

"*Dearest, darling, David,*" it began. "*Yes, I know, you probably want to wring my neck right now. I would beg you not to, since it's still tender from your kisses last night. But that is precisely the point, my love. Nothing like that can ever happen again. We were utterly reckless, as I knew full well we would be. We two are completely incapable of being cautious in bed, in spite of knowing how absolutely necessary it is. We want each other too deeply, and our tastes are far too exotic for any sort of mundane congress. In short, just as I suspected all these years, we are incapable of restraint. And in this particular matter, that lack of self-control will be fatal.*

"*So I'm leaving. I'm already gone. I'll spare you the platitudes of how this is for your own good and you will find someone else to love who is far less of a danger to life and limb than I am. If you love me anything like the way I love you, there will never be anyone else. You have not only filled my heart, you are my heart. I love you more than I thought it was possible to love anyone. I love you beyond sense and reason, beyond thought and feeling, with everything that I am and everything that I could have been. I love you so much that I will forever hear your voice in my mind, forever see your smile, forever have the scent of you in my nose and the feel of you in my fingertips. I love you so much that I cannot stay and wait for the inevitable day when this wretched disease spreads to you. I won't destroy you that way.*

"*Yes, I know you're fuming right now—*"

"Bloody right I am, you arse," David growled aloud as he read.

"*—but don't try to come after me,*" he read on. "*You know this is for the best. All my love forever, or at least for as long as I have left, Lionel.*"

David swore under his breath and was tempted to rip the letter to shreds, if only to vent his frustration. He should have known Lionel would try to run after giving in to what they both wanted at last. It was exactly the sort of noble and horrifically misguided stunt Lionel would pull. And the bastard was probably just using the possibility of infecting him as an excuse to mask how vulnerable giving his heart away made him feel.

Well, he wouldn't just stand around and let Lionel walk out on him. David crushed the letter in his fist and marched across the hall to his own room. He threw the balled-up letter into his wardrobe as he took out clean clothes for the day, his mind already at work. There was no telling when precisely Lionel had left, but he couldn't have been gone for more than a few hours. Hull wasn't as bustling a town as London or Manchester, so there were likely only a few trains departing per day. With any luck, Lionel would still be lingering around the train station, waiting to take the coward's way out and flee.

But Hull's train station was nearly empty when David arrived. He jogged from one end of the platform to the other, searching for any sign that Lionel had been there already. The departures board beside the station office only displayed trains that would leave later in the day.

"Excuse me," David asked a porter who stepped up onto the platform just as panic was swelling anew within him. "When did the last train depart?"

The porter flinched, as though the last thing he expected was to be accosted by a Londoner so early in the morning. "Last night," the man said. "About eleven o'clock."

David huffed out a breath, scrubbing a hand over his face. "Lionel, you fucking martyr, where are you?"

LIONEL CHECKED HIS WATCH, COMPARING IT TO THE clock that ticked away above the window where he'd purchased his passage on *Poseidon's Treasure*. The steamer would depart within the hour. He stepped away from the ticket office, following the sleepy stream of people boarding or waving goodbye to their loved ones. *Poseidon's Treasure* was an ambitious name for the squat and serviceable vessel. What it lacked in the grandiosity of its namesake, it likely made up for in serviceability, though. It would take him far away from David, which would keep the man he loved safe.

He knew it was the right thing to do. He didn't trust himself anymore where David was concerned. It was a rash and sudden decision to run, but now that the cat was out of the bag, he knew he wouldn't be able to do what was right and restrain himself. David would only encourage him to put them both at risk. It was far, far better for him to leave and never see David again. He would make a quick trip back to London to gather his belongings, then he would flee to the continent, and perhaps on to the orient or some other place David would never think to look for him.

The plan was so simple and so direct, and yet, he couldn't make himself move any closer to the ship than the railing where loved ones were waving to their soon-to-depart friends. He was the worst sort of impulsive idiot. The gangplank was only a few yards away, but Lionel's feet felt stuck to the dock, as if his body were betraying the impulse of his brain.

He loved David. He'd always known he did, almost from the very first moment he'd laid eyes on the man. He'd somehow fooled himself into thinking he could love David with his heart only and that would be enough. But the moment he'd loved David with his damaged and infectious body, he knew that it was all or nothing. And it couldn't be all.

He sighed. "Who would have thought that love could be so maudlin and redundant," he muttered to himself.

"Sorry?" a man standing close behind him asked.

"I was talking to myself," Lionel informed him.

The man blinked. "Oh. Well, move along, then."

Lionel stared incredulously at the man. "This is not the line to board," he said, wondering how people could be such fools.

"Oh. Sorry." The man edged around him and continued on to the gangplank.

Lionel shook his head, but within seconds, he felt like even more of a fool than his fellow passenger. He should have been in line. He should be moving toward the ship and toward his escape. He should be taking himself as far away from David as he could, but he kept glancing back over his shoulder, hoping, praying that David would—

A man in an unseasonably long, thick coat with the collar turned up rounded the corner from the ticket office and started toward the gangplank. He held a small suitcase in one hand and tugged his hat low over his face with the other. The gesture would have been suspicious on its own, but the coat was of the finest wool, and the man's shoes were a thousand times more expensive than any of the scuffed fishermen's boots or worn shoes that the rest of the departing passengers and their friends wore. Lionel's heart shot to his throat. It had to be Chisolm.

Lionel grasped his suitcase tighter and surged forward, putting himself on a path to intercept Chisolm before he reached the gangplank. He didn't know Chisolm well, even though the man was single-handedly responsible for the bitter course of his life, but Lionel had seen the man before. He was certain it was him as their paths came close to intersecting. He picked up his pace, moving in such a way that Chisolm was forced to steer to one side in order to avoid him. Once he did, Lionel shifted to stay in front of him, blocking his path.

"Get out of my—" Chisolm's eyes flashed with recognition. His mouth remained open in shock, even though he didn't finish his sentence. "Mercer?"

Hearing his name on Chisolm's lips, seeing the full impact of shock in the man's eyes as they came face to face, caused something to snap in Lionel. He dropped his suitcase, not caring that it spilled to its side, balled his fist, and slammed it hard across Chisolm's jaw. Pain radiated through his knuckles and up his arm, but he hardly cared. The blow was worth it.

Gasps rang out from the people milling around the dock as Chisolm stumbled to the side. Thankfully, no one rushed to intervene.

"That's the least of what you deserve, you bastard," Lionel hissed, bracing himself for what he hoped was a fight as soon as Chisolm recovered from the shock of the blow.

Chisolm recovered, but not in a way Lionel anticipated. He straightened, holding a hand to the side of his face, and chuckled. "That's quite a blow for a prissy little queer."

A rage filled Lionel like nothing he'd ever felt before.

"I am capable of much more than you could ever dream of, Chisolm."

"Yes, I expect you're quite the entertainer at country house parties," Chisolm drawled.

Lionel knew enough from Everett about the sort of country house parties Chisolm once threw to take the insult for what it was. The utter dismissiveness in Chisolm's tone only fired his fury. He meant so little to the man that Chisolm wasn't taking him seriously. It was a fatal mistake, as far as Lionel was concerned.

"As delightful as it would be to make some grandiloquent speech about how you destroyed my life as part of your own, disgusting games, I have neither the time nor the inclination to give you one further second of consideration in my thoughts. I just want you dead."

Chisolm started to chuckle, but Lionel grabbed him by the front of his coat with his left hand and landed another punch hard across Chisolm's face with his right. He didn't stop there. As soon as Chisolm was off-balance, he wrenched him to the side, causing him to stumble and drop to his knees. That wasn't enough either. All the rage of the half-life he'd lived since Chisolm had used him to strike at Everett filled Lionel. He flung himself on Chisolm, kneeing him hard in the groin, then pinning him on his back.

"Did I mention that I spent a delightful few weeks in Malta with a champion prize fighter as part of my misspent youth?" he panted, then threw another punch, cracking Chisolm's nose. "The skills I learned then have proven invaluable," he went on. "Men like me have to protect ourselves from men like you." He let loose one last punch before shaking his hand out and deciding the pain wasn't worth it.

Chisolm groaned and writhed under him, as though he wanted to make some sort of reply. He didn't get a chance. A police whistle sounded from the far end of the dock. Within seconds, the crowd that had gathered to watch the fight parted, and a pair of Hull police officers charged the scene.

Lionel pulled back, pushing himself to stand. "Arrest this man," he said before the officers lunged toward him, assuming he was the criminal. "This is Lord Chisolm. He's wanted for kidnapping and child trafficking, among other things. He's also a first-rate bastard who enjoys ruining lives for fun." He addressed his litany of accusations to Chisolm himself, but turned to the officers to say, "I believe my business associate, Mr. David Wirth, spoke to your office yesterday about the whole matter?"

The officers blinked in confusion. "You wouldn't be Lionel Mercer, would you?"

"I am." Lionel stood taller, tugging at the cuffs of his jacket and straightening his tie.

"Don't listen to him," Chisolm growled, struggling to get to his feet. "He's—"

"What are you going to say I am?" Lionel snorted, brushing his sleeves and tilting his chin up proudly. "I am a friend to the friendless. I am a confidant and a shoulder to cry on. I am a lover of all people and a man who will give his life to make a friend smile. I am a man who has and will always fight for those who have been used, as you used me, and Everett, and the children you bought and sold." He took a step closer to Chisolm. "You don't frighten me at all. You are nothing."

Chisolm blinked, shutting his mouth. His lip was cracked and bleeding, and the side of his face swelled from Lionel's blows. Lionel might have been the sick one, but Chisolm was the mess.

"We have been advised to be on the lookout for Lord Chisolm," one of the officers said cautiously. "Mr. Wirth did say he would attempt to sail out of Hull today, and we received a telegram from a Lord Clerkenwell with Scotland Yard late last night."

Even with his mangled face, Chisolm managed to look alarmed at that bit of news. He glanced to the officers, then attempted to dart away from them. With his injuries and the encroaching crowd, he only made it a few steps before one of the officers caught him by the arm.

"At the very least, sir, we should take him to the station and try to sort this mess out," he said to the other officer.

"Agreed," the first officer said.

"The ship is getting ready to sail," someone shouted through the crowd.

In an instant, the men and women who had been watching the altercation scattered, dashing toward the gangplank as the ship's crew began to dismantle it. The sleepy feeling was gone from the dock as people scrambled aboard. A porter from the dock retrieved Lionel's suitcase and handed it to him.

"Are you coming with us to the station?" the first officer asked Lionel.

Lionel gripped the handle of his suitcase hard, glancing to the gangplank. He narrowed his eyes and stared hard at Chisolm. As easy as it would be to run away and tell himself it was for his and David's own good, his business with Chisolm wasn't finished yet. It wouldn't be until the man stood before the House of Lords, along with Eastleigh and Castleford, and received the punishment he deserved.

"Let me just return to the inn first to drop off my things and—" He paused, swallowing the dread that suddenly welled up in his gut. "And inform my partner about Lord Chisolm's arrest," he finished in a hoarse voice.

The officers nodded and led Chisolm away. Lionel sucked in a deep breath, turning toward the end of the platform and the road that would lead him back to the inn. He started forward with even more reluctance than he'd had to board the ship. David was going to flay him alive for attempting to leave, and there was a fair chance that he deserved it.

CHAPTER 18

By the time David returned to the inn, there was a telegram waiting for him from Lord Clerkenwell. Castleford was secure in a prison in London, and Lord Clerkenwell and a few men were on their way to Hull. David had to admire the man's determination. He probably hadn't had a moment's rest or seen his wife and family for days. But David understood the drive behind Lord Clerkenwell's restless pursuit of justice. It was a drive he'd lived with for most of his life.

And for the first time in his life, that drive seemed unimportant when half of his heart was missing. He wanted to make Chisolm pay as much as the next man, perhaps even more, but Chisolm wasn't the prize he was after.

"And you say Mr. Mercer hasn't returned to the inn since he departed before dawn?" David asked the young man behind the front desk after reading the telegram.

The young man bore a distinct resemblance to the young woman who had been there the day before, leading David to believe they were members of the same family that owned the inn.

"No, sir." The young man shrugged and shook his head. The lad couldn't have been more than fifteen. His face flushed and he looked sweetly guilty as he admitted, "He asked me to delay any efforts you might make to go after him if I possibly could."

David huffed out a breath and clenched his jaw, frowning. The young man flinched as though he were the object of David's ire. "A word of advice," David growled to the young man. "If you go into business, be certain you choose a partner who isn't a vain, sanctimonious, self-righteous prick and a colossal pain in your arse."

"Why, David, you do say the sweetest things."

Every fiber in David's body snapped taut at the sound of Lionel's voice behind him. He whipped around to glare at the bastard, ready to let loose with every expletive he knew, in spite of the tender ears of the young man behind the desk.

Lionel stood in the inn's doorway, his suitcase in hand—a hand that was bruised and swollen around the knuckles. His sandy-blond hair was tousled by the sea breeze, and spots of pink stood out on his cheeks in sharp contrast to his pale skin. Lionel's blue eyes were bright with guilt, and a dozen other intense emotions David couldn't quite put his finger on. As furious as David was, his gaze instantly dropped to the blush of Lionel's lips as he remembered their taste, then on to the subtle mark low on Lionel's neck that wasn't quite hidden by his collar. The thought struck David that it probably wasn't wise of him to leave that sort of a mark where everyone could see it, but it filled him with a possessive pride all the same.

The jumble of emotions and lust that assailed David quickly coalesced into frustration. He marched across the lobby to Lionel, wanting to take the infuriating man into his arms and shake sense into him, then kiss him into utter submission. It took a supreme effort of will not to tug Lionel into his arms with the young man behind the desk, and who knew who else from the street, watching them.

"Where have you been?" he growled instead, trusting Lionel would feel the impact of all his emotions, whether he acted on them or not.

"Nowhere," Lionel said with a casual shrug, his eyes blazing with excitement. "I had a daft idea that I would go sailing—"

"Daft is right, you blessed idiot," David rumbled, dropping his voice as he stepped closer to Lionel. "Don't you ever think of leaving me like—"

"And as it happened, I ran into an old friend at the dock," Lionel went on, his voice growing louder and rising half an octave.

David's mouth was already open and ready to tear Lionel to bits with scolding, but it stayed open as Lionel grinned victoriously at him.

"Chisolm?" he asked, nearly choking on the word.

Lionel nodded, eyes brighter than ever.

David continued to gape at him. "Only you are mad enough to make a coward's retreat from a situation more important than life itself to the both of us, only to run smack into the very man we came here to apprehend."

"I have a knack for the surreal," Lionel said, hoarse with irony. Uncertainty filled his expression as he tilted his head slightly, as if trying to gauge just how furious David was with him. "I punched him in the face," he went on, shifting his suitcase into his other hand so he could hold up his bruised hand the way a child would show off an interesting rock he'd collected. "Multiple times." When David merely stood there and gaped at him, he went on with, "It was uncommonly satisfying. I also did a satisfying amount of damage to his useless groin."

"Unbelievable," David muttered, shoving a hand through his hair. He hadn't thought it was possible to love Lionel more than he already did, but the paradoxical blend of pride and humiliation in his eyes had him wanting to kiss Lionel so hard he forgot his name...right after he lectured him into next Sunday. "And where is Chisolm now?" he asked, one eyebrow raised.

"The Hull police just happened to be on the scene," Lionel said with pretend casualness, stepping carefully away from David and setting his suitcase on a chair closer to the lobby's fireplace. "They received a telegram from Lord Clerkenwell, alerting them that Chisolm might make an appearance at the docks today. I'm afraid my altercation with Chisolm caused a bit of a scene, but it only served to draw the police in. Once I explained who I was and who Chisolm was, they arrested him and hauled him off to jail to await whatever Scotland Yard cares to do with him next."

David followed Lionel with his eyes as he crossed the room. "Let me guess. As you prepared to board a ship with the expressed intent of leaving me, you spotted Chisolm attempting to board as well. And you decided it would be a good idea to confront and assault the man right then and there."

"More or less," Lionel admitted in a quiet voice, lowering his head.

"You." David crossed his arms. "Lionel Mercer. Clever fashion plate, London man about town, ever the debonair dandy, who prides himself on pulling strings behind the scenes while maintaining perfect poise in every public situation."

"That sounds like me." Lionel attempted a cocky grin. It ended up making him look more vulnerable than ever.

"You punched a man on a dock in front of a crowd of people."

"It was surprisingly satisfying," Lionel said, his mouth twitching into a different sort of grin.

David was beside himself with a dozen different kinds of emotion. He had no idea what to do with the infuriating, amazing, idiotic man in front of him. All he knew was that he couldn't do it in the lobby of an inn. He surged forward, grabbing Lionel's suitcase from the chair and marching toward the stairs.

"Those are my things." Lionel chased after him, scrambling up the stairs as David took them two at a time. "I need them."

"You don't need them right now, because right now, you're not going anywhere," David said over his shoulder, turning a corner and continuing up to their attic rooms.

"I checked out of my room this morning," Lionel told him, keeping close behind David. "So I don't know where you're going to put them."

"I do," David said.

He reached the top of the stairs and paused to unlock his room, then stormed inside. He tossed Lionel's suitcase into the corner of the room with more force than he needed to, then spun back to face Lionel.

"Careful," Lionel snapped, jumping into the room. "That poor case has been through more than enough already."

David ignored him, crossing past Lionel to shut and lock the door. Lionel opened his mouth to say more, but David stepped into him, clasping Lionel's face in his hands, and slanting his mouth over Lionel's in a kiss designed to silence every protest, every word, and every thought Lionel could possibly have.

David had never kissed anyone out of anger, but there was definitely something to be said for it. He invaded Lionel's mouth and clamped his body close in a way that brooked no argument. He took what he wanted, showing Lionel with his lips, teeth, and tongue that arguing or resisting him was an exercise in futility, that he was the one in control of the both of them, and Lionel would do well not to forget that. Ever.

Lionel gave in within seconds, moaning deep in his throat and going slack against David. His eyes rolled back as David showered kisses across his jaw and nibbled on his neck before returning to plunder his mouth again. It didn't matter how much David took or how powerfully he mastered Lionel, the fear of almost losing Lionel, the possibility that Lionel might try to run again, only made the potency of everything David felt hotter and harder.

"All right, all right," Lionel panted, gripping David's jacket as it for dear life. "I'm sorry that I tried to leave without consulting you about it. But if this isn't proof that we cannot be trusted to act sensibly—"

"Shut up," David growled against Lionel's mouth, unbuttoning his jacket and shoving it off his shoulders. "I don't want to hear another word from you."

"If you aren't willing to hear sense—"

"Sense?" David jerked back, hands gripping Lionel's waistcoat as he began to unbutton it. "From a man who attempted to run away like a thief? From someone who got into a fistfight with an earl on a dock in Hull?"

"Yes, well, you may have a point about—"

David silenced him with another searing kiss that left Lionel groaning and limp. He made quick work of Lionel's waistcoat, then pushed his suspenders off his shoulders and tugged Lionel's shirt from the waist of his trousers. The quicker he had the man naked under him, the better. He would show Lionel everything he stood to lose by painting himself as a martyr and everything he stood to gain by sharing whatever bad hand life had dealt him with a man who loved him.

"David, please, please," Lionel pleaded between kisses as David yanked his shirt off over his head. "You're killing me. I can't resist this anymore."

"Then don't." David pulled him into his arms, raining kisses along his neck and nibbling his shoulder. Lionel had the most exquisite neck of any man David had ever known, and he intended to mark every inch of it as his.

"Please," Lionel continued to protest, though the way he begged had the exact opposite effect on David than he intended. "I don't want to hurt you."

David wrenched back, letting go and glaring at Lionel. "Then why did you run out on me? Or did you think that wouldn't hurt?"

"I—" The tension quickly drained from Lionel's face, and he lowered his head. "You are without a doubt the most stubborn man I've ever known."

"No, love, you are," David said, glowering at Lionel with what he was sure was a heady mixture of frustration and lust. "You act as though you're doing me a favor by keeping your distance from me. Aside from the fact that I'm still not convinced you received a correct diagnosis—"

"David—" Lionel stared flatly at him.

"—you're denying me the right to make decisions about my own life," David rode over him. "And isn't that precisely why you clocked Chisolm across the face earlier? Because the man's deceit denied you the right to make your own decisions about whom you choose to sleep with and when?"

"Actually, I could make whatever decisions I want about that," Lionel said in a practical tone that was utterly at odds with the way he stood, shirtless, his trousers tented, a superior look on his face. "But I'm not a monster who doesn't care about his fellow men."

"Neither am I," David insisted, unbuttoning his jacket. Before he shrugged out of it, he reached into one of the pockets and pulled out an entire handful of French letters he'd purchased on his way back to the inn from the train station.

"Good heavens," Lionel gasped, his eyes going wide and bright, as David tossed the lot of them on the bed. He shifted to stare at David as he tossed his jacket aside and made quick work of his waistcoat and shirt. "Are you certain?"

David paused in the middle of unfastening his trousers, letting out an irritated breath and letting his shoulders drop. "Lionel, you are the single most aggravating man in England. What has this whole episode been about if not my absolute certainty that I want to spend the rest of my life with you, loving you in every way possible."

"That life might not be long if you—"

"Will you *please* shut up," David said, his patience at an end. He stepped closer to Lionel, grabbing his face and planting a kiss so hard on his mouth that it would likely bruise Lionel's tender lips. "You bloody aggravating fool," he said between kisses. "Don't you know that without you, my life isn't worth living? You are my life. You are my work and my pleasure. You are my heart and my soul. And I am yours. So if you don't stop resisting what we both know to be true, I won't be responsible for my actions."

"You won't?" Lionel asked breathlessly, heat and expectation glittering in his eyes.

"No," David said, staring hard at him. "So don't you ever try to run away from me again." He reached for the fastenings of Lionel's trousers, quickly working them loose and sliding his hand along the hot length of Lionel's cock.

"I'll admit, it was a terrible idea to run," Lionel gasped, jerking into David's touch. "And you did purchase quite a few fine-looking preventatives. It would be a shame to waste them." He gasped and shuddered as David stroked him, reaching lower to cup his balls. "And I suppose that lovely ointment you bought for my rash would be effective enough as a lubricant."

David hadn't thought of that. He was suddenly glad Lionel had left the jar behind—either accidentally or to prove a point—and that he'd rescued it from the other room. It sat conveniently on the table beside his bed now. He grinned wolfishly as he crushed his mouth over Lionel's in a demanding kiss.

"I am going to make you mine," he growled against

Lionel's ear, earning a satisfying shudder that shook Lionel from head to toe. "You won't even be able to think about leaving me after I'm done with you. You won't be able to get the feeling of me inside of you out of that pretty little head of yours for the rest of your life."

Lionel glanced up at him, sparks in his eyes. "Promise?" he asked with so much mischief that it sent bolts of lightning through David's body.

He answered by yanking Lionel close and kissing him so hard Lionel went limp in his arms. Which was perfect, as far as David was concerned, he lowered a hand to caress Lionel's backside, pushing his trousers down as he did. Lionel gasped and moaned as David fingered his arse, giving him a taste of what he was about to get.

It was so wonderful to have Lionel eager and panting in his arms that David simply couldn't hold out and tease Lionel the way he wanted to. He fumbled his way out of the rest of his clothes as Lionel shed the last of his. The two of them spilled, naked, across the bed, grabbing whichever of the French letters reached their hands first, opening them, and putting them on. Even with sensation slightly dulled, David knew he wasn't going to be able to last forever.

"I love you," he told Lionel as he rolled him to his back, kissing his mouth, his neck, and his chest. "Even though you aggravate the hell out of me, I love you."

"And I love you," Lionel panted, smile on his beautiful face, eyes hazy with passion, the picture of surrender. "I would have to love you to put up with your stubbornness and your mood swings."

"*I* have mood swings?" David arched one eyebrow, propping himself above Lionel.

"Of course, you do, love." Lionel grinned as though he had never been happier. "You're a stodgy, moody prick most of the time."

God, how he loved Lionel. Even when he was being an insufferable arse. *Especially* when he was being an insufferable arse.

"I'll show you prick," David growled, reaching for the jar on the bedside table.

The look of absolute joy and flushed anticipation that came over Lionel was enough to make David wonder why he hadn't fucked him much, much sooner. He'd heard Lionel say for years how much he enjoyed sex, but seeing that enjoyment firsthand, experiencing the erotic tension in Lionel's body and the sounds of excitement and abandon he made as David kissed him everywhere he could possibly think of, was a heady experience. It carried him away, increasing his own anticipation and enjoyment as he shifted Lionel to his side and fit himself behind him. As lovely as it would have been to make love to Lionel face to face, David loved the idea of being able to go deep and wrap his arms around the man he loved.

Which was exactly what he did. Lionel gasped and sighed as David pushed carefully into his arse. It took immense willpower not to simply pound into Lionel until they were both mad with passion, but the urge to be careful was still foremost in David's mind.

"Are you trying to drive me mad?" Lionel panted as David filled him slowly, making certain their bodies fit well together.

"Aren't you the one who wanted to hold back and be careful?" David asked him in return.

"Forget I ever said that," Lionel gasped, moving against him urgently. "Fuck me like you mean it."

David didn't have to be told twice. He jerked against Lionel, finding a satisfactory rhythm, then doubling it in speed and intensity. Lionel responded with enthusiasm, moving with David and making the most delicious sounds. Lionel added a few, charming expletives as David reached around to stroke his cock as he thrust. Lionel was the perfect blend of submissive and demanding as David sped toward his climax, obviously and vocally enjoying everything they were doing. It made absolute sense that Lionel had been in such high demand years ago. Who wouldn't want such an enthusiastic partner? But instead of jealousy, David took incredible satisfaction in the absolute certainty that Lionel was all his in every way from that point onward.

"I love you," he repeated as his body tightened and heated in preparation for what he could feel would be a powerful orgasm. "I love you so much."

Lionel responded with a moan, his body tensing with orgasm. David felt it fully, inside and out, and it pushed him over the edge. He growled against Lionel's shoulder, clutching him tightly as he jerked and spilled deep inside of him. It felt so good to come that way, almost in unison with the man he loved, that pleasure reverberated through him long after the initial burst was done.

It kept David feeling as though the two of them were deeply connected, even after they both dissolved into a limp, panting pile. He gathered Lionel closer in his arms, turning him so that they faced each other, limbs entwining, as they stole lazy kisses. The afterglow of making love had never felt so good.

"I won't ever leave you again," Lionel promised, closing his eyes and nestling against David. "It was a stupid idea in the first place."

"It was," David agreed, stroking his hair.

Lionel's kiss-swollen lips twitched into a grin. "The office would fall apart without me anyhow."

David laughed. "Dream on, love," he said, sliding his thigh between Lionel's and holding him close. Their life was a dream he didn't ever want to wake up from.

CHAPTER 19

*I*t was a gross abdication of responsibility. One Lionel was certain he would come to regret.

Later.

He stretched slowly as the haze of the nap he'd fallen into after he and David made love began to lift. His body felt absolutely wonderful in every way. He was warm and loose. His skin pressed against David's in a thousand different ways and places as they lay tangled up in each other. Best of all, his arse was just sore enough to feel decadent where David had been inside of him. Lionel adored the sensation of being used, but knowing David was the one who had found pleasure in him, and vice versa, brought a whole new level of enjoyment to his heart as well as his body.

"This bed is entirely too small," he sighed, still groggy from sleep, as he wriggled against David.

He was already well on his way to being fully

aroused again. Cleaning preventatives was a loathsome task, but David had purchased enough of them that they might not have to worry about it just yet. He wanted to laugh at himself for how drastically his mind had changed toward intimacy since that morning, but the cat of sin and seduction was already out of the bag where he and David were concerned. He'd been motivated by fear just hours before, but pummeling a sworn enemy into a pulp and watching him being carted off to jail did wonders for a man's confidence. Or perhaps he'd just been hungry for David for so long that his moral compass had broken. A repeat performance of their earlier activity wouldn't make things more dangerous than they already were.

"The bed isn't the problem," David grumbled, sounding mostly asleep himself. He, too, stretched—causing a world of delicious friction between their bodies—and groaned before rolling to his back.

Lionel rolled with him, perching atop David and positioning himself straddling David's legs. It was an eye-opening position that made him rethink his preference for being on the receiving end of sexual congress. He folded his arms across David's chest and rested his chin on the back of his hands as they rested over David's heart. Or at least started to until he remembered how battered his hand was from punching Chisolm.

"This is foolish, you know," he told David with one eyebrow raised.

David sighed, stroking his hands across Lionel's sides

to caress his backside. "Lionel, if I hear one more word out of you about me putting myself in danger by loving you, I'm going to tie a gag around your mouth."

A giddy thrill wriggled through Lionel, sending blood straight to his cock. "I could be amenable to that sort of play," he said, shifting to both bring his face level with David's and to rub his stiffening erection against David's belly. "There isn't anything I haven't tried before, and a little light bondage is quite stimulating, when one has the right partner."

David's eyes snapped fully open. He gaped at Lionel with a charming hint of trepidation.

"I take it you've never experimented with anything out of the ordinary before," Lionel went on with a sly grin. He dipped down to steal a kiss from David's swollen lips. "We'll soon change that," he promised in a purr.

For a moment, he indulged in that kiss, sucking in a breath when David's hands tightened on his bum, spreading him, David's fingertips stroking against his hole. Lionel made a sound of acquiescence that David answered with an aggressive groan.

At least, until he stopped and said, "Wait, I thought you were just saying that this is foolish."

Lionel propped himself above David with a sanctimonious look. "You interrupted me before I could finish," he said. "What I was about to say is that it is extraordinarily foolish of us to engage in blatant buggery in a hotel room with the window open in the middle of the day." He shot a glance toward the open window in the slanted ceiling above them. "This isn't London, you know. They'll be out there with pitchforks and torches if we make too much noise."

David started laughing before Lionel finished his warning, grabbing Lionel's face and pulling him down for a lingering kiss. It was heaven, as far as Lionel was concerned. Yes, his conscience still burned with the physical danger that the two of them being together presented, but David had a point that Lionel couldn't refute when he asserted that it was his choice to take the risk. And after the hour they'd just spent, even Lionel was willing to concede that the benefits might be worth the risks.

His mind was already whirling with all the adventurous practices he wanted to teach David—even while he was quickly losing the will to do anything but let David mold him in whatever way he wanted—when the sound of footsteps coming up the stairs to the attic rooms shook him. David went suddenly still and stiff as well. The two of them held their breaths, waiting to see if the footsteps were a maid or a new guest at the inn or worse.

Lionel's worst fears seemed confirmed for a moment when there was a knock on the door.

The knock was followed by a man clearing his throat. "Wirth, Mercer," Lord Clerkenwell's voice sounded from the tiny hall. "I'm going to assume that the two of you are in there, based on the information the gob-smacked young man at the front desk gave me, and that I don't want to intrude."

Lionel glanced down at David, eyes wide with guilt and humor, swiftly losing his battle not to crack into laughter.

"We're in here," David called to the door, his face going red.

"Well," Lord Clerkenwell began again, a hint of humor in his voice, "I'll be downstairs. So finish up, if you please, and join me there."

"Yes, my lord," Lionel called, breaking down into giggles and hiding his face against David's chest as Lord Clerkenwell's footsteps retreated.

"Stop laughing," David ordered Lionel, sitting and bringing Lionel with him.

The movement left Lionel in the intriguing position of straddling David's lap, his knees digging into the mattress on either side of him, his arms slung lazily around David's shoulders. It was a perfect kissing position, so Lionel bore into him, indulging in a long, lingering kiss. David was too startled to do anything but kiss him back for a moment before snapping to his senses.

"What are you doing, Lionel?" He planted his hands firmly on Lionel's sides, as if he would push him away. "Lord Clerkenwell is waiting downstairs."

"Lord Clerkenwell said to finish up here first," Lionel hummed, flexing against David and kissing him again.

David's hands slipped down to Lionel's backside, and he slanted his mouth over Lionel's, their tongues dancing for a moment, before he pulled back again. "Lord

Clerkenwell could have us arrested under the Labouchere Amendment," he said with a frown.

Lionel wasn't deterred, although he knew they weren't going to take things any further than teasing just then. All the same, he kissed David as if he planned to continue and said, "Lord Clerkenwell was born to a whore and raised in a brothel. I'd wager he knows more about what we're doing than you do, and that he doesn't care one wit where we put our cocks."

David made a sound of consideration deep in his throat that Lionel covered with an open-mouth kiss. The moment didn't last, though.

"We need to wrap up this investigation once and for all," David said with a sigh, pushing Lionel away from him at last. "Once business is taken care of, we can sort everything else out."

"Ever the pragmatist," Lionel sighed, climbing off of him and stumbling out of bed. He was just as eager as David to put Chisolm and the rest far, far behind them. Once all of that was out of the way, he and David could settle on how exactly they were going to meld their mad lives, and all of the dangers they presented, together.

They washed and dressed as quickly as they could with all the temptations that being half aroused and no longer keeping their distance from each other brought with it. Lionel was convinced it would have been easier for the two of them to get each other off as simply as possible so that they could move on to other things, but doing so would probably only take their minds even further from settling the last of the business with Chisolm than they already were.

Even so, the look on Lord Clerkenwell's face when they finally made it downstairs, dressed and groomed with surprising fastidiousness, proved that the enigmatic man knew exactly what they'd been up to.

"So Chisolm was arrested at the dock," Lord Clerkenwell began with a teasing grin as Lionel and David headed out the inn's front door with him.

"It was a miraculous act of heroism on my part," Lionel said, feeling extraordinarily content with himself for a variety of reasons. "I singlehandedly ferreted him out, subdued him, and made certain he was arrested."

"Lionel accidentally noticed him while attempting to run away," David told Lord Clerkenwell with a sardonic look. "He apparently then flung himself at Chisolm and beat him to a pulp before almost being arrested himself by officers who just happened to be on the scene. Did I get that right, Lionel?" he asked, one eyebrow arched.

Lionel tilted his chin up, heat splashing his face. "Chisolm was arrested. That's all that matters."

Lord Clerkenwell chuckled and shook his head. "I cannot wait to take statements from witnesses."

Lord Clerkenwell's amusement and Lionel's sheepishness vanished in an instant as they turned the corner onto the street where Hull's central jail stood. A small crowd had assembled outside of the building, and several officers pored over the scene, shouting orders for the onlookers to stay back. Lionel had no idea what was going on until a pair of men rushed out of the building carrying a stretcher between them. Even from a distance, it was clear that the man in the stretcher was bleeding profusely and not moving.

"What happened here?" Lord Clerkenwell asked, falling into natural command as he strode forward, David and Lionel hurrying behind him.

"There's been a jailbreak," one of the women watching the scene said as though reporting on the latest stage melodrama.

"An officer's been shot," another woman said.

It took a moment for the three of them to push their way past the crowd. Lord Clerkenwell had to take out his Scotland Yard credentials before the officers at the periphery of the scene would let them past. In the process, Lionel got a good look at the man in the stretcher. It was the younger of the two officers who had arrested Chisolm at the dock, and as far as Lionel could see, the man was dead from a gunshot wound to the head.

"What happened?" Lionel asked, feeling faint.

The Hull officers weren't in a hurry to answer until Lord Clerkenwell pushed his way inside the jail, David and Lionel behind him. The older of the two officers who had been at the dock recognized Lionel and stood from the chair where he'd been weeping.

"That man, Chisolm," he said. "He got away."

Lionel's stomach twisted and bile rose in his throat. "What do you mean he got away?"

A younger officer whom Lionel didn't recognize

stepped forward. His uniform bore the insignia of a man in charge, as did his demeanor. He glanced at the credentials Lord Clerkenwell still held and decided Lord Clerkenwell was the man to speak to.

"Officer Nyman," he said shaking Lord Clerkenwell's hand.

"Lord Clerkenwell, Assistant Commissioner, Scotland Yard," Lord Clerkenwell introduced himself. "And my associates, Mr. Wirth and Mr. Mercer."

Officer Nyman's eyes went wide for a moment before he snapped straighter, saluted Lord Clerkenwell, and launched into an explanation. "Lord Chisolm was taken into custody at eight-thirty this morning, my lord. He was processed and locked in cell three. Officer Kinney was set to guard him. At some time after nine-thirty, a gunshot was heard. Officer Ingersoll and myself rushed in to see what had happened. Officer Kinney lay dead in cell three. Lord Chisolm was gone."

"Escaped through the window in there," a young officer who stared at Lord Clerkenwell with wide eyes said, pointing through a doorway to what looked like the cellblock.

Officer Nyman glared at him for a moment before continuing with, "Lord Chisolm is believed to be on the loose, my lord. And he appears to be armed. Officer Kinney's sidearm is missing, as are three other pistols."

"Chisolm is on the run again, and he's armed," Lionel said in disbelief, pushing a hand through his hair. Remorse ate at him. He should have stayed at the jail to make certain Chisolm was handled correctly. The Hull officers must have been lulled into complacency by Chisolm's title and noble demeanor. He never should have returned to the inn to face David, never should have—

No, he didn't regret going to bed with David for an instant, no matter what the consequences were. Which said far more than he wanted to think about at the moment. Catching Chisolm had to come before his twisted and guilty conscience.

"He can't have gone far," David said, as businesslike as David always was. Lionel loved him for it.

"My men are already out searching," Officer Nyman said. "He hasn't been gone that long. He can't have gone far."

"He'll either try to leave by train or by sea," Lord Clerkenwell said, gesturing for David and Lionel to follow him back out to the street. "Chisolm will want to get as far away from here as fast as possible."

Lionel shook his head. "He'll hide," he argued. "He knows we've found him and that we've already guessed his plans to leave the country. He'll lay low until we stop searching, and then he'll move."

"I'm not so sure," David said with a frown as they edged their way past the crowd that was still gathered around the jail, eager for news. "He doesn't have friends around here. Not according to the woman we spoke to when we first arrived."

"What woman is this?" Lord Clerkenwell asked as they strode toward the center of town.

"Her niece worked at the house where Chisolm was staying," David said. "Chisolm received a telegram from George Eastleigh, warning him that Eastleigh was apprehended."

Lionel's thoughts spun back to the day before as David told the story. It was true, Chisolm had no friends in Hull, but he did have them in London. Which meant he would try to return to London as soon as—

He stopped, grabbing David's sleeve as another part of the day before struck him. "If Chisolm is smart, he'll be hiding in the smuggler's caves."

"Smuggler's caves?" Lord Clerkenwell asked.

David's expression lit with inspiration and determination. He turned toward the sea. "There are a series of cliffs with caves in them off that way." He pointed through the buildings as though they weren't there. "Lionel and I explored a small portion of them before...." His words trailed off.

"Everything after 'before' isn't important," Lionel picked up the story. "I would be willing to bet my eye teeth that that's where Chisolm has gone. It's the perfect place to stay out of sight until the furor dies down."

"We should at least check the area," David agreed. He glanced to Lionel. "Do you think you're up for it?"

Lionel let out an irritated breath and shook his head. "You're the one who can't swim," he said, starting on at a faster pace. "And I'm the one who singlehandedly wrestled Chisolm to the ground and incapacitated him earlier today."

David's mouth twitched into a grin as the three of them charged on. "Why do I have the feeling that story is going to grow with each retelling?"

Lionel was about to make a witty reply when Lord Clerkenwell said, "You can embellish the story until it includes angels flying down out of heaven to bestow a magical shillelagh on you that you used to bash Chisolm's head in, as long as we catch him first."

CHAPTER 20

A strange sense of déjà vu filled David as he, Lionel, and Lord Clerkenwell made their way past the shops and houses at the edge of Hull and continued along the path that skirted the sea, heading toward the cliffs and the smugglers caves.

"If I had known being a solicitor would involve prolonged chases through the countryside and spelunking in seaside caves, I would have put more time and effort into athletics," he said, sending Lord Clerkenwell a sideways look as they picked up their pace.

"You're no average solicitor," Lord Clerkenwell reminded him with a grin.

"And there's certainly nothing wrong with your physique," Lionel added from David's other side.

David shot him a warning look as Lord Clerkenwell tried to hide a grin, but Lionel was staring straight forward and barely noticed. David was tempted to make a crack about Lionel's surprising strength and dexterity, considering that Lionel believed himself to be on death's door, but the pinch of Lionel's brow and the way he raised his hand to his forehead to focus on something in the distance distracted him.

"I think that's Chisolm," Lionel said, his voice rising with excitement.

David snapped his glance forward, squinting to see what Lionel saw. It was the middle of a sunny, balmy day, and the path they walked was far from abandoned. Holiday-makers and fishermen ambled along the walk, even a few children out with their caregivers. It was a peaceful scene overall, accented by the salt tang in the air and the sounds of the surf and gulls circling above. But one figure sped along the path faster than any of the others, heading for the cliffs.

"Come on," Lord Clerkenwell said, picking up his pace.

The three of them broke into a jog. David's heart pounded with the exertion, but even more with the swirling anticipation of what would happen when they reached Chisolm. In just a few minutes, after months of searching and effort, the whole episode would be over and, if he had his way, Chisolm would be brought to justice. It seemed simple enough, but a deeper trepidation pulsed through David's gut. Something far greater than the end of a case was about to happen.

"He sees us," Lionel said as they darted past a group of young women who were foolishly trying to get their attention by posing and preening. "He's headed for the stairs to the beach."

"He won't get away now," Lord Clerkenwell vowed.

David prayed the man was right. He prayed that Lionel's strength would keep up as they switched to a full run, gaining on Chisolm slowly but surely. Lionel's face had gone red with effort, but his gaze was locked on Chisolm with enough determination to bring the stars down out of the sky.

"Stop!" Lord Clerkenwell shouted when they came within earshot of Chisolm. "Lord Chisolm, you are under arrest by order of Her Majesty's police."

Chisolm had nearly reached the stairs. He jerked to a stop, spinning to face the three of them as they sprinted closer. David was surprised at the change that had come over the once refined and mighty lord the moment he saw Chisolm's face. Gone was any sign of smug authority. In its place was pure fear and a feral look of desperation. It was the look of a man who knew he was caught.

Rather than charging down the stairs, Chisolm ran on, fumbling for something in his jacket.

"Where is he going?" David asked aloud, picking up his pace.

No one answered, and Chisolm sprinted ahead as the ground sloped up slightly, dashing for the far end of the cliffs. Perhaps there was a second set of stairs on the other side, a boat that would—

Without warning, Chisolm stopped, whipped to face them and fired a gun that was suddenly in his hand.

David remembered the warning of the officer from the jail that Chisolm was armed as the crack of the gun startled him. His foot hit a rock on the path, and he stumbled, crashing to his knees.

"David!" Lionel screamed behind him. "Oh, God, no, David!"

Lionel flung himself to his knees by David's side, throwing his arms around David and sheltering him as though Chisolm would fire again and he was the only thing standing between David and death. David could feel Lionel's entire body shaking as he embraced him.

"No, no, no," Lionel wailed, fumbling to pull David up straight and raking his hands over David's chest and arms, looking for injuries. "I'll kill the bastard if he hurt you. Please don't die."

"Lionel," David panted.

"I can't live without you." Lionel gasped for breath.

"Lionel," David raised his voice.

"If he shot you—"

"I tripped," David admitted.

Lionel froze, his mouth open in a sob and his eyes bright with sudden tears. His expression widened to incredulity.

"I tripped," David repeated, wrenching himself to his feet and bringing Lionel with him to prove it. "I'm not shot."

Lionel snapped his mouth shut, his brow furrowing. "As soon as I am finished with Chisolm, I'm going to kill you too," he promised in a hoarse voice, then turned to sprint off after Lord Clerkenwell.

Lord Clerkenwell had continued the chase when David fell. Chisolm hadn't stopped running, and as he neared the edge of the cliff, he turned to fire again. Lionel flinched as he ran ahead of David, but Lord Clerkenwell didn't miss a step. He reached into his jacket and pulled out a pistol of his own, taking aim at Chisolm and firing.

The shot couldn't possibly have been aimed to kill, otherwise Chisolm would have dropped on the spot. Instead, Chisolm merely jerked to a stop, spinning to face Lord Clerkenwell. His arms shook visibly as he held his gun out toward Lord Clerkenwell. David and Lionel caught up to Lord Clerkenwell's side.

"Let me go," Chisolm shouted. "I can make you all wealthy men. I have contacts, influence."

"You have a warrant out for your arrest," Lord Clerkenwell told him. "Your accomplices in the child kidnapping ring have already been captured and are awaiting trial. Come quietly and the House of Lords may be lenient with you."

"I seriously doubt that," Lionel muttered by David's side with a ferocity David rarely heard from him.

"I'm not a fool," Chisolm said with a hysterical laugh. "If I surrender to you, my life is over. Don't think I don't know how these things work. The second I have my back turned, you'll stick a knife in it and call it an unfortunate accident."

"That may be the way you operate," Lord Clerkenwell said with an ominous scowl, "but that is not how officers of Scotland Yard conduct themselves."

"And what about them?" Chisolm shifted to point his gun straight at David's heart.

David raised his hands instinctively. He'd never had a loaded gun pointed at him by a man with murderous intent. It was far more unnerving than he expected it to be.

"They won't harm you either," Lord Clerkenwell promised.

"Speak for yourself," Lionel said, surprising everyone by lunging for Lord Clerkenwell's gun.

Lionel's movement came as so much of a surprise to everyone that he was able to snatch the pistol from Lord Clerkenwell's hands and aim it at Chisolm before anyone could stop him. Lionel's hands shook for only a moment before he adjusted his grip on the gun, bared his teeth in a snarl, and narrowed his eyes at Chisolm.

"Lionel, put the gun down," Lord Clerkenwell ordered him with practiced calm. "You don't want me to have to take it from you."

"Listen to Lord Clerkenwell, love," David said, inching closer to Lionel.

"It's long past time you paid for your crimes, Chisolm." Lionel stared straight forward, blue eyes wide as he stared Chisolm down. "You've ruined more lives than can be counted, and it's time for you to stop."

"Those are brave words, coming from a rent boy," Chisolm flung back at Lionel with a vicious smile.

Lionel ignored the taunt. "You've destroyed the lives of innocent children in your lust for money and a false sense of power," he went on. "You tried to destroy Everett simply because you thought it would be fun. No man should ever be reduced to a plaything for another."

"Only a fool would give his heart away to a weakling like Jewel," Chisolm laughed.

"Everett is and always has been my friend," Lionel raised his voice. "I don't need to be in love with him to care about his life and his person. But you would know nothing about true friendship or true love. You used me as a tool of revenge." Lionel's voice took on a bitter edge as tears trailed down his red face. "You crippled my heart and damaged my body out of spite, as if I don't matter, as if the love I have to give doesn't matter."

"It doesn't." Chisolm shrugged. "You don't matter. You made yourself into a tool long before I came along, and you know it."

"You're wrong," Lionel seethed, taking a step toward Chisolm.

David exchanged a glance with Lord Clerkenwell, who nodded. They were both ready to put an end to the whole thing, but only after Lionel had a chance to exorcise his demons.

Lionel stood straighter, chin tilted up, gun aimed with perfect precision at Chisolm's heart. "You're so very wrong," he repeated, taking another step forward. "I am a man with a heart, and you have none. I most certainly matter. I matter to myself. I matter to the man I love. I matter to my friends." He arched one eyebrow. "Can you say the same?"

"I—" Chisolm backed away from Lionel, reaching the edge of the cliff.

"Do you matter to anyone, Chisolm?" Lionel went on, his voice returning to its usual, calm, otherworldly power. "Will anyone come to your defense when you're standing before the House of Lords at your trial? Will your friends step forward to speak for you the way that mine would speak for me? Or will you face what is coming completely and utterly alone?"

Lionel's eyes blazed with intensity as he stared Chisolm down. Chisolm seemed transfixed by him, unable to look away.

"I know who I am," Lionel went on. "I am a man with friends. And I know who you are. You know it too." He paused. Chisolm's face went ashen and he lowered his gun, but he couldn't pry his eyes away from Lionel's. "You are a dead man," Lionel said at last.

Chisolm transformed before David's eyes, the life leaving his expression as he surrendered. Panic filled David, and for a moment he was certain Lionel would fire, killing the man. But without even looking to see what he was doing, Chisolm took a step back, tumbling over the edge of the cliff. He didn't make a sound as he plummeted to his death, either crushed by the rocks below or swallowed by the sea.

The color quickly drained from Lionel's face. He blinked at the horizon before slowly lowering his arms and Lord Clerkenwell's gun. He sucked in a breath, then turned away from the cliff's edge.

"I'm terribly sorry for taking your gun," he said in a vague, wispy voice, stepping over to Lord Clerkenwell and returning the weapon.

Lord Clerkenwell took it silently as Lionel walked on, heading back toward the path—which was littered with spectators who had rushed to see what was going on. Lionel only made it a few steps before collapsing into a heap and bursting into pitiful tears.

"Lionel!" David rushed forward, sinking to a crouch at Lionel's side the way Lionel had done for him when he thought David had been shot. Neither of them had been pierced by bullets, but they had both been wounded by the whole experience.

Lionel twisted into David's waiting arms, sobbing uncontrollably and shaking. David closed his arms tightly around him, cradling him close.

"Ssh, ssh, love, it's all right. It's over." David smoothed his hand over Lionel's head, not caring who saw the two of them locked together in such an intimate position. "What's done is done."

"It's so unfair," Lionel sobbed before gulping in a few breaths and burying his face against David's shoulder. "I can't get back the lives he stole."

"None of us can," David tried to soothe him. "But you did your best. Think of all the children we've saved by thwarting the ring when we did."

Lionel nodded against David's shoulder, breathing

hard. He pulled away slightly, straightening his back and squaring his shoulders as best he could in an effort to regain some semblance of dignity. "Do you know," he began with an attempt at sounding above it all, "I didn't think I would be half this emotional about bringing an end to Chisolm's reign of terror. It's incredibly disconcerting."

David couldn't help but laugh as he brushed the tears off of Lionel's cheeks with his thumbs and clasped the sides of his face. "You're allowed to be disconcerted after such a traumatic experience," he said, going so far as to steal a quick kiss, regardless of who was looking on.

"Well, I don't like it," Lionel said, gently shaking David off and pushing himself to stand. David stood with him, helping Lionel to his feet. Lionel made a disgusted noise. "I hate making a spectacle of myself like this."

"Nonsense." David grinned from ear to ear, brimming with love and affection as he brushed Lionel's suit off. "You adore making a spectacle of yourself whenever possible."

"Yes, but not because I've transformed into a blubbering idiot for no good reason," Lionel protested, attempting to straighten his hair by brushing his hands through it.

"You have a very good reason, love," David said, squeezing his arm and staring hard into his eyes. "I only wish I had known how badly Chisolm had wronged you sooner. I would have broken into his house and slit his throat in the dead of night if I had."

"No, you wouldn't have," Lionel said with a flat look, returning to his old self, but with a look of resolution in his eyes that hadn't been there before, as if a chapter of his life had been closed and a new one had begun. "You cannot slit a man's throat without getting blood everywhere, and you abhor the sight of blood."

"Who said I can't stand the sight of blood?" David protested, taking Lionel's hand and walking with him to where Lord Clerkenwell had moved to the path and was speaking to a pair of Hull police officers and several men who had likely watched the scene unfold. David noticed a stream of people heading down to the beach as well, likely to retrieve Chisolm's body.

"Darling," Lionel said, pursing his lips for a moment. "You cut your finger while opening a letter a few weeks ago and nearly fainted. I had to apply the plaster because you'd gone too woozy to do it yourself."

David shrugged. "Perhaps I just wanted you to lavish me with attention and bind my wounds," he teased.

"I wouldn't put it past you." Lionel rolled his eyes, but the gesture was accompanied by a grin that told David that, at last, everything would be all right.

CHAPTER 21

he Concord Theater was as busy in the afternoon a week after Chisolm's death as it normally was before a performance, and Niall Cristofori's new musical wouldn't open for another few weeks at least. Lionel was fascinated by the buzz of rehearsal and the bustle of sets being constructed, costumes sewn, and scenery being painted as he and David were shown into the backstage area by the no-nonsense stage manager.

"No wonder so many of our sort take to the theater," he told David as they dodged out of the way of a shirtless, muscular young man carrying a load of lumber over one, well-formed shoulder. "There's so much to see and do here."

"Kindly keep your eyes in your head," David said with a wry grin, pushing Lionel on toward the hallway with the dressing rooms, though Lionel caught him looking as well.

"Love, the very point of theater is to give people something to look at," Lionel argued, chin tilted up superiorly. "I'm merely appreciating the scenery the way I'm supposed to."

David hummed doubtfully and pointed toward a door down the hall with the name "Everett Jewel" emblazoned on it.

Lionel treated David to a saucy wink before moving on to face what he'd come to the theater for. He was eternally grateful to David for accompanying him on that particular errand, and for being a fussy, hovering, mother hen since they arrived back in London several days before. Though the very last thing he would do was admit to David that he not only enjoyed the man's constant nagging and presence, he needed it. He wasn't sure he would be able to have the conversation that needed to happen with Everett unless David was there to hold his hand, metaphorically, if not in actuality.

He paused before Everett's door, taking a deep breath and knocking. The door stood open, but Lionel waited for Everett's call of, "Come in," before crossing into the room.

Everett stood in the center of the dressing room in nothing but his drawers, of course. His arms were held out to the sides as a young woman with a pencil tucked behind her ear measured him with a tape. Lily Logan stood a few feet away, dressed in boy's clothes, writing down the measurements on a small clipboard. Patrick Wrexham sat on the stool in front of Everett's wardrobe, staring at Everett's backside and looking as though he were lost in a world of inappropriate thoughts. Patrick straightened and cleared his throat loudly as soon as Lionel and David entered.

"Why am I not surprised to find you mostly naked in a room full of people?" Lionel asked, crossing his arms and smirking. Though there was far less malice in his expression than was usually there when talking to Everett. Their rivalry seemed ages in the past now.

"Why, if it isn't London's most obnoxious popinjay," Everett greeted him with a wry grin. "Come to eat your heart out over what you can't have?"

"Why would I want gristle when I already have steak?" Lionel replied, sliding closer to David's side and sending David a particularly fond smile.

Everett burst into laughter. "It's about bloody time," he said, exchanging a glance with Patrick. "You owe me five quid."

Patrick shook his head, crossing his arms. "You'll get yours," he muttered.

"Now, now," Everett pretended to scold him. "If you start talking like that, there's no way Jenny will be able to properly measure my inseam."

"Just take a measurement and subtract three inches," Lionel told the costumer sarcastically.

"That's not true and you know it," Everett snapped back, one eyebrow raised.

Lionel's mouth twitched with the urge to smile. He'd forgotten how much fun it was to bicker with Everett when they didn't hate each other.

"Lily," David spoke over whatever bantering reply Lionel was tempted to make. "It's a pleasure to see you settled in at the theater."

Lily lit up at the sight of David and Lionel. "I can't thank you enough for finding me a position here, Mr. Wirth," she beamed.

"It was Lionel's doing, not mine," David said, crossing the room to hug the young woman.

"And it was my doing, not Lionel's," Everett added. "Any sister of Joe Logan's is a friend of mine."

"Are you enjoying your new employment?" David asked Lily. "Have they found suitable accommodations for you?"

"I love everything about it so far," Lily said. "I'm sharing a flat with Jenny and her sister, but it's simply lovely after...." Lily lowered her head, the same haunted look she'd worn last time Lionel saw her, at The Silver Serpent, taking over her expression. She shook it off, though. "Joe and Alistair wanted me to stay with them, but I'm happy where I am. I'd feel so out of place in Alistair's grand townhouse."

Lionel's brow flew up. He wondered if Lord Alistair Bevan had ever imagined a day when the stagehand sister of his low-born, male lover would refer to him in casual conversation by his given name. Then again, the world they all inhabited in the shadows had its own set of rules.

"Why are you here, Lionel?" Everett asked as Jenny stepped away, giving Lily a few measurements to write down. "Do you have something to tell me, or have you come to bask in my presence?" He moved to the over-stuffed sofa on one side of the room and draped himself over one end in a pose that was more or less obscene, considering he still only wore his drawers.

Jenny rolled her eyes at Lily, and the two of them left the room. Knowing full well what they'd come for, David followed them, shutting the door and affording the four of them that remained the privacy they would need.

Lionel instantly lost his flippant attitude. "Chisolm is dead."

Everett dropped his coquettish demeanor as well. "I know." He sat straighter. "I heard."

"I'd like to say I killed him for you," Lionel went on, moving gingerly to the sofa and taking a seat at the far end. David moved to stand beside him, resting a steadying hand on Lionel's shoulder. "I'd like to say that, but truthfully, I killed him for me."

Everett's eyes popped wide.

"You didn't kill him, Lionel," David said in a gentle voice, squeezing his shoulder.

"Didn't I?" Lionel twisted to glance up at him. "Would he have jumped if I hadn't implied he should?"

"Yes," David said. "I believe he would have. He knew his time was up."

"Because I pointed it out to him rather effectively," Lionel said, glancing down at his hands for a moment.

Hands that had aimed a loaded gun at Chisolm. A gun he couldn't say with certainty he wouldn't have fired if it came down to it. David could attempt to make the sordid situation as pretty as he wanted—just as he continued to insist on glossing over Lionel's illness by pushing the theory that it was a misdiagnosis and a reaction to harsh laundry detergent—but Lionel knew the truth.

"Either way," Lionel went on, glancing up at Everett, "Chisolm is dead. You won't ever have to worry about him again."

Everett glanced across the room to Patrick with a surprisingly vulnerable smile. The look that the two exchanged spoke volumes, though neither said a word. Lionel was happy for them, truly and genuinely. Just as he was happy that David still squeezed his shoulder, and likely would until the day they died, whenever that would be.

"Everett, there's something I have to tell you," Lionel said with a sigh, resting one of his hands over David's on his shoulder. "Something I should have told you a long time ago."

Everett glanced back to Lionel, his brow lifting in puzzlement. "I thought we'd said everything there was to say to each other."

"Darling, we haven't even begun saying the things we should have said, that I should have said, years ago." Lionel found himself closer to tears than he wanted to be. He and David had talked about the necessity of explaining everything to Everett, but he hadn't bargained on it being so emotional. "I need to tell you about my connection to Chisolm, about why I broke things off between us."

"So you admit it was you who broke things off?" Everett asked, flickering into a teasing grin for a moment before turning serious again. The seriousness took over his expression as he studied Lionel. "I wasn't aware you knew Chisolm apart from the stories I told you about him."

Lionel swallowed the old lump of guilt in his throat. "It's a far longer story than I have the heart to tell, now that the man is dead and gone, but the important bit is that he attempted to use me to hurt you."

Everett's brow knit in confusion. "I can believe Chisolm would use every method in his power to hurt me, but how could he use you?"

David's hand felt heavier than ever on Lionel's shoulder as he drew in a breath and raised his eyes to meet Everett's. "He knew we were lovers. He also knew I needed money. So he arranged for me to be a paid companion for a time to a man whom he knew to be riddled with syphilis. I wasn't aware that Chisolm was behind the arrangement, or that the man in question was ill, until it was too late."

"What do you mean, too late?" Everett asked. A moment later, understanding dawned in his eyes. "Oh, God, Lionel. Are you ill?"

"Yes," Lionel admitted, lowering his head.

"That has yet to be determined," David said.

"Yes," Lionel repeated, stronger, sending David a frustrated look. He turned to Everett, who seemed surprisingly stricken by the news. "I broke things off with you as soon as I realized how I'd been manipulated. I didn't want to infect you."

"You were ill," Everett said, his expression haunted by the memories of their past that he must have been sifting through. "I remember when you came home from that house party. You were positively awful to be around and then you—" He stopped, gaze unfocused, mouth hanging open for a moment, before focusing on Lionel with a look of deep pity. "You were ill," he said with complete understanding. "And I shouted at you, called you all sorts of horrid names, and left. Oh, Lionel, I'm so sorry."

Everett lunged across the sofa, wrapping his arms around Lionel in a hug that carried so much sorrow and regret with it that Lionel could feel the emotion down to his bones. And yet, it was an embrace filled with healing and forgiveness as well. He closed his eyes, letting out the breath he felt as though he'd been holding for years. His secrets were out, and letting go of them banished whatever remaining resentment he had for Everett not reading his mind, for not staying, all those years ago.

"I forgive you," he sighed against Everett's shoulder, then pushed himself straight, holding Everett at arm's length. "As long as you can forgive me for being such an arse and purposely driving you away so I didn't have to admit how stupid I'd been."

"Forgive you for being an arse?" Everett said, mouth pulling into a grin that was as cocky as it was fond. "Perhaps when you stop being such an arse, I'll consider it."

"My behavior has been learned from my company," Lionel said, straightening and tilting his chin up. "You always were an arse."

"Finest arse in London." Everett stood and caressed his backside. "As two of the three men in this room well know." He sent David a saucy wink. "Care to make it all three?"

"No, thank you," David said, rolling his eyes and blushing at the same time. "I've made a pledge to care about just one colossal and annoying arse for the rest of my days."

"How uncharacteristically romantic of you, Wirth," Everett said with an approving smile. "And here I thought you were all business all the time."

"And speaking of business," David said, clearing his throat. "Lionel and I have a bit more to take care of today."

"Do we?" Lionel stood, grateful for the excuse to leave the overly emotional situation and to spend some time with just David. Even though the kidnapping ring case had been over for days, Lionel felt as though it would take weeks of him being with David alone to recover fully from it.

"Just because the kidnapping ring has been foiled

doesn't mean we don't have a pile of cases waiting for us at the office," David said, seeming to thwart Lionel's hopes for time off. "We'll be up to our eyeballs in disputed wills, property quarrels, and members of The Brotherhood who are being treated unfairly by everyone from Her Majesty to their mothers for the foreseeable future."

"Then by all means, go take care of that," Everett said, waving a hand dismissively. "I'm too fabulous and important for the likes of you anyhow." He grinned at Patrick, who winked in return.

"Niall Cristofori writes one show for you and now your head is as swollen as a melon," Lionel sighed, heading for the door. "Just remember who introduced the two of you."

"I knew Niall long before you invited him for supper that time," Everett called after them as Lionel left the room.

David followed, chuckling over the scene they'd just exited. "Did you really introduce Cristofori and Jewel?"

"Of course," Lionel said with a casual shrug. "I've introduced everyone of any importance to everyone else they need to know. It's what I do, love."

David laughed, reaching for his hand and holding it until they left the theater and started down the street. David hailed a cab, and they headed home to David's modest townhouse in an up-and-coming area of Kensington. Lionel had moved into the townhouse immediately after they returned from Hull. There hadn't been any discussion. There hadn't needed to be discussion. David would have packed up Lionel's entire flat and carried all of his belongings to Kensington on his back if Lionel had put up even a hint of a fuss. But Lionel had gone more than willingly.

He hadn't even protested when David summarily fired Lionel's laundress, lecturing the woman on the caustic substances she'd been using to wash Lionel's things. If David wanted to continue to believe his rash and sores had been the laundress's fault, then Lionel would let him believe it. And in truth, his body had been in perfect condition since purchasing new clothes. Perhaps there was some truth to David's insistence that he wasn't sick after all. Lionel certainly didn't feel sick anymore. Far from it. But the blasted nature of syphilis was such that only time would tell.

"So, do you truly have business to discuss with me or was that merely a ploy to get me away from Everett?" Lionel asked once they were home.

"I truly have business to discuss with you," David said, gesturing for Lionel to follow him upstairs. "I have something I need to discuss with you and something I want to show you."

"Something you want to show me upstairs?" Lionel asked, following David into their bedroom, excitement bubbling within him. "In here? I can only imagine what it is." He unbuttoned his jacket in anticipation of wiling away the afternoon in his absolute favorite way. After years of reluctant celibacy, and after coming to terms with David's insistence on putting himself in danger, Lionel was determined to make up for lost time. And David had been more than willing to indulge him.

"First things first." David crossed to the wardrobe and opened it, taking out a small, flat box.

Lionel's heart beat faster as he tried to imagine what wickedness the box contained. "Generally speaking, love, when one is planning on proposing, the box is smaller and square."

David laughed, returning to Lionel but keeping the odd-shaped box closed. "You know I'd marry you tomorrow if I could, but you might not want to marry me once I tell you what I have been holding back for the past few days."

Lionel lost his smug grin even as he shrugged out of his jacket and tossed it aside. "Oh, dear. You're keeping secrets from me already?"

David's face pinched with a guilty look. "I haven't had a chance to tell you about the conversation John and I had in Manchester." Lionel's face lost even more of its humor, but David went on before things could get any more uncomfortable. "John would like to move back to London and take up the law here again. His partnership in Manchester isn't working out, professionally or personally, and he wants to come back."

"To London," Lionel said in a flat voice.

"But not to me," David emphasized. "I let him know in no uncertain terms that I am with you, fully, completely, and forever."

314

Lionel smiled in spite of his jealousy. There was no point in being jealous, he knew, but old habits died hard. "What a sweet thing to say."

"I want to do more than say it," David went on. "I want to make a fairly large change."

"A change?" Lionel arched one eyebrow and started in on the buttons of his waistcoat. "Do tell."

David cleared his throat as Lionel shrugged out of his waistcoat and pushed his suspenders off his shoulders. "To avoid any confusion once John opens his new law office, I wanted to do this."

David opened the box and took out a shiny brass plaque. It bore the words "Wirth & Mercer".

Lionel froze halfway through tugging his shirt out of his trousers. He blinked at the plaque, then glanced up at David.

"I want you to be my partner," David said.

"I don't have a law degree," Lionel said, his voice heavy with sentiment. He traced their names on the plaque, then took it from David, gazing at it as though it were the largest and most expensive diamond in the world.

"You have more experience and have been of more use resolving most of the cases that have come through the office for the past few years than anyone with a law degree could ever have," David went on, his voice soft and tender. "But we both know this isn't about the law. I want our names together for all to see. I want us bound together legally for the rest of our lives, and if a business partnership is the only way to make that happen, then that's what I want."

"Oh, David," Lionel sighed, blinking away the tears that sprung to his eyes. "Only you could make something as pedestrian as a business contract into the most beautiful and romantic gesture a man has ever made."

"What do you say?" David asked, hope and expectation filling his eyes. He took the plaque from Lionel's hands and set it and the box on the windowsill nearby, then took both of Lionel's hands in his. "I promise that I will spend the rest of my days driving you mad by working too hard and getting involved in hopeless cases that require both of us to bash our brains out in search of clever solutions."

"You would," Lionel sniffled, giddy with joy.

"I promise to hound you to take care of yourself and to make you crazy by insisting you visit as many physicians as possible until you get a proper diagnosis."

"David—"

"And in the meantime, I promise to keep you in a state of near constant arousal and to seduce you on a daily basis, then satisfy you beyond your wildest desires, all done with the utmost care and protection for both of our persons. Because now that I've had you, I don't think I could possibly restrain myself," he added with a wicked look.

He stepped into Lionel, sliding his arm around Lionel's waist. Lionel was immensely grateful for his foresight in beginning to undress already, because it enabled David to slip his hands under his shirt, against his skin, as he pulled him close. And there was nothing Lionel wanted more than to be skin-to-skin with David whenever possible, no matter how daft it was. When he was with David, their bodies, hearts, and souls entwined, it was easy for him to believe that the world was exactly as it should be.

"I love you, you irresponsible darling," Lionel sighed against David's kiss.

"And I love you, you stubborn dolt," David growled, tugging Lionel flush against him. He leaned back long enough to stare into Lionel's eyes. "So, what will it be?"

Lionel laughed, looping his arms over David's shoulders and playing with his hair. "Of course, I'll marry you, you silly man."

"It's a business partnership, not a—"

"I know what it is." Lionel arched an eyebrow and leaned in for another kiss. "And the answer is yes."

"Good," David said, kissing him with a smile that Lionel felt through to the center of his being. Any risk they took would be entirely worth it as long as they took it together.

EPILOGUE

*N*iall Cristofori had a thousand things to do and very little time to get any of them done. The curtain was set to rise on his new musical in less than a month, the sets weren't finished, the cast was under-rehearsed, and he wasn't happy with half of the musical numbers his composer had thrown together. There was so much to do that he refused to let himself wave to David and Lionel as he spotted them leaving Everett's dressing room and heading out of the theater. If he stopped to say hello to them he would fall into an entire conversation about the arrests of two of the men responsible for the child kidnapping ring and the death of the third.

All of London was buzzing about the wicked noblemen and how they'd gotten away with so much for so long. Niall was as riveted by the story as the next man, but the next man didn't have a major theatrical production on his hands or connections to one of the criminals' brother.

"Everett, I have that new scene for you," Niall said, striding into Everett's dressing room with barely a knock on the doorframe to announce himself.

He should have been more considerate, as he ended up walking in on Everett with his arms around Patrick and his head resting on Patrick's broad shoulders. Niall immediately turned and started to walk out again before realizing that his two friends weren't in the midst of a passionate embrace after all.

"Is something the matter?" Niall asked, hesitating instead of leaving.

Everett let out a heavy breath and straightened, turning away from Patrick. He wore nothing but his drawers—which wasn't entirely out of character for Everett—but the sorrow in his expression was anything but salacious. "I've just received some emotional news is all," Everett said with a sniff, attempting to downplay his show of emotion.

Niall glanced over his shoulder at the door. "It doesn't have anything to do with Lionel and David, does it? Or the investigation they just concluded?" Niall knew enough about Everett's past after the trip they'd all made to Yorkshire a few weeks before—a trip that had dredged up more than a few ghosts from his own past—to know the investigation into the child kidnapping ring was more than gossip for Everett.

"Lionel and David had some information about

Chisolm's death that isn't public knowledge," Patrick answered on Everett's behalf, sending Everett a look as though asking whether he should say more.

When Everett didn't add anything, Niall nodded carefully. "I suppose you're happy to have that chapter of your life closed."

"More than you can know," Everett sighed. He scrubbed a hand through his hair and shook his shoulders, as though banishing the last of those demons for good. "And you'll be happy to know that Lionel and David have thrown in their lot together at last."

Niall grinned with unexpected joy. "I guess he took my and Percy's suggestion after all."

"I beg your pardon?" Everett's expression shifted to curiosity.

Niall's grin widened. "We advised David to get on with things and seduce Lionel to put them both out of their misery. Apparently, the suggestion worked."

"Apparently," Everett echoed. "Now all that remains is for you to take your own advice."

"And seduce whom exactly?" Niall laughed.

"Why, that dashing, confused friend of yours from Yorkshire," Everett said with a wink. "Patrick here tells me the poor dear is consumed with regret for the way things ended between the two of you."

"Er, that wasn't exactly something Lord Selby intended for me to share," Patrick added, his face going red.

Niall lost his grin. "It would be a fruitless effort," he

said. "What Blake and I had was lovely and special, but it was also painful, and it is most certainly over."

"I highly doubt that," Everett said with a playful twinkle in his eyes. "Not with the way the man looked at you when we were in Leeds."

"It's over," Niall said in no uncertain terms. He marched up to Everett, slapped the pages with the new scene he'd written against Everett's chest, then turned to march out of the room. "Learn your lines, Jewel. And get dressed. Rehearsal starts in half an hour."

Niall stormed out of the room, wishing his heart didn't hurt every time Blake was mentioned. Ten years, and he still couldn't get the man out of his heart or out of his mind. Ten years, and he still tossed and turned at night, remembering how sweet it had been to make love to the man. Even though Blake had rejected him, married, and produced three children. Everett had been imagining things if he thought Blake wanted any part of him now.

"A letter arrived for you, Mr. Cristofori." Lily Logan dashed across backstage area where Niall walked, caught up in his thoughts.

Niall took the letter from her with a frown. "Who on earth would send me a letter at the theater?" he wondered aloud.

Lily shrugged, looking perfectly charming in her boy's clothes, her dark hair caught up under a cap. "Your name is on the marquee out front, sir," she said before dashing off on whatever other errand she had.

Niall grunted. She was probably right. The envelope was unmarked, so he opened it to reveal the answer to his question.

As soon as he saw the neat, looping handwriting, his heart caught in his chest. Blake.

"*Dearest Niall,*" the letter began. "*I will be blunt. Since seeing you again after such a long and bitter separation a fortnight ago, my life and my world have utterly fallen apart.*"

Niall sucked in a breath, glancing around to see if anyone was watching him. The backstage area was cacophonous with activity, so he refolded Blake's letter and hurried along until he found a quieter spot, just outside of the stage door in the alley behind the theater. When he was certain he wouldn't be disturbed, he reopened the letter and kept reading.

"*I don't know how to explain the heaven and hell that my life has been for the last ten years—heaven because it has brought me three wonderful children, whom I love more than life itself, and hell because I have been forced to spend those years without you. Oh, Niall, I was so wrong to pretend that you didn't matter to me and that what we shared was nothing more than the folly and experimentation of youth. Not a day has gone by when I haven't remembered you with a smile...or more. Seeing you again after so long only proved to me that my self-inflicted wound of a decade ago has not only failed to heal, it has only gotten worse.*

"*And now the unimaginable has happened.*

Annemarie has uncovered the truth at last. She puzzled out who and what I am and where my heart truly lies. And she has taken the children. I am beside myself. I don't know where they have gone. I haven't been able to eat or sleep in days. It feels like the last of my soul has been ripped from my body. I am terrified that Annemarie will take the children to her father's home in America, in which case, I may never see them again.

"I don't know what to do, Niall. I don't know who else to turn to who will fully understand the position I am now in. I need you, more than I have ever needed anyone. I knew it the moment I saw you again. Please, Niall, please come to me. Please forgive me for turning my back on you by helping me now. I don't think I can go on without you. Yours, truly, Blake."

Niall let out a breath and sagged against the theater's wall. He glanced up at the hazy London sky above the rooftops, feeling as though all the wounds Blake had inflicted years ago were bleeding again. He'd waited so, so long for Blake to reach out for him, for the only man he had ever truly loved to say that he needed him. He'd dreamed of the moment. He just wasn't sure he had the strength left in him to heed Blake's call and fly to him.

I HOPE YOU HAVE ENJOYED DAVID AND LIONEL'S story! So. Does Lionel truly have syphilis or was it a misdiagnosis and an allergic reaction? I'll leave that up to you, the reader to decide. But one of the things that has always frustrated me about romance novels is the way they tend to ignore just how prevalent syphilis and other STDs were in the age before antibiotics and how many "active" men and women were afflicted with it. Condoms had been around for centuries before the 19th century, but they were considered scandalous and associated with prostitution. The whole concept of safe sex was foreign to most people of the era. So it wouldn't have been out of the question for someone with a past like Lionel's to be sick.

Beyond that, the sad historical fact is that gay men were shunned by the medical community in the 1890s... just as they were in the 1980s at the dawn of the AIDS epidemic. Any illnesses they contracted, especially of a sexual nature, were seen as punishments from God for their sins, and treatment was denied at worst and shoddy at best. It boggles my mind to think that that draconian viewpoint has existed within my lifetime, and still exists today in so many ways, particularly with the trans community.

When I first conceived of Lionel and David's story, what was foremost in my mind was exploring the question of how love can flourish and be expressed when syphilis, or AIDS, is an undeniable part of the equation. Being in love and finding your soulmate isn't about sex at all, and it frustrates me that so much of gay romance, and about the way we tend to see the LGBTQ+ community, is about sex and not love. But love is LOVE. And yet, how do you express love with a deadly disease as part of the picture? It's a question that's still on my mind and that probably will be for a while.

Part of my inspiration for this story was the 2014 film *The Normal Heart*. If you haven't watched this movie about the early days of the AIDS epidemic, the race to figure out what it was and seek a cure, and the emotional toll it took on the gay community, I urge you to seek it out and watch it soon! But bring tissues, because you'll need them.

So what about Niall and Blake? Will Niall answer Blake's call and help him locate his children and get them back? And will their old flame be rekindled again? You can find out in December with *Just a Little Heartache*, which is available for preorder now!

If you enjoyed this book and would like to hear more from me, please sign up for my newsletter! When you sign up, you'll get a free, full-length novella, A Passionate Deception. Victorian identity theft has never been so exciting in this story of hope, tricks, and starting over. Part of my West Meets East series, A Passionate Deception can be read as a stand-alone. Pick up your free copy today by signing up to receive my newsletter (which I only send out when I have a new release)!

Sign up here: http://eepurl.com/cbaVMH

. . .

ARE YOU ON SOCIAL MEDIA? I AM! COME AND JOIN the fun on Facebook: http://www.facebook.com/merry-farmerreaders

I'M ALSO A HUGE FAN OF INSTAGRAM AND POST LOTS of original content there: https://www.instagram.com/merryfarmer/

Click here for a complete list of other works by Merry Farmer.

ABOUT THE AUTHOR

I hope you have enjoyed *Just a Little Seduction*. If you'd like to be the first to learn about when new books in the series come out and more, please sign up for my newsletter here: http://eepurl.com/cbaVMH And remember, Read it, Review it, Share it! For a complete list of works by Merry Farmer with links, please visit http://wp.me/P5ttjb-14F.

Merry Farmer is an award-winning novelist who lives in suburban Philadelphia with her cats, Torpedo, her grumpy old man, and Justine, her hyperactive new baby. She has been writing since she was ten years old and realized one day that she didn't have to wait for the teacher to assign a creative writing project to write something. It was the best day of her life. She then went on to earn not one but two degrees in History so that she would always have something to write about. Her books have reached the Top 100 at Amazon, iBooks, and Barnes & Noble, and have been named finalists in the prestigious RONE and Rom Com Reader's Crown awards.

ACKNOWLEDGMENTS

I owe a huge debt of gratitude to my awesome beta-readers, Caroline Lee and Jolene Stewart, for their suggestions and advice. And double thanks to Julie Tague, for being a truly excellent editor and assistant!

Click here for a complete list of other works by Merry Farmer.